Aubrielle's Call

I0556051

by C. Marie Bowen

Aubrielle's Call by C. Marie Bowen
Copyright © 2016 C. Marie Bowen
All rights reserved.

ISBN-13: 978-1-945215-025 Paperback
ISBN-13: 978-1-945215-032 Ebook

Edited by Liette Bougie
Published by Pixler Publications

Discover other titles by C. Marie Bowen at
www.cmariebowen.com

Dedication

For my father, Eugene Nelson Pixler.

Dad was born in Benkelman, Nebraska on July 30, 1923. He moved with his family from Benkelman to Denver, Colorado in the late '30s, during the Great Depression so his father and brothers could find work.

When he was seventeen, he joined the Civilian Conservation Corps and worked out of Morrison, Colorado from July to December 1940. He listed his occupation as a cabinetmaker.

After the attack on Pearl Harbor at the end of 1941, like all patriotic young men, Gene joined the service and volunteered for the U.S. Navy. He was honorably discharged as a Seaman 1st Class on October 25, 1945.

He married Inez Christopher on November 12, 1944, in Englewood, Colorado. My brother, Jerry Eugene, was born in August 1945, and my sister, Rama Lee, was born the following year, in September.

On August 25, 1950, he reenlisted and served during the Korean War as a Steelworker R 2nd class in the Seabees at the U.S. Naval Construction Battalion Center. He was honorably discharged on April 12, 1953. I was born in December 1958.

Dad was a stainless-steel worker and owned his own kitchen installation business. He and mom built a cabin in the mountains where the family spent many wonderful holidays and weekends.

He rebuilt player pianos as a hobby. He loved to sing and watch science fiction. He had a kind heart and gentle disposition. I think he would have liked this story.

Dad died on April 9, 2002, in Denver from Alzheimer's disease. Forever missed.

CONTENTS

Acknowledgments

The research for this story took me down many unexpected paths. Each time I thought my hero would do something simple, like board a ship from America to England, he was thwarted by facts. It made for interesting turns, letting John solve the impediments I discovered while combing through historical documents. John made intriguing choices. And while that enhanced the story, it always involved additional research.

Thank you to the *Banque de France* for answering questions about banking before—and during—the first part of WWII and for providing me with banking regulations used during this time.

Many of the descriptions and incidents I describe during the evacuation at Dunkirk were fashioned from eyewitness accounts.

A big thank you to my wonderful editor, Liette Bougie. You're amazing. Your knowledge and love of language is impressive. I'm grateful to have you on my team. *Merci beaucoup.*

A special, heartfelt thanks to my critique partner, C.A. Jamison. To have someone know and care about my writing as much as you do lifts me when I am down and struggling to get the words onto the manuscript. I'm lucky to have you as a critique partner and honored to call you my friend.

And lastly, to my husband, Todd Bowen. Your knowledge of all things nautical and military kept me on the right track. Your unwavering support and love made this story, and all my writing possible. I wouldn't be able to do this without you.

Chapter 1

John Larson

September 1939

Able Seaman John Larson swung onto his lower rack as the overhead light in the seamen's quarters winked off, and the red light came on. *The Yankee Dream* would make Boston Harbor the day after tomorrow. The run from Panama should prove profitable for the small merchant vessel. Lucrative enough, the shipmaster had hinted, that there might be a bonus to the crew's regular wages.

John closed his eyes and prayed for a dreamless rest. A nightly ritual ever since the death of his wife, almost twenty years ago. How long would her face haunt him?

Until the magic beckons and I find her again.

As memories edged into dreams, he watched his wife call flame to her hand. In the glow of the fire, her perfect silhouette stole his breath. Her smile and sparkling eyes nearly broke his heart.

Alyse, my love. How I miss you.

Emotion closed his throat, and he clenched his teeth, awake once more.

John hunched his shoulders and rolled to his side. A seaman's rack didn't fit a man his size. To curl his six-foot-five frame onto a six-foot long bunk became another nightly torture. Still, work on a ship offered enough change from working cattle. These reflections only plagued him at night.

After he had lost Alyse, he buried the man he'd been beside her. He chose a new name. A new profession. A new life. The in-between years stretched before him. The years, decades, centuries, after his soul mate's death.

What if I never feel her call again?

The recollections of their recent life together were still too raw and painful to bear. Eventually, he would cherish the memory of Alyse as he did all the lives she had lived, back to the beginning.

Back to Agaria.

Agaria sim Biraci.

My life changed forever because I loved Agaria and rejected another.

As if summoned, the sharp specter of the Druidess Nescato scraped across his mind. Her jealous, contorted face encircled by the Biraci tribe's most sacred pelts. The embodiment of evil. Bitter with envy, she raised her staff to the heavens, spoke her curse, and then pointed the staff at him and Agaria.

Nescato cursed his soul to endure the centuries alone, unable to love another. Bound forever to await his soul mate's rebirth, for a threat to her life, and for the magical summons that would draw him to her side. Not always able to reach her or save her, he would forever be compelled to try.

He pushed the image of the sorceress away and rolled to his other side, seeking a comfortable spot, both on the bed and in his heart.

"Hey, Big John, you're rocking the rack," Elmer Jones called down from above.

"He's rocking the ship," Fred Harmon said from across the way.

"Sorry," John muttered.

Lie still. Rest.

The motion of the ship relaxed him, lulled him to sleep. At first, a deep, restful emptiness soothed and replenished his mind and body.

And then he dreamed.

He stood the first watch, waiting in a darkened room. Silent as the night, Alyse joined him, slipping her small hand into his.

Further back.

Alyse laughed when she took his arm, and he escorted her to the family dinner table.

A sweet reminiscence.

Their first kiss. A promise made a hundred times over. *I love only you.*

His dream darkened.

He waited inside a circle scored in the dirt. The intense heat of a summer sun beat down on his shoulders. Others fought beside him, but dust obscured his vision. He wiped a sleeve across his eyes, and Alyse stood before him. Fire cradled in her hands. Hatred bled from her eyes like tears.

Out of the shadows crawled a monster. The threat to his beloved's life. The reason for his summons. This prophetic evil had threatened Alyse since the day she'd been born.

John raised his rifle and took aim. The name he once called himself rang through the apparitions of sleep. *"Jim, wait!"*

"Wake up, son." Fred nudged John with his boot. "It's time for morning muster."

John rolled from his rack and stretched, pressing his palms against the overhead steam pipes. Most of his shipmates had already dressed and headed aft for breakfast. He pulled on his dungarees, buttoned his shirt, and followed Fred up the ladder to the main deck.

At muster, Bosun Garza assigned John to mend the mooring lines damaged while in Panama. When he finished that task, he was to chip and paint the bollards with young Elmer.

Clear blue sky and southerly winds stayed with them as they sailed up the coastal waters. The crew moved about their tasks with a light heart. Tomorrow they'd make port.

At evening mess, John consumed a bowl of soup and a slice of bread.

"Will you join us in town tomorrow night, John?" Elmer asked.

"Of course, he will." Fred dabbed at the last bit of soup in his dish with a crust of bread. "We'll unload the ship, collect our pay, and depart. Ain't that right, Big John?"

John shook his head at his friends. "How can I argue with the two of you?"

Elmer, a farm boy from Nebraska with a large head and a shock of white hair, rubbed his hands together in anticipation.

The oldest of the three, Fred took a sip of his coffee and laughed at Elmer.

After another night at sea, the morning found them moored in Boston Harbor. The long task of unloading the cargo and waiting in line to see the ship's purser took most of the day. They crossed the gangway at dusk and headed for Gull's Tavern.

Early evening customers filled the bar. The friends found a small table near the back.

"I'll buy the first round," Fred said and made his way through the jam-packed bar.

Elmer pointed. "There's a barmaid."

The buxom server shoved mugs of brew across a table filled with sailors. She pulled a pencil from her curls, prepared to take their orders.

"She's busy." John pulled out a chair. "Let's wait for Fred."

On the shelf behind them, a radio played a swing melody. As the song ended, a Glen Miller tune began to play.

"Look, they're dancing." Elmer nudged him and pointed at three couples near the bar.

Fred wove through the crowd with mugs of beer and set them on the small table. "Drink up, shipmates. Next round's on John."

"Are we going back to Panama, have you heard?" Elmer asked Fred.

Fred took a swig from his mug and wiped the foam from his mustache. "Seems likely. Bananas, coffee, and sugar sell well in the States. Master Riley welcomes the profit, and so my friends, do I." He smacked his lips and took another drink.

The music changed to a slower song and a woman's lilting voice crooned about the memory of a lost love. John's stomach clenched each time they played this song. It reminded him of Agaria. He drank his beer in silence and watched the dancers.

"Will you stay on *The Dream*, Big John?" Elmer asked.

He shrugged. "No reason not to. The master is fair and the pay, as you say, is good."

The barmaid offered to bring another round.

John pulled a bill from his pocket. "My turn."

As the dark-haired server returned with their mugs, the radio changed from music to news. Several patrons shouted for her to switch the station to dance music, but she hesitated, listening to the announcer.

"News today from Great Britain. German forces have invaded Poland. German planes have bombed Polish cities, including the capital, Warsaw. The attack came without any warning or declaration of war. Britain and France have declared war on Germany in support of Poland. They have mobilized their forces in preparation to wage war on Germany for the second time this century."

A cold chill ran down John's arms.

The barmaid reached for the dial. "I hate those lousy Krauts," she told John with a smile and a wink as the first notes of a jazz tune played on the radio. She let the music play and took an order from the next table.

The noise in the bar became muted and distant. A familiar high-pitched whine bled into John's brain.

His mouth went dry as his heart thundered alongside the shriek in his ear. A cold sweat plagued his brow.

It's been only twenty years since I buried Alyse.

5

He shook his head and stared at Elmer and Fred.

The in-between always lasts longer.

The men talked and laughed. Elmer nudged Fred and pointed across the bar, but when they spoke, John heard nothing.

The call has come so soon. She must be a child.

His stomach twisted with certainty as pain pierced between his eyes and shot through to the back of his skull. John set his mug on the table and missed. Released from his hand, the beaker fell and then slowed to a stop in mid-air. The beer's foamy head froze in its splash toward the floor. His hand, a hairsbreadth from the handle.

In the next instant, time resumed.

The mug shattered, and the barmaid spun in surprise.

The pressure in his head expanded, pushing outward until his vision filled with white light. As the glare faded, the pain contracted to a single point above his right eye.

"I'll get that." The barmaid pulled a towel from her skirt pocket and tossed it over the spill.

"You feel all right, John?" Fred raised an eyebrow and took another swig.

John squeezed his eyes shut and pressed the heel of his palms against his eyelids "I'll be all right." He lowered his hands. When he moved, the point of pain sliced across his forehead. He tilted his head the other way until the sting settled between his brows. He didn't have to step outside to know he faced east-northeast.

Across the sea, Agaria calls

Chapter 2

John Larson

Is she in Poland?

John nodded to the barmaid as she replaced his beer.

She used her shoe to sweep the towel and glass across the floor, away from the dancers.

The stinging point on his forehead would be a distraction until he set eyes on Agaria.

Or whoever she is in her new life.

The adrenaline spike in his chest would ease once his journey toward her began.

He brushed a hand along the back of his neck. There would be no way to reach her for days, even weeks, and he had no idea where to find her.

His heart clenched.

Damn.

John gripped the handle of his mug and raised the foamy brew to his lips.

The white-haired young sailor emptied his glass and chuckled at the dancers. He elbowed Fred and pointed. "See the blonde? I knew a girl in Toledo who moved like that."

John drank his beer and watched the blonde dancer. He remembered a conversation he'd had with a curly-haired blonde, a lifetime ago. She had claimed knowledge of the future and warned of wars that would encompass the entire world. Wars fought with weapons that didn't exist in the late nineteenth century. She'd been right.

He and Alyse had learned of events in the Great War by reading newspaper reports from the safety of their Denver home. Thankful for once, they could never conceive a child.

The second war, his friend had warned, would sweep across Europe in what the Germans would call a blitzkrieg. The death toll would be astronomical, especially in Poland.

John drank his beer. If his love dwelt in Poland, she could already be beyond his reach. Even so, she lived. As long as her heart continued to beat, he would feel her call, and the direction he must follow.

He scrubbed his hand over his face. *I'll have to cross the Atlantic.*

Once in Europe, he'd have a better idea where to find her.

Fred cleared his throat and raised an eyebrow. "You're less than fine, I'd say. What's on your mind, son?"

John pressed his lips and took a deep breath. "I won't be sailing on *The Dream* to Panama." He leaned back and ran his hand through his hair. "I need to find a ship making a North Atlantic run."

"What?" Elmer set his mug down hard. "Are you mad?"

"Why rush off to war?" Fred narrowed his eyes and put his beaker on the table.

John shook his head. "Not war. Not for me." He waved his thumb at the radio. "But war means more ships sailing to Europe, more profit."

"Could be." Elmer shrugged. His attention returned to the dancers.

"I'd guess you have family in Europe?" Fred held his gaze and sipped his brew.

John rolled his shoulders and gave his friend a slow nod. "I do."

He looked away and rubbed at a point on his forehead. "And I can't just listen to radio reports and speculation. I need to find her." He glanced at Fred. "Find them."

Fred tipped his head toward one of the tables filled with men. "Ask those shipmates where they're bound." He gave a nod to several men at the bar. "Those men, as well. The Gull is as good a place as any to find a ship across the pond."

John gave Fred a pat on his shoulder and rose from his chair. There were five men at the table dressed in sailor's dungarees. He stopped beside them and nodded. "Good evening, mates. I'm looking for work on a North Atlantic run to Britain or any port along the European coast."

Five ruddy faces lifted to John.

"Nothing goes to Britain now, because of their tariffs." A husky man at the table jutted his chin at John. "You a stoker?"

John shook his head. "Deckhand."

"Talk to the men at the bar." One of the sailors pointed over his shoulder.

"Thanks." John scanned the bar.

Two mariners threw down bills for their tab and rose to leave.

"Gentlemen," John said. "I heard you might have a berth for a deckhand heading to Britain."

One sailor shook his head and shrugged into his jacket. "Sorry, mate."

The other man narrowed his eyes at John. "You might ask at some of the taverns on the south end of the pier." He winked and left the bar.

John returned to their table.

"No luck?" Fred asked.

"No." John picked up his mug. "But they suggested I try south along the pier."

Young Elmer drained his glass, stood and rubbed his hands together. "I'm going to dance with the blonde. Wish me luck." He two-stepped his lanky frame away from their table. His focus on the dancers.

Fred shook his head at the younger man. "That boy needs watching. Have a seat, son. You can ask around tomorrow. The south end's no place for a lad alone at night."

"This can't wait." The adrenaline punch to his gut kept John on his feet. He couldn't sit still. "I'm going to walk down the pier and ask around." John threw down money for their next round and ducked outside into the night.

The sharp point of pain on his head swung around his skull like a compass arrow spinning north. He crossed the street and headed south along the pier. To his right, warehouses and darkened alleyways lined the waterfront, a counterpoint to the brightly lit harbor. Past the warehouses, music, and bawdy laughter echoed down a side street. He put his back to the pier and walked up the dead-end road. All around, the scent of the harbor hung heavy in the night air.

Three taverns competed in the cul-de-sac. Several men passed by, headed to the dock. They gaped at John, commented on his height and then burst into laughter.

John ignored their amusement.

As he entered the first bar, the shatter of glass in the cul-de-sac caught his attention.

From the tavern across the way, a mariner fell backward into the street.

A group of men pursued him out the door and stood on the sidewalk, mocking the fallen man.

Without hesitation, John turned from the doorway and into the street. His long stride took him to the man who lay on his back rubbing his jaw.

"Are you injured?" John asked.

The man's eyebrows rose as he looked up at John's face.

"I'll do, friend." He raised his hand and John hoisted him to his feet.

The men, clustered on the sidewalk, followed their leader into the street. "Found a friend, Sweeney?"

"He's no part in this, Taylor. Hell, I've no part in this." Sweeney brushed his hands along his thighs and reached down to grab his cap. "She asked me to dance. I didn't know the whore belonged to you."

Taylor charged Sweeney and came to an abrupt halt against John's hand.

"Easy, shipmate," John said to the thick-necked man.

Taylor's face flushed. "She's not a whore," he yelled at Sweeney. Spittle flew from his mouth, and he wiped the back of his fist across his lips.

"I bet she's wondering where you've gone," John said in a calm voice. "You should take your friends back inside and buy your lady friend a drink."

Taylor's bloodshot eyes focused on John. "This doesn't concern you, mate."

"Not yet. I only offer you a bit of good advice." John eyed Taylor's friends as they moved to flank him and Sweeney. "You don't want this fight."

"Screw you, Goliath." Taylor barked and swung wildly at John. He missed by four inches. He swung again, but John's arm held him further than the burly man's reach.

"Tell your friends to step back," John demanded.

Sweeney shuffled up beside John—fists raised. "Leave off, Taylor. You'll get us thrown in the brig over a whore."

"Get 'em," Taylor yelled, and two of his friends stepped to either side of John.

John lifted Taylor and tossed him into his nearest man. Both went down with a grunt and rolled in the dirt.

At John's side, Sweeney dealt Taylor's other comrade a hard right to the nose and a left uppercut to his gut. The man sat down and gasped for breath.

Taylor's friends on the porch took a step back, spun on their heels, and raced into the bar.

The muscular man struggled to his feet and glared at John. "I'll remember you." He shook his finger at John as he hastened back into the bar, his friends close behind.

"We'd best move on." Sweeney brushed his clothing and walked toward the pier. "Shore Patrol will be around." He stopped at the end of the street. "Come along," he called to John. "There's a quiet bar round the corner. I owe you a drink."

John cast a last glance at the doorway where Taylor and his friends had entered. "John Larson, able seaman on *The Yankee Dream*." He held out his hand and fell into step beside Sweeney.

"Bosun Sweeney on the *Giselle-Marie* but my friends call me Pete." They walked south along the pier. "*Yankee Dream*? Is she docked on the south end?"

"No." John shook his head. "We docked north. We're just in from a Panama run. I expect Master Riley will make a return run as soon as *The Dream* is loaded."

"What're you doing on the south pier?" Sweeney pointed down the next street, and they changed direction.

"Looking for work on a ship bound for Europe."

Sweeney opened the door of a quiet tavern and ushered John inside. They ordered a draft from the bartender and found a seat at an open booth.

When their drinks arrived, Sweeney took a long draw on his mug and gave John an appraising look. "No ships are bound for Britain or France, mate. Their tariffs make it unprofitable, and now, their declaration of war makes it illegal."

"Illegal?" John ran his hand through his thick dark hair. "I thought they would want to buy American arms."

"I'm sure they do." Sweeney set his mug on the table and cocked one eyebrow at John. "But the U.S. doesn't trade with belligerent nations, at least not according to Roosevelt and Congress." He wiped at a wet spot on the dark wood tabletop. "A little thing called the Neutrality Act makes transporting goods, passengers, and arms to a country at war a federal crime."

"You're saying there's no way to sail to Europe?" John rubbed at the stinging spot on his forehead. "I can't accept that."

"No, mate. I'm not saying you can't sail to Britain or France. I'm saying it's illegal." Sweeney rested his arm along the back of the bench and eyed John. "Able seaman, you said, and good in a fight, by my own eyes. Tell me—" Sweeney leaned forward, elbows on the table. "If I knew a master, who wanted to help the Brits and Frogs, and make a bit of cash for his crew on the side, would you be interested?"

"Aye," John replied without hesitation. "I would."

Sweeney grinned. "That's good, mate." He paused as two sailors entered the bar and moved to a table in the back. "It's too crowded this early," Sweeney said in a low voice into his half-empty glass. "Come back at midnight. Tell the bartender you're to meet with me. He'll give you directions." He finished his beer and set the mug down hard on the table. "Don't be late." He turned his collar up and slipped out the door.

Chapter 3

John Larson

John finished his drink and waved off the barmaid who walked his way. He dropped coins on the table to cover his tab and headed into the night. Men hurried along the wharf in groups of two and three, most moving away from the ships for the evening. He passed the quay where *The Yankee Dream* had moored and continued north to Gull's Tavern.

Fred and Elmer were still in the little bar, both cutting a rug on the dance floor. The waitress eyed him as he sat at their table.

"Same as before?" she asked over her shoulder as she cleared the table beside his.

"Yes. Thank you."

She nodded and made her way through the crowd carrying an armful of empty mugs.

The slow, plaintive melody ended. Fred and Elmer escorted their dance partners back to the table.

"You're back." Elmer pointed to the young blonde woman on his arm. "This is Marge."

Fred seated his tawny-haired date and pulled over another chair. "Charlotte, this is John. He's a friend of ours." Fred scooted his chair up to the table and held up four fingers to the waitress. "John wants to find a ship to Britain."

"We asked some sailors about a North Atlantic run after you left. They said there were no ships bound for Britain." Elmer thanked the waitress and took a gulp of beer.

John nodded greetings to the ladies. "I may have found a vessel," he said to Fred and Elmer. "A line on one at least. I meet with the bosun tonight."

"Be careful, John." The silver glistened in Fred's hair as he shook his head. "I'd hate for something bad to happen. Not all masters are good ones."

"I'll be all right, Fred," John reassured his friend. "If all goes well, I'll be leaving *The Dream* in the morning, so I wanted to buy the table a round of drinks tonight." He reached over and gave Elmer's back a pat. "You've been good mates, the best a man could ask for."

Before long, the ladies urged Fred and Elmer to return to the dance floor.

John finished his drink and signaled to the waitress. He bought the table another round and handed the young woman a tip for her service.

"I get off at midnight." She smiled at him and tucked the bill into her blouse.

He winked at her and slipped on his coat. "You take care walking home, miss."

The clear fall night had grown colder, and he pulled up his collar to the wind as he hurried back down the pier. He still had an hour, but Sweeney's warning about being late rang in his ears. He passed the rowdy cul-de-sac and turned up the next street.

Inside the quiet tavern, the bartender leaned against the counter and made soft conversation with a woman at the bar.

John slipped into the same booth he and Sweeney had shared earlier. He waved when the barkeep glanced his way.

Instead of greeting him, the man behind the bar returned to his conversation with the woman.

John didn't mind. He had experience with waiting, even when

anxiety clawed a hole in his heart.

After several minutes, the bartender stopped in front of John's table. "What'll it be?" The man's white bib apron stretched over broad shoulders, the ties knotted tight around his ample waist. Despite his midsection, the barman's biceps bulged as he wiped his hands on a large bar towel.

Perhaps he's the reason this tavern is quiet. "I'm waiting for someone. We were here earlier and planned to meet again at midnight."

The bartender finished with the towel and set his fists on his waist. "Sweeney?"

"Yes."

Without a word, he returned to the bar, filled a mug of beer, then caught John's attention by tipping his head toward the back of the room.

John grabbed his knit hat from the seat and followed. He paused as the bartender set the beer on a table before the furthest booth. When the man walked away, John's gaze locked with the same woman who had been seated at the bar earlier.

She nodded her head and flicked the ashes from the cigarette attached to the end of a six-inch holder. "Sit," she said and pointed to the bench seat across the table.

John slid into the seat as the barman drew a gauze-black curtain across a high-hung rod.

Her almond-shaped gray eyes studied him. A delicate oval face made her appear younger than her silver-veined auburn hair would put her. Coiffed impeccably, her streaked locks rolled back from her forehead, pinned and adorned by a silver flower hairpin. She inhaled from her cigarette holder and blew the smoke in the air. "Sweeney said you were tall."

John stroked his chin, then shoved his hat in his pocket and picked up his beer. "My name's John Larson."

"I know." She flicked her ashes and smiled.

"You have me at a disadvantage, Miss…?"

"Master Keats." She dipped her head but never lowered her eyes. "Tell me, have you ever worked for a woman, John Larson?"

Surprised, John chuckled and ran a hand over his face. "Yes ma'am, I have."

"You don't look old enough to have done much of anything at all."

"I'm told I have an old soul."

Her laugh echoed across the empty bar. "We shall see, Mr. Larson." She pulled the stick from her martini and drew an olive down its length with her teeth. She chewed the olive and swallowed. Her eyes narrowed as she studied him. "Where are you from?"

"Most recently, Denver."

"No oceans to sail in Denver."

"No, ma'am."

"Stop with the ma'am nonsense. You make me feel old." She opened her bag, pulled out a two-foot line of hemp and tossed it on the table. "You may call me Keats, or Master Keats. If—and this is a big if—I decide to bring you aboard, you will address me as sir." She raised the martini in front of her and took a sip. "Tie a sheep-shank."

John twisted the rope into a long loose knot and tossed it back.

She pulled it straight. "Now, a chain hitch."

"On?" John picked up the line and looked around. He pushed back the gauze curtain and wrapped the chain hitch knot around the rod.

"Very resourceful. Untie that and sit down."

John pulled the knot free, drew the curtain closed and took his seat.

Keats removed the cigarette butt from the holder and crushed it in the ashtray. "One last test." She peered at John from the corner of her eye. "A double fisherman's."

John shook his head. "You know as well as I do, a double fisherman's knot takes two lines."

She gathered the rope from the table and shoved it into her bag. "Can you use a compass?"

"I can."

"Can you navigate by the stars?"

"Yes. And I know port from starboard, fore from aft."

"Are you familiar with weapons?"

"I am. Both new and old. I'm also a fair to good medic in a pinch."

"Very impressive, Mr. Larson."

"We've talked about what I can and will do. Now I must tell you what I won't." John leaned forward and took a short breath. "I won't kill a man if disabling him will do, and I don't kill at all without a damned good reason."

"A master's orders aren't reason enough?"

"No, sir." John closed his eyes for a moment. The truth could cost him this opportunity.

It doesn't matter. I won't lie about taking a man's life. If need be, I'll find another way.

He opened his eyes and stared directly into hers. "I'm not telling you I won't kill a man. I have before, and most likely will again, but I need to know the right of it for myself."

"So, you would not kill for me?"

"To protect your life, the lives of my mates, and the ship I serve, I wouldn't hesitate."

"My husband would have liked you, Mr. Larson. Such honor and honesty are rare commodities these days." She rapped her knuckles on the wall.

In a moment, the burly bartender pushed the gauze curtain back. He held open her coat and handed her a matching slouch *chapeau.*

She settled the hat on her head. "My ship, the *Giselle-Marie*, is moored at the southernmost pier. We sail on the morning tide. Should you care to join us, Mr. Larson, you would be welcomed." She faced the barman and kissed his cheek. "Thank you, Steven. We should be back in about six weeks if all goes well, but don't be overly concerned should it take longer." She navigated the long barroom gracefully and vanished into the night without a backward glance.

John tore his gaze from the door and found the barkeep's eyes narrowed in his direction.

"You'll mind your manners and guard her back," the man said and blinked moisture from his eyes and sniffed.

"Aye." John offered his hand, and the man shook it. "I can promise to do both." John pulled on his hat as he crossed the bar to the door.

Fred and Elmer's berths were empty when John entered *The Dream's* crew quarters. He removed his dungarees, organized his small trunk, and swung into his berth.

The point of pain moved to the top left side of his head, a stinging sensation both loathed and cherished. God forbid that prick of pain should cease before he set eyes on Agaria again. He held the stinging spark like a lifeline as he fell asleep.

The next morning, Fred and Elmer slept as John made his way from their rack. He spoke with Bosun Garza and collected his seaman's papers and letter of discharge from *The Yankee Dream*. With his small trunk under one arm and his duffel bag over his shoulder, he headed down the gangway toward the *Giselle-Marie*.

Chapter 4

John Larson

The three-island tramp steamer, *Giselle-Marie*, had been more than well-cared-for. Someone loved this ship. The proud older lady wore a new coat of red paint on her hull, with only a slip of black showing above the waterline—a sign of a nearly full hold.

John stopped at the gangway and studied her deck. She boasted a single center steam stack with two lookout masts, one forward, and one aft. Each pole supported two davit cranes to load cargo. Painted white, the deck, and masts gleamed in the morning sun. A single stripe of hull red around the stack adorned her alabaster skin. A beautiful lady indeed, like her master.

On the deck, Bosun Sweeney directed men in preparation for departure. When he glanced down and recognized John on the pier, he waved him aboard with a broad grin on his narrow, tanned face. "Glad you decided to join us." He gave John a pat on the back. "The bunks are aft—two mates per cabin—when we run a full crew, that is."

John accompanied Sweeney to the back of the ship while the bosun called instructions to the men. They passed two harbormasters, escorted down from the boat deck by the second officer.

Sailors worked the lines with practiced determination, ready to cast off for the *Giselle-Marie's* imminent departure.

Sweeney directed John past the open cargo hatch and beneath the aft housing. Down an inside hallway, a cabin door stood open. Sweeney stepped inside. "Have you ever served aboard a tramp?"

John ducked through the cabin door. "Aye. *The Dream* is a tramp—older than this lady and larger. Her stack is aft, not midship." John tossed his bag onto one of the bunks and pulled his papers from his back pocket. "*The Dream's* cargo holds are forward." He tipped his head at the adjacent bed as he handed Sweeney his papers. "No bunkmate?"

"Not for this trip," Sweeney replied. "We're running with a reduced crew."

John dropped his trunk at the foot of his rack "Why's that?"

Sweeney shrugged. "Master Keats will explain it to you, or not, as she sees fit." He tipped his head forward. "Now that you're aboard, she'll want to speak with you in her office."

John nodded and went with Sweeney down the short hall, across the deck and up a flight of stairs to the master's suite.

The *Giselle-Marie* moved slowly away from the dock. The tug guided her through the harbor channel to the opening in the breakwater. The cloudless autumn sky promised clear sailing.

John's chest remained tight, and his senses tingled, even as he moved toward his goal—one step closer to the woman who bound his heart. The pinprick sensation on his head remained true as a compass, pointing north-northeast of their forward direction.

Sweeney stopped at an open door and knocked.

Inside, Master Keats sat across from the first officer. A map spread between them on the desk.

Keats looked up as she pulled the chart across the desk and folded it closed. "Enter."

"Seaman John Larson, as you requested, sir," Sweeney reported, stepping aside for John.

"Thank you." Master Keats tipped her head to the bosun. "That will be all, Mr. Sweeney. Come in, Mr. Larson"

John entered the office under the scrutiny of both the master and the first officer. He greeted them with a nod and stood silently by the door.

"Mr. Rice, this is the man I met on Bosun Sweeney's recommendation—Able Seaman John Larson." The master gave her first officer a quick glance and inclined her head at John. "Mr. Larson, this is my first officer, Kenneth Rice."

Older than Master Keats, Mr. Rice's full white beard matched the new deck paint. He nodded to John. "Mr. Larson. I'm glad you decided to join us."

"Thank you, sir."

"Before we clear the harbor, I want there to be an understanding between us, Mr. Larson." Keats steepled her fingers as she studied John. "This run will be our first wartime effort, and we've found the North Atlantic passage dangerous already."

John nodded. "Yes, sir."

Master Keats appeared a different woman from the one he'd met last night. Her braided auburn-gray hair was pinned tight to her head, and she wore an officer's uniform with Captain's pips on her epaulets. A master in command of her ship. A remarkable woman.

She tapped one long finger to the closed map on her desk. "We plan to make a stop in Nova Scotia and take on cargo we're unable to obtain in the States—arms and ammunition for our countrymen in Europe."

John looked from her fingertip to her calm gray eyes. "And my role?"

"You'll accompany Mr. Rice when we make the exchange. You'll be armed, of course, but your size alone is rather intimidating. More importantly, you've shown to have a cool head under pressure. That's what I need most." She grinned and relaxed back in her chair. "Perhaps it's that old soul you spoke of, but I need your instincts and knowledge of how men react."

"I'm more than willing to help." John straightened his

shoulders. "However, you need to know this is a one-way trip for me. I'll leave your service when we dock in Europe."

Keats pressed her lips. "I'm surprised and disappointed with this information. I'd hoped to make you a permanent member of my crew."

"At another time, it would be my wish as well." He spread his hands. "The Maginot Line won't stop Hitler from invading France." He ground his teeth. "And I have loved ones in Europe I must find."

"Where are they?" Keats leaned forward. "In France?"

"I'm not sure." John rubbed the back of his neck. "I'll know more once we reach Europe. Where is your buyer?"

Master Keats and the first officer exchanged glances. "I won't share that yet." She plucked a brown Captain's hat from her desk drawer and secured it on her head. "We should be close to the breakwater. Mr. Rice, I'd like you in the wheelhouse."

"Yes, sir."

Mr. Rice rose and withdrew from the room.

Master Keats stared at John, elbows on the desk, her hands folded beneath her chin. "You'll take your watch assignment from Mr. Rice. Unless you hear otherwise from either Mr. Rice or myself, Bosun Sweeney will assign your duties."

John tipped his head. "Yes, sir."

Keats nodded. "You'll be paid before you leave the *Giselle-Marie*." She eyed him a moment as if trying to see inside his mind. "I hope you find who you're looking for in Europe, Mr. Larson. Carry on."

"Aye aye, sir." John closed the door as he departed to find Mr. Rice.

* * *

John stood forward watch from ten 'til two for the next three nights. Headed north for an illegal arms exchange, the *Giselle-Marie* ran lights out and silent. They had waited two weeks for the rendezvous date, sailing just beyond sight of the Nova Scotian beaches.

Alone in the darkness, urgency pounded through his veins, and a pinprick reminder pressed against the side of his head, fueling his memories. Agaria's many lives stayed with him—haunted him—in a theater of love and loss. Her name and face changed, but she remained the only woman John had ever loved. His teeth clenched as he remembered. *Elena limping through a castle, or in repose, laughing beside a stream. Alyse, on horseback, as they raced across the open prairie.* Those were but two of the lives they'd shared.

Each time Agaria's soul passed from life—his grief—and his purgatory, would begin. Forced to wait for the next calling, and the race to reach her side in time.

He turned his head and placed the urgent sting of her direction between his brows and leaned his shoulder against the forward housing as he stared into the night. The myriad of constellations disappeared at the black line of the horizon.

She's out there—my Agaria—she's alive. Her danger real. Her life forfeit should I fail.

The tap on his shoulder startled him, and he stood to face the man behind him.

"You're wanted in the master's suite." Sweeney bent his shoulder to the wind and lit a cigarette. In the flare of the flame, he looked at John and spoke from the side of his mouth, "I'm to finish your watch."

"Aye aye, Bosun."

Sweeney grasped John's arm. "Be careful tonight." His words muffled against his hand as the ember from his cigarette lit his face for a moment. "We've never dealt with these men before." He exhaled smoke above his head. "Everyone's likely to be a bit jittery."

"I understand," John's quiet tone, matched Sweeney's. "I'll be all right, and I'll take care of the others."

"That's good." Sweeney nodded, the cigarette tight between his lips. "Carry on, John."

In the master's suite, Mr. Rice issued John a snub-nosed .38 special with a shoulder holster, as well as a Thompson sub-machine gun. John checked the ammunition for each weapon and slipped off his coat to strap on the holster. He nodded to Mr. Rice when ready.

John, Rice, and two seamen John didn't know moved to the port side of the ship. Beside one of the rafts, men stood prepared to lower the smaller vessel by a winch. The armed men climbed into the raft, and it dropped to the surface of the sea. The *Giselle-Marie's* engine had come to a stop, and the anchor chain rattled as its length slipped out of the housing.

Storm clouds were banked above the mainland, blocking the stars but reflecting the light of the late rising moon. John and Rice sat silent guard duty while the two sailors paddled the boat.

A slight breeze, sharp as a shard of ice, slipped beneath John's jacket collar as he strained to see the shore.

Coves dotted the long seaward edge of Nova Scotia. Hundreds of tiny harbors with thin sandy beaches surrounded by a thick indigenous forest.

This area hasn't changed much in a thousand years.

Near the beach, John vaulted over the side of the raft, knee-deep in the moonlit foam. He guided the boat onto the sand with one hand while his other held the machine-gun high above his head.

They were the first to arrive. The four men stood silently in the chill darkness beside their craft and waited.

"There," Mr. Rice breathed.

John scanned the rolling waves and caught sight of a small vessel, similar to theirs, riding the swells to shore. Two men jumped from the boat, both armed, and pulled the craft onto the sand.

The leader of the other group stepped from the boat and walked in their direction. His gaze met John's, then slid to the first officer. "You have the payment?" His English thick with a French accent.

"Aye. As agreed." Mr. Rice pulled a bulky envelope from his inside pocket.

"Give it here." The man held out his hand.

"You have our merchandise?" Rice moved toward the smuggler, but John slipped in front of him.

"Let me," John whispered to Mr. Rice. "*Montrez-moi,*" John nodded at the smuggler.

"*Tu parles français?*" The smuggler's eyebrows lifted.

"You have the merchandise, no?" John replied, matching the smuggler's heavy accent. "We see it first." He held the Thompson with both hands and stared at the smuggler.

"Louie—" The smuggler waved his hand.

Two men lifted a long trunk from the boat. They set the crate on the sand near John and went back for another.

"Your merchandise."

"Marv, take a look," Rice instructed.

The seaman beside John crossed the sand. He slung the strap of his machine-gun over his shoulder and knelt to unlatch the trunks. After the second lid had fallen open, he turned to Rice and nodded. "They're all here."

"As agreed," the smuggler said. "Now, the money."

"Give this to our friend." Rice handed the envelope to the other crewman. "And help Marv move the trunks to our boat."

The smuggler's feet remained planted while he counted the money. "I would have asked for more, as the price for weapons have risen since I met with your master." He nodded to his men, then walked past the trunks filled with small arms to their boat. "But for a fellow Frenchman, this I will accept. *Bonne chance, mes amis,*" he said over his shoulder as he boarded his watercraft.

Marv and the crewman loaded the guns while the smuggler's small craft move away from the beach.

"Let them get well away from the beach," John said to the first officer.

"I didn't know you spoke French," Rice brushed sand from his hands.

John waited for the voices of the Frenchmen to disappear. "I have family in France."

"That's right."

"They're gone." John slung the gun strap over his shoulder.

"Step sharp, men. Master Keats will be pacing the deck." Mr. Rice sat on one of the trunks while the two seamen manned the oars.

John kept watch into the darkness, listening for danger while the sting of urgency rode against the side of his head. To the west, lightning flashed through the cloud.

Chapter 5

Aubrielle Cohen

October 1939

Aubrielle arranged an assortment of colorful lilies, roses, and lavender sprigs in her market wagon and secured the awning. She leaned against her pony, Éclair, and scanned the *Champ-de-Mars* for customers. Few tourists remained in Paris at this time of year, especially now, after France had declared war on Germany. The exodus of tourists over the last two months left the streets empty. Everyone wanted out. Only soldiers and a few desperate vendors populated the park in the morning chill.

She pulled her old coat tight at her throat and allowed her sight to drift to the top of the Eiffel Tower. If she didn't make a few sales soon, she wouldn't be able to refresh her floral stock. Greenhouse flowers came at a dear price this season, and Papa's decline had left his millinery shop floundering—their savings nearly gone.

Although Papa had stopped using the poisonous mercury to shape felt hats years ago, the damage had already been done. Often, his hands shook so badly he could hardly eat. Thank God her mother's best friend, Mae Moroney, lived next door. She kept an eye on Papa and brought him lunch while Aubrielle tended her flower cart. If not for *Tante* Mae's kindness, Aubrielle would not be able to make her daily trip to the park with Éclair.

At lunchtime, she ate a croissant with cheese, then split her apple with Éclair as she walked the pony and cart around the park. At their slow pace, the long circuit filled most of the afternoon. The sun played peekaboo with passing clouds, but the rain stayed away. Unfortunately, there were no tourists who wanted to purchase her flowers.

As she rounded the corner, near the Tower at the park exit, a young couple approached and purchased a small bouquet of lavender. They were Americans on their honeymoon, and obvious about both details.

"We're leaving for New York at the end of the week," the man told her, hugging his bride close to his side. "We don't want to get caught in France when the Germans attack."

"The Germans can't attack us. They won't get past the Maginot Line." Her assurance, a repeat of what Papa told her every night at dinner while they listened to the latest broadcast news on the radio.

"The Maginot Line?" the American girl asked as she sniffed her bouquet.

"*Oui.* A line of defense my country built along the German border after the Great War. We are safe," Aubrielle assured the couple before they hurried on their way.

When they left the park, she walked with Éclair beside the Seine and crossed over the *Pont de l'Alma,* or Alma Bridge as the American couple would have called it. She passed the *Grand Palais* then turned down the side alley behind her father's hat shop, not far from the *Avenue des Champs-Élysées,* in the *Le Marais* district.

Aubrielle pushed open the wide gate and Éclair pulled the cart into the yard without prompting. She saw to her pony's comfort first, then changed the water in each of the vases in the wagon. She refilled the flower jars with her mother's particular water mixture of bleach, sugar, and vinegar. A loose tarp protected the delicate merchandise from Paris's unpredictable fall weather.

As Aubrielle opened the back door, the aroma of freshly baked bread and braised beef filled her senses, and her stomach rumbled. Music floated down the hall from the radio in the sitting area. She hung her coat on a hook and slipped her shoes off in the cloakroom.

"Aubrielle, is that you?" Her father called over the music.

"It is, Papa." She kissed his forehead as she came into the kitchen. "Is that dinner? It smells delicious." She untied the scarf that covered her thick dark hair and smiled at *Tante* Mae. "Did you close the bakery early?"

"Aye, darlin'. Not a customer since noon." Mae Moroney rolled her R's and stretched her vowels with her Irish brogue. She'd kept the bakery open after her husband's death in '25 with persistent hard work and determination. Her beloved husband, Oscar, had fought in the Great War, like Aubrielle's father, and had inhaled mustard gas in the trenches. Oscar came home from war a sick man and never fully recovered. Their decision to relocate to France to be near her dear friend Marguerite and her husband, Lou, never gave her a moment of regret.

Mae set a plate of braised beef and mashed turnips in the center of the table. "Could you get the place settings, Brie?"

"Of course." She and Papa spoke English more than French these days, even to each other. *Tante* Mae spoke only her own peculiar English, as did the wealthy American tourists, who had become the largest portion of their meager income.

Now, even those sales have dried up.

Aubrielle set the table for three and filled her father's plate. "Here you go, Papa."

"I'm going to open the shop tomorrow," her father announced. His hand shook as he brought the fork to his mouth. He raised his brow at Aubrielle as he chewed and swallowed. He pointed the empty fork at her to emphasize his word. His thin, spotted hand trembled. "I've decided to take on an apprentice."

"An apprentice?" Aubrielle exchanged a guarded look with *Tante* Mae. "Papa, people are too frightened of war to spend what little money they have on a new *chapeau*." She shook her head. "How will we pay an apprentice?"

"Any boy who wants to learn a trade will work for free." Papa's dark eyes glared disappointment at her. The spots on his bald head showed stark against his white skin in the overhead light.

Aubrielle huffed in annoyance. "We would need to house and feed him." She lifted both hands in despair and shrugged her shoulder. "How would we feed an apprentice? Where would he sleep?"

Mae settled at the table and folded her hands. Her soft black hair, highlighted with several silver strands had been pulled back into a tight bun. Hazel eyes closed, and she bowed her head and spoke loud enough to still the heated conversation. "May God bless this food and all who share his bounty. Amen."

"Amen." Aubrielle's head came up. She pushed her thick dark hair over her shoulder and picked up her fork. "I only sold one bouquet today." She stirred the turnips on her plate and eyed her father as he ate.

"That reminds me," Mae said. "The young man you buy your flowers from came by earlier today."

"Henri?" Aubrielle looked up from her plate. "What did he want?"

"He didn't say." Mae's eyebrow rose. "It could be about your flower order."

"I don't like that boy," Papa stated, never raising his eyes. "A boy his age should be in the military defending our borders, not selling flowers to young girls in the park."

"There won't be new merchandise this month," Aubrielle said. "Greenhouse flowers are too expensive." She took a small bite of beef, chewed and swallowed. "I still have last week's flowers, and they won't last much longer." She shook her head and raised an eyebrow at *Tante* Mae. "When the flowers are too wilted to sell,

I'll be finished selling until next spring."

"Perhaps that's for the best." Mae nodded. "Two young women have been attacked in the hedgerows beside the park. It may be time for you to stay home with your Papa."

Aubrielle lifted one shoulder. "I'm not concerned."

They ate in silence and listened to the *Radio Normandie*, broadcast in English, a mixture of news and American band music.

Aubrielle rose and carried her plate to the kitchen sink. "I'll clean up."

"Don't bother," Mae said. "I'll take care of the dishes. Your Papa and I haven't finished yet." She waved Aubrielle toward the hallway. "Go on, with you. Set your curlers. The kitchen won't take but a moment to tidy."

Aubrielle paused in the hall and looked back at her loved ones. Sometimes, Papa acted as though he didn't remember who she was. At least tonight he hadn't called her Marguerite, her mother's name.

In her small room, she put her hair in rollers in front of her spot-stained mirror. Outside, the rain beat against the roof. It would be clear again by morning, and the tarp would keep her flowers safe.

Her dark eyes stared back from the mirror. There had been whispers in the park about Hitler's *Mein Kampf*, and she'd felt the burden of antisemitism before, even in Paris. Her dark hair and eyes, along with the surname of Cohen, labeled her and Papa as Jewish, regardless of her faith. If the Germans came, they would be detained, or worse.

She blinked at her reflection and put another roller in her hair. Concern over Hitler would have to wait. Henri Vogl would insist she purchase more of his greenhouse flowers, and she could not. She took the few coins from her sale today and set them on her dresser. Little enough to buy meat and bread. She intended to repay *Tante* Mae's generosity before purchasing any more of Henri's flowers.

Chapter 6

John Larson

Dark, turbulent clouds hung low and threatening above the *Giselle-Marie*. The storm over Nova Scotia had pursued them across the Atlantic. As though fleeing bad fortune, the sturdy ship ran swift before the approaching tempest. They rode the outer edges of the front, pushed ahead of rougher seas, for close to a week.

Tonight, rain would find them. John could smell it in the air. He wore the yellow rain gear Bosun Sweeney had handed him after dinner. Although John appreciated the slicker, it only reached to his forearms and barely covered his backside. The headcover fit well enough and would keep the rain from running down the back of his neck.

Lightning danced across the gray sky, accompanied by a sudden crack of thunder. As though that were a signal, the sky opened wide, and rain pelted down.

The popular rumor among the crew said Master Keats sailed for Portsmouth Harbor, but John knew better. Even if the steamer flew French colors, they risked being recognized in the busy British port.

Keats will seek a sheltered cove, perhaps along the French coast, to complete her business.

The call from the wheelhouse rang out instructing a course change. They'd tried to outrun the weather but could not. Now they would turn and face the storm to ride it out. The all hands klaxon sounded to alert the crew. Yesterday's preparations had left the ship ready to battle the weather. Hatches battened, cargo secured, and the deck cleared for rough seas.

As the ship came about to face the wind, the sting of Agaria's urgent call sliced across John's scalp and pressed against the back of his head. He lifted closed eyes to the pelting rain.

Soon, my love.

Ahead, the ship nosed down into a trough and the sea broke over the bow of the vessel, swamping the forward deck. In the next instance, the *Giselle-Marie* surged upward in a race toward the crest of the next wave.

Keats turned the ship into the storm at the last possible moment.

The swells grew as the tempest rolled over the stalwart vessel. John rode the sea, back pressed to the wheelhouse, memories crashing over him with each wave.

He had no fear of the storm or concern for himself. He'd been cursed with incredible fortune since before he'd stopped aging. The fear in his heart had always been for those around him. His current shipmates, and of course, for Agaria.

For five days, the steamer faced into the rolling waves. The *Giselle-Marie* and her crew rode the tempest until the angry sea and sky calmed.

Unfortunately, the unfavorable weather had blown them off course, driving them south of their original heading. They put in at *Marina d'Angra* on Terceira Island in the Azorean Archipelago to take on fuel. Although several of the crew members were native Portuguese, when Master Keats discovered John spoke the language, she called upon him to negotiate with the harbormaster for oil.

They reached the coast of France two months past the date of their original assignation. Master Keats weighed anchor offshore from their rendezvous location until their contact with the French smugglers could be reestablished.

Off duty, John waited in his cabin until called to accompany the cargo to shore. He'd spread several precious items on the bunk before him, examining each one.

Hurried footfalls on the deck and a call to prepare the small craft for departure alerted him. He scooped up his treasures and placed them back into his leather drawstring pouch one at a time. A silver wedding band, inscribed. A small brass key, with the number seventeen, etched into the head. The tarnished silver key tied with yellowed lace would open the front door of the house in Denver. He dropped a smooth black stone, painted with a protective rune, into the pouch beside the ring and keys.

Memories.

He pulled the bag closed and laid it alongside his papers in a hand-tooled wooden box.

At the knock on his door, he placed the box back in his small sea chest and closed the lid. "Come in."

Taylor poked his head into the small quarters. "Master Keats wants you." Sober, the stocky sailor displayed a dependable and friendly persona. Despite their initial meeting, Taylor and John had become friends.

"I'll be right up."

Taylor nodded and pulled the door shut.

John tucked in his shirt, ran a hand through his hair and pulled on his coat. Outside his cabin, the wind blew sharply out of the north. Above the wheelhouse flew the French Tricolor. He crossed the deck with long strides, double-stepped the stairs and knocked at the master's office door.

"Come."

John entered as Master Keats looked up from her desk.

Her silver-veined braid, pinned neatly to her head, crowned her master's uniform. "Please, have a seat, Mr. Larson." She nodded at the chair across the desk and slid the pen she held into its holder.

"We're in radio contact with our buyers and will rendezvous with them in a few days."

"Yes, sir." John unbuttoned his coat and sat across from Master Keats.

She studied him. "I wanted to make sure you hadn't changed your mind and still intend to leave us when we land."

"I must." John shifted in the chair and gave a small shrug. "I'm—compelled to walk this path, sir. Otherwise, I would stay on the *Giselle-Marie*."

"In that case, I want to pay you now." Master Keats opened the top drawer, withdrew an envelope, and pushed it across the desk. "We may not have another moment to speak in private before you depart."

Inside the envelope, John found both American dollars and French francs. His eyebrows arched as his gaze rose to Master Keats. "You appear to be overly generous."

"Smuggling is a profitable venture." She grinned at John. "That is no more than your share. Besides, I have a soft spot for ambitious endeavors, as you may have noticed."

John chuckled and put the envelope into his inside pocket. "Yes, sir." John stood as Master Keats came to her feet.

She held out her hand. "I wish you the best of luck, John Larson. Godspeed in locating your family."

He took her hand. "Thank you, and luck to you as well, sir."

"My given name is Giselle. It was my husband's ship, after all." She released his hand and shoved hers deep into her pants pockets. "If you'd be interested in sailing with us again, once your family is safe, leave a message at the tavern where we met. Steven, the owner, was my husband's brother. He'll know how to contact me."

Should I warn her about the coming war? There would be too many explanations needed and not enough time. "Sir? Giselle? The Nazis won't be satisfied with Poland." John pressed his lips. "Be careful."

"I will, John. You take care, as well." She gave John a nod and returned to her desk. "Carry on."

"Yes, sir." John backed from her office and closed the door behind him.

Later that night, Bosun Sweeney tapped his shoulder while John stood watch. "The master needs you in the armory. I'll stand your watch."

John paused as he walked past the Bosun. "Thank you, Pete, for recommending Keats bring me on board."

"Aye." Pete nodded and leaned against the bulwarks. "You're a good man, John Larson." He grinned at John with a matchstick clenched between his teeth. "Be safe tonight."

* * *

John sat point in the small boat, his duffel and sea chest tucked behind him. He held the Thompson tight against his chest and carried the unfamiliar weight of the .38 strapped to his side, beneath his jacket.

The swells remained high, and the rough surf pounded against the boat, rocking the men and the cargo.

Mr. Rice echoed the instructions Keats had given the men before the winches lowered the small craft to the sea. "We'll make three trips with the four boats." The hushed tone of his voice reached only the men in the small craft. "John and I will stay on the beach and guard the cargo while you return to the ship for the rest."

"Aye." Four whispered voices acknowledged the first officer.

Clouds scuttled across the moon and cast the shoreline in an eerie darkness. A brief flash of light caught John's eye. "Starboard two ticks."

Mr. Rice raised his flashlight and gave a signal to the boats that followed. They adjusted course.

The clouds parted, and moonlight reflected off the beach.

Several armed men and two trucks waited for them.

"Master Keats knows these men?" John whispered to Rice.

"Aye. You'll be safe enough."

John chuckled. "I wasn't worried about me, sir." He vaulted over the side of the craft into the thigh-high surf and guided the bow of the boat onto the shore. The other craft from the *Giselle-Marie* came to rest beside them.

John stood watch as Mr. Rice spoke with the leader of the Frenchmen. Rice hunched his shoulder to the wind to light a cigarette, nodded and shook hands with the man, then hurried back to the rowboats. "They'll help us unload." He nodded across the beach to the furthest craft. "Stow your weapons and transfer the cargo—everyone except John." Rice grinned at John. "You can take your gear and be off if you like."

"I'll stay and stand watch, sir. If you don't mind." John shouldered the machine-gun and grabbed his duffel. "If they'll give me a ride to the nearest town, I'll leave with your friends."

The Frenchmen loaded the textiles, wine, and tobacco into the back of their trucks. Before the moon set into the sea, the large trunks of arms were hauled from the shore boats and loaded as well.

The man Mr. Rice had spoken with crossed to John as the boats returned to the *Giselle-Marie*. "*Monsieur* Rice said you might need a ride into town." He held out his hand. "François."

"I'm John, and yes, I'd appreciate a lift."

"Our first stop is at Caen." François smiled and held out his arm toward the open door of his truck. A blond-haired smuggler watched from the cab. "Billy and I shall make room."

The last boat cleared the beach. Mr. Rice raised his hand to John in farewell.

John had returned the machine-gun, but Rice had told him to keep the .38. A parting gift from Master Keats. The gun's weight pressed against John's side as he waved back to the first officer then followed François to the vehicle. "Caen will be perfect. Thank you."

* * *

In Caen, John took his leave from the smugglers and sought a tailor to purchase civilian clothes. The garment-maker agreed to lengthen the dark slacks and double-breasted jacket to fit John's height. While he waited for the alteration, John bought shoes from the shop down the street. A new overcoat, two new shirts and ties, and a fedora completed his transition from mariner to civilian. The tailor had his clothes sized and ready by late afternoon, as promised.

John changed in the tailor's dressing room and hurried to the train station. Three months had passed since he first felt Agaria's call.

It's taking too long to reach her.

When the station came into view, anxiety twisted in his chest.

Both British and French soldiers filled the station's benches and slept beside their duffel bags along the outer wall of the building. Inside, the crowd was worse. Men packed the small building, sprawled wherever they could find.

The man behind the window shook his head when John inquired about a ticket to Paris. "*Non.*" He indicated the soldiers who waited along the platform and shrugged. "The next two trains are filled as well. *Désolé.*"

"*Merci.*" John nodded to the tired ticket attendant and paused to study a map of France tacked to the wall beside the window. His love was still to the west, but how far away remained a mystery. She could be as near as Paris, or as far as Munich.

I've no way to know.

He left the train station and looked down the road in the direction of her call. With no choice remaining, he walked.

Outside of town, a convoy of military vehicles forced him off the road. He waited until they passed before he returned to the road. He waved at two other cars as they passed, intent on begging a ride, but the drivers never slowed.

John's shadow faded before him as the sun slipped below the horizon.

I'm a fool. I could have taken a room in Caen for the night and sought transportation in the morning. As it is, I'll sleep in a ditch.

Headlights on the road behind him brought his long shadow back to life. Instead of stepping to the side, he stopped and faced the vehicle.

A lift to the next town isn't too much to ask.

He shielded his eyes as the vehicle slowed to a stop.

A man stuck his head out of the truck window. *"Bonjour, monsieur."* The driver called, then opened the door. "John, is that you?"

It took John a moment to place the voice. *"François! Bonjour, mon ami."* He approached the vehicle.

"What are you doing in the middle of the road?"

John chuckled. "I couldn't get on the train to Paris."

"So you thought to walk?" François laughed, shaking his head with amusement. "You Americans. You never said you were going to Paris, or I would have offered a ride. Hop in."

John set his bag and chest into the back of the truck with the remaining items from the *Giselle-Marie*. He recognized the two crates of weapons, secured and covered by a canvas tarp. He opened the passenger door. "Thank you."

"You've changed your clothes." Billy moved to make room. "I wouldn't have recognized you except for your size."

François put the truck in gear, and they picked up speed. "You must tell me, are all Americans as big as you?"

* * *

The sharp urgency pointed toward his love slid across his scalp from above his right eye to behind his ear. The sensation woke him, and he blinked several times as he sat upright and looked out the window. The truck moved slower, and the world had disappeared into a cloud. "What time is it?"

François glanced at John and chuckled. "Early, *mon ami*. The sun should have risen, but today..." His shrug finished the sentence.

"Where are we?" John re-centered the pinprick between his brows. Past his reflection in the side window, he could just make out a river beyond the fog.

Billy blinked and cleared his throat. "Is this Paris?" He rubbed his eyes and yawned.

"Yes." François pointed at the river. "This river, she is the Seine. She winds her way through the city."

"I need to get out." John set his hat firmly on his head and straightened his coat."

"Now?" François's brows rose.

"Yes. Right now." John indicated the curb ahead. "Pull over and let me out here."

When the truck stopped, John reached over Billy and shook François's hand. "You've been a lifesaver. *Merci, mon ami.*"

François released his grip. "*Vous êtes le bienvenu*, my American friend."

John closed the door and pulled his duffel and chest from the back. He turned his collar up and hurried down the street to the bridge. Agaria was close. He could sense her movements on his forehead.

Chapter 7

Aubrielle Cohen

Aubrielle led Éclair across the Alma Bridge toward the *Champ-de-Mars* in the morning fog. A cold mist had moved across Paris overnight. This morning, a thick cloud snaked along the Seine spilling outward over the banks and across the city. The heavy sky hid the top of the tower from view as she crossed the street to the park entrance. She stopped near the tower and looked back along the empty street.

Footsteps, unheard until now, echoed through the mist and then stopped.

"*Bonjour?*" The vapor confined the light from the streetlamp into a bright globe above her head and allowed little illumination of the street behind her. "Is someone there?" Her voice, dampened by the moist air received no response.

Uneasy, she held tight to Éclair's lead and continued beneath the tower. The squeak of the wagon wheels and the muffled beat of her pony's hooves were the only sounds inside the cloud. When she reached her usual morning spot, she gave Éclair his feedbag and lifted the cover from her merchandise to study her wares. The lilies and lavender still looked fresh, but the roses all bowed their heads as though in prayer.

No one will buy these.

She plucked the roses from the containers, tossed them in the wagon, and rearranged the display to look as full and inviting as possible.

She paused, long stem in hand, as a tingling sensation passed across the nape of her neck. To her right a bell chimed.

The low clouds carried the moist fishy scent of the river and masked her view of the tower. The nearby trash receptacle, a smudge of darkness, appeared to move as vapor shifted. For a brief moment, the shadowy outline of a tall man appeared. When the gloom thickened, he vanished into the mist.

Close by, in the other direction, the pastry vendor sat beside his pushcart filled with croissants and sipped a warm beverage. Steam rose from his cup and blended with the fog. He never glanced her way.

Aubrielle shivered. *What's wrong with me?*

She finished grooming her display, muttering to herself as she pulled a stool from the wagon. "I should have stayed home." There would be no tourists in the park with this weather. Still, it would be shameful to let what remained of her merchandise fail, undisplayed in the backyard. Besides, Papa had refused to get out of bed this morning and had called her Marguerite, her mother's name, several times.

That's another reason I'm unsettled.

As soon as *Tante* Mae had arrived with fresh baked bread, Aubrielle had hurried out the back door.

I should have brought a piece of bread with me.

She cast another glance at the pastry vendor and felt for coins in her coat pocket. *No luck.* She'd left them on her dresser at home.

"Your neighbor said I would find you here."

The voice beside her ear startled her, and she came to her feet. Hand to her chest, she spun and faced Henri Vogl, her flower broker. "Henri. You frightened me."

He laughed and ran his hand down the arm of her wool coat. "I see that. Why so nervous, *ma petite fleur?*"

Aubrielle shrugged off Henri's hand and stepped back. Henri could always make her uncomfortable. His thick blond hair and flirtatious manner annoyed her. Although other women might find the broad-shouldered man attractive, Aubrielle did not. "What do you want?"

Henri's grin widened, and his scrutiny drifted down her coat to her legs then made its way back to her face. One brow lifted. "That depends on you."

Aubrielle shook her head. "I cannot restock again this season." She held out her hand to the empty park. "The petals fade before I can sell them. Besides, I have not the funds to buy more."

"We could work something out, *mon petit bouton de rose.*" Henri's eyes narrowed as he grasped her arm again. "Walk with me."

"Leave Éclair and my flowers unattended?" She jerked her arm from his grip. "*Non.* I will not."

* * *

John Larson

The urgent pain between John's eyes dissolved as his gaze rested on a young park vendor. *A flower girl?* He strained to see her through the mist as she arranged her floral display in the back of an old wagon. Her well-worn coat spoke of hard times, but the bright red triangle scarf tied over dark hair made John smile. Now that she stood only a few yards away, he hesitated.

She won't know me. I've made that mistake before.

The young woman pulled a stool from her wagon and sat beside her wares, casting furtive glances at the bread vendor a few paces away.

She's hungry.

John gulped the moist air as his heart contracted. Driven by a will not entirely his own he moved forward, and then came to an abrupt halt as a gentleman crept up behind her. The blond, broad-shouldered man bent and whispered in her ear.

A friend? A lover?

John cursed the clouds that blocked his view and crossed the pavement in time to see his flower girl jerk her arm back in anger.

A threat?

"*Non.* I will not." She addressed the blond-haired man with a sharp tone.

The weight of the .38 pressed against John's side as he grasped a handful of her flowers. "Excuse me—"

Both heads turned toward John.

The girl's eyes widened in confused recognition.

The man's eyes narrowed. His glare rose to John's face.

"I hope I'm not interrupting," John murmured and grinned down at the man.

"No, no. Not at all." The girl brushed past the man's shoulders. "*Au revoir*, Henri."

Henri gave the girl a long look then stalked away.

"A friend of yours?" John asked as he handed her the coins for the bouquet.

"Not really." She refused to look him in the eye. "A business acquaintance." The coins slipped into her empty coat pocket without a sound. "*Merci.*" Her smile didn't reach her wary dark eyes as she pulled the wedge from beneath the front wheel and tossed her stool in the back of the wagon. "Enjoy your day." She tugged her pony's lead and led her cart away.

* * *

Aubrielle Cohen

Aubrielle walked Éclair toward the exit and passed beneath the tower near the footing.

I was right.

45

The tall man had been watching her. She'd seen his large, unmistakable outline in the mist. Between Henri's odd behavior, and the giant in the fog, her knees shook as she led Éclair onto the street. *Tante* Mae's warning about attacks on young women near the park prompted her to hurry home.

She glanced over her shoulder.

Was he following her?

She quickened her pace beside the Seine and onto the Alma Bridge. At the top, she paused and brushed a hand along Éclair's withers while she searched the shadows behind her. The clouds had begun to lift in the park, but along the river, the fog remained thick. She couldn't see past the edge of the water to the street. With a tight grip on her pony's lead, she made her way over the bridge. The further she moved from the river, the brighter the day became. Once she locked the backyard gate, she felt foolish at her fears and chuckled at herself. Never before had she allowed her imagination to pull her reason out by the roots.

She stopped in the kitchen and listened to the house. Papa's shallow, even wheeze told her he slept in his room down the hall. On the kitchen table, Mrs. Moroney had left her a handwritten note. A bank official had come to the house and asked about the mortgage payment. Their finances had been in arrears for several months, ever since Papa had stopped working.

Aubrielle crumpled the note and shoved it into the pocket of her coat. Cold metal brushed her knuckles. She pulled the coins from her pocket and stacked them on the table.

I cannot make hats, but I can sell flowers.

She would go back to the park tomorrow, try harder somehow. Be friendlier. She shook her head as she walked to her room and lay on her bed. The tall stranger must think her unhinged, the way she had run off. She closed her eyes thinking about him.

Firm hands shook Aubrielle awake. She sat up in bed and blinked at *Tante* Mae. "What time is it?"

"Just a wee bit past five. I've sent my baker lads home and

brought supper for you and your Papa."

Aubrielle nodded and scrubbed her hand across her face. "I didn't mean to fall asleep."

"And sound asleep you were, too." *Tante* Mae held out a paper document. "I found this taped to the shop door."

Aubrielle took the document and pulled it open. She read the text and her gaze rose to her neighbor. "We've been evicted." Her hand trembled as she read the notice through tear-filled eyes. "It says we are eight months in arrears and have to be out of the shop and apartment by the first of the New Year."

Tante Mae eased her hips onto the narrow bed beside Aubrielle. "I know, darlin'. I've been expecting this."

"You have?"

"Aye." The older woman nodded and pushed an errant black curl streaked with gray from her forehead. "Your Papa can't keep the shop. It's a hard truth he'll have to understand."

"But—where will we go?" Aubrielle sniffed.

"You'll both move in with me, of course. I rattle around in an empty apartment. Besides, I'm over here more than at home." She nodded and pulled Aubrielle close.

Aubrielle clung to the dear woman as equal parts defeat and relief washed over her. "Why would you do that for us?"

"Here now, enough tears." *Tante* Mae pushed Aubrielle's dark hair from her face and kissed her forehead. "Your Mama was my dearest friend for many years. She held my hand when my beloved Oscar died." Mae lifted Aubrielle's chin and met her gaze. "She and I swore to take care of each other, and before she passed, I promised her I'd watch over you and your Papa."

"Are you sure?" Aubrielle shook her head. "How can we impose like that?" Tears slipped from her eyes, and she hung her head.

"Ah, my sweet Brie. It would be easier for me to have you close so I can tend to Lou." She lifted Aubrielle's chin with her finger. A smile lifted the corner of Mae's lips. "There is even room for

Éclair in the back if need be. You could still sell your flowers."

Aubrielle wiped her face and grinned at *Tante* Mae. "I am done with selling flowers. Soldiers do not buy them, and the tourists have left Paris."

"Well then, you'll have to sell something else. How about baguettes and croissants? I have plenty and soldiers need to eat."

"That's true, but there is another *boulangerie* selling croissants in the park."

"There will be room for two. It is a very large park."

Chapter 8

John Larson

John held his sea chest beneath his arm. The flowers in one hand and his bag in the other. He admired the dark-haired beauty.

My love!

She was young, but certainly no child.

In his heart, John made a solemn vow, one he made each time his eyes first rested on his soul mate's new face.

I will love and protect you all the days of your life.

The flower vendor barely glanced at him as she pocketed his coins. She kept her chin tucked, and her eyes downcast while she unblocked the pony cart and led it away.

John clenched his teeth and took a slow breath as she vanished into the fog. He shoved the bouquet of flowers into the trash receptacle, and with renewed determination, he pursued her into the cloud bank.

I don't even know her name.

Far enough behind to remain hidden by the fog, but near enough to reach her should a need arise, John kept pace with the young woman. He could do nothing else. From the end of an alley, he watched as she closed the gate behind her cart. As soon as she climbed the stairs to her house and disappeared inside, John circled the block. She lived on a winding street of vendors, above a millinery shop. He passed the busy *boulangerie* next door, and the smell of fresh bread followed him around the corner.

On the street of shops behind her house, he found what he wanted—a sign in the butcher shop window. *Appartement à louer.* Inside the store, John spoke to the owner about the apartment rental.

From the third-floor living room window, John's view was of the back of the bakery. Next door to the *boulangerie*, Agaria's covered flower cart stood beside the small stable.

"There is a box to receive mail at the bottom of the stairwell." The butcher walked through the living area and stopped in the kitchen. "The furniture comes with the apartment unless you have your own."

"I don't." John inspected the bedroom and water closet. "I'll take it."

"For how long, *monsieur?*" the butcher inquired.

"Indefinitely, *mon ami.* I have business in town."

"That is good for us both, no?" The butcher stopped outside the door. "There are two keys in the kitchen drawer. You may pay your rent on the first."

* * *

Aubrielle Cohen

Aubrielle turned off the light in her father's room and softly closed his door. She made her weary way down the dark hall to her room and stood at the window overlooking the back gate. Papa grew worse each day, one moment anxious and the next angry, unable to follow a simple conversation. At times, he believed Aubrielle to be her mother. They could not afford a physician, and even if they could, there was no cure for Mad Hatter's disease.

Tomorrow she would sell the last of her flowers. Truthfully, she intended to give them away if there were no buyers. No doubt

Henri would attempt to persuade her to continue to sell his wares, but she would be firm. *Tante* Mae's offer to let her sell baked goods appealed to her. What she didn't sell could be put in the day-old bin in the store. No more dying flowers to throw away.

Across the alleyway, a light came on in an upstairs room and caught her attention. The familiar outline of a tall man stood framed in the light.

Aubrielle gasped and drew back from the window even though he couldn't see her in the darkened room. She pulled the curtain closed and peeked around the edge.

The tall shadow paced away from the window, only to return a moment later.

Unwilling to turn on her light, she undressed in the dark and crawled between the sheets.

Had the tall man followed her?

She rolled over and stared at the closed curtains.

I must be imagining things.

She would keep a look out for the man tomorrow, and if she saw him, she would report him to the *préfecture de police.* Although she tried, she couldn't remember the details of his face.

The next morning, she left the house just after *Tante* Mae arrived with a basket of croissants. Folded into a napkin, the flaky pastry Mae had given her warmed Aubrielle's pocket as she crossed the bridge and walked along the river with a lighter heart. Yesterday's fears had evaporated like the fog. She didn't care that her flowers had wilted a bit more overnight. She would give them away if she had to. Today would be the last day she and Éclair would sell dying flowers in the park.

After Éclair had his feedbag, Aubrielle pulled the pastry from her pocket, broke off a small piece and popped it in her mouth. As usual, the park was empty except for the vendors and a few residents enjoying the bright morning. The man she had glimpsed in the third-floor window last night remained a mystery, his large form nowhere to be found. At noon, she handed out small bouquets of flowers to soldiers and homemakers cutting through the park.

She took her time in the afternoon, walking the half-circle paths that meandered to the edge of the park, beneath the colorful autumn trees before returning to the avenue. Aubrielle and Éclair waited for two cars to pass, then crossed the roadway and continued in the direction of the *École Militaire.* There would certainly be more soldiers near the military school to present with flowers.

With her cart nearly empty, she turned Éclair north, along another arching path, toward the exit to the park and home.

"Aubrielle!" Out of breath, Henri jogged up to her cart and graced her with his most flirtatious smile. "I didn't know to look this far from the tower. I couldn't find you." He gestured to her depleted flower display. "You've had a good day?"

"*Non.* I gave them away." She took Éclair's lead and scratched the mane between his ears. "I've decided not to sell flowers anymore, Henri. I'm sorry."

"What do you mean?" Henri paced away, then turned back as he pushed his shock of blond hair back from his face. "You cannot quit. If I do not sell the remaining stock, I will lose my broker position." He inhaled deeply, rested his hands on his hips and softened his voice. "Aubrielle, the petals of these lilies are so exquisite, their fragrance so rare, that their scent will make you cry. I promise you, people will fight to have a bouquet from your cart."

"Who will fight, Henri?" She shook her head. "There is no one here. Besides, I have no means to buy your exquisite greenhouse flowers."

"You don't understand how important this is for me." Henri gripped her arm. "My uncle—"

"*Arrêtez*, Henri." Aubrielle pulled away and put Éclair between them. "You have been my friend, but this behavior must stop."

Henri's jaw clenched as he glared at Aubrielle. Without another word, he stalked away around the curved walkway.

Aubrielle glanced around. Henri's words and actions were out of character. Threatening.

Is there no police nearby?

She had come a third of the way around the long arching walkway. The path had become too narrow to turn Éclair and the cart around. The bright day and the colorful leaves overhead no longer lifted her spirits.

What if Henri refuses to leave me alone?

Just past the apex of the arch, she spotted the croissant vendor. He rested on the curb beside his pushcart rubbing his leg.

"Are you all right, *monsieur?*" Aubrielle left Éclair and hurried to the injured man.

"*Oui. Oui.* It is just the *petit chien.*" The man looked up at Aubrielle and shook his head. "My employer insisted I bring his new puppy to the park with me today. Now he's run away." The seller massaged his right leg and grimaced. "I injured myself chasing him through the bushes." He waved his other hand behind him.

Along the edge of the park grew thick rows of hedges lined by trees—intended to shield the park from the city and give the illusion of an oasis amid the busy Parisian downtown. Narrow steps led up to the street, a small landing at each plateau.

"Oh no! Is he friendly?" Aubrielle hurried up to the first landing and bent to look beneath the hedge. The hedgerows were planted far enough apart to allow gardeners to walk between them. "Will he come to me?"

The vendor limped up the steps behind her. "He ran that way." He pointed between the row of bushes.

"What is his name?" Aubrielle eased between the break in the handrail and took several steps along the hedgerow. She crouched down to peer beneath the bushes.

"Gullible."

Aubrielle turned her head toward the vendor just as he shoved her to the ground.

The weight of his knee pressed her body into the soft loam. One hand gripped her face, covering her mouth while he pulled her head back at a painful angle. "I've watched you, *jolie fleur*, every day for months. Selling your blossoms. Smiling at soldiers."

The tall bushes shielded her from both the park and the street. Mrs. Moroney's warning flashed through her mind as the man's nails scraped up her thigh beneath her coat.

"Shall we open the petals of your *fleur secrète* and touch your sweet dew, *ma chère?*"

She tried to bite his palm as she struggled to throw his weight from her back.

"Bitch." He slammed her face into the ground. "I shall enjoy this."

Dirt and twigs filled her mouth, and she screamed. Cold air chilled her skin as he held her head down with one hand and yanked up her skirt and coat with the other.

Chapter 9

John Larson

From his bedroom window, John watched his new Agaria leave for the park. He slipped his arms into his overcoat as he hurried out the door, down the stairs, and into the street. Near the tower, he purchased a newspaper from a boy while keeping an eye on her cart.

She stopped where he had first seen her, along the edge of the central walkway, not far from the park entrance.

He chose a bench on the other side of the expansive concrete entryway from where she set up her cart and shook open the paper. He pretended to read the newsprint while he kept his attention on his love.

Although John could read and speak French like a native Parisian, he wasn't sure about current French law. He'd been conscripted into military service before and had no intention of getting caught up in the war he knew was coming. To pose as a Brit, or continue as an American entrepreneur, like he had told the butcher, would gain him the advantage of citizenship abroad. He held no personal loyalty to any nation. He'd seen too many come and go. His only concern was the well-being of the lovely flower girl.

I must learn her name.

Foolish didn't begin to describe the situation. Throughout their many first meetings, he had never encountered this problem. She wouldn't look at him or speak to him. The only thing he could do was remain close enough to intercede on her behalf. Confident the Polish invasion was what had triggered the magic, he had time. Time to make her acquaintance. Time to convince her to love him again. Time to stalk her around the large Paris park.

When she unblocked her cart and led her pony south along the plaza, John rose and followed. He watched the dark-haired young woman as she handed out bouquets to passersby.

She's giving away her flowers.

He saw the way she smiled and chatted with strangers.

Something has changed for her. Her heart has lifted.

She crossed the street that cut through the square and continued toward the war college on the far side of the *Champ-de-Mars*.

John used his long stride to get ahead of her. He took a seat beside a cadet on a park bench, shook his newspaper into place, and peered over the top as she came near the corner where he sat.

She paused in front of the college and gave away two small bouquets to young servicemen. After they had left, she turned the cart in the direction of the tower and led her pony up the long arching walkway that curved toward the edge of the park.

He folded his paper, prepared to follow when the blond-haired man she had spoken with yesterday rushed up the path and disappeared around the pony cart. John clenched his jaw and rose to his feet.

The cart stopped along the passage, but the curve in the walkway hid most of it behind by bright autumn foliage.

When the vehicle moved, John stepped around the bench to follow. Any moment, he would lose sight of the flower cart altogether.

A woman with one arm around a grocery bag pulled a child across his course.

The little boy stared upward at the red helium-filled balloon floating above his head.

"Allons, viens avec moi, Tomas." The woman turned to tug the child's hand, and several apples slipped from the top of her bag.

A bone-deep shiver crawled along John's spine.

No!

The woman's lips moved without sound.

John attempted to take a breath, but the winter air caught in his throat. His heart pounded rapidly in his chest. Time wound to a standstill and the familiar high-pitched whine underscored the piercing pain that shot through John's head.

Three apples hung suspended in their fall to the ground. Her tug had loosed the balloon from the little boy's hand, and the string hung just beyond his pudgy fingertips.

A second call?

A small corner of the flower cart remained visible on the path, as the crushing pain in his head coalesced between his eyes.

He began to run as soon as the magic released time. The mother's exclamation and the young boy's cry fell behind him as he raced up the path. He reached the front of the cart and stopped. No one stood on the walkway except the pony. The urgent sting on his forehead pointed to the steps up to the street. When he ducked around the small horse, he caught sight of movement in the bushes.

Long bounds brought him to the landing on the steps. Two people struggled in the dirt between the hedgerows. Anger boiled from his chest in a primitive cry of rage. He hopped the handrail, grabbed the man on the ground by the hair and lifted him up and away from the woman.

From the corner of his eye, he saw her move on the ground. The pain on his forehead dispelled as his fist landed a solid blow to the man's face. With his second blow, the cartilage in the stranger's nose dissolved. The third blow sent him into the bushes to collapse in an unmoving heap on the ground.

John clutched the man to finish him. Her whimper made him

hesitate.

Leaves and dirt clung to her face and mixed with the blood that ran freely from her nose. She had backed against the bushes, both hands covering her mouth as if to smother her anguish. Her wide eyes captured him. Dark irises swam in tears, until the liquid spilled, scoring a trail through the grime on her cheek.

John's heart surged with sympathy and sadness.

My Agaria.

He thrust the man into the dirt behind him, ignoring the curious people who gathered on the landing drawn by his savage cry.

He dropped to his haunches before the dark-haired flower girl, his hands on his knees.

She pushed her heels into the dirt, pressing herself further into the bushes.

"I won't hurt you." He kept his voice low and calm, although rage and terror clawed at his throat. "You know that." He raised an eyebrow and smiled. "Somewhere inside, you know I'll never hurt you."

Her gaze found his, then flicked to the man who lay behind him in a heap.

"Don't look at him, *ma chère*. He will never harm you again." John held his hand out to her. "Look at me, instead."

The shrill rattle of a whistle sounded nearby.

"The police are almost here." John swallowed back the endearment on his tongue and in his heart. His words would only confuse and frighten her more. "You are safe. Let me help you stand."

Ma bien-aimée.

Her terrified panting had slowed. She lowered her hands from her mouth and tipped her head to one side. Her lips trembled as she spoke. "He said he lost the puppy."

"It was a ruse. A trick." He wiggled the fingers of his open hand. "Come. I'll take you home." He could sense more people had gathered on the steps behind his back, yet he refused to look away from her eyes. "My name is John."

"John," she breathed. "John." She reached for his hand, never taking her gaze from his. "I don't... How do I? Do I know you, John?" Her scraped and torn hand touched his.

For the second time in the last few minutes, John's breath caught in his throat. He swallowed and nodded as he took a firmer grip on her hand and helped her stand. "In a way."

"*Reculez, s'il vous plaît.*" The commanding voice shouted beyond the crowd.

Her eyes widened as she peeked around John's arm.

He pulled a handkerchief from his inside coat pocket and handed it to her. "Are you injured, *ma chère?* Should I ask the police to call a doctor?"

She wiped her forehead and nose. "No. I'm not injured." She shook her head as her dark eyes filled with tears. "Thank you, John. I... He..." Her breath caught in a sob.

"You're safe now." John put his arm around her heaving shoulders as she leaned into him. "No one will harm you, I promise." He pushed his back into the bushes so she could see around him. "The police will want to speak with you. If they ask me your name..."

"Aubri—" She coughed and ducked her head. She wiped her face again. Her attention strayed to the crowd of curious faces. "Aubrielle Cohen."

On the ground between them and the landing lay Aubrielle's attacker. The merchant pushed himself to his hands and knees raising his hate-filled glare to Aubrielle.

When the vendor moved, Aubrielle gripped the lapels of John's unbuttoned coat.

The officer broke through the crowd and stared at the merchant on the ground. Then his attention shifted to Aubrielle's terrified grip on John's jacket. With a toss of his chin, he spoke to John, "What happened here?"

"The man," John spoke in English, his words hoarse with pent-up emotion, "attacked this woman. When she cried out, I came to her aid."

Aubrielle turned her face away from the staring crowd.

"Is she injured?" The officer walked around the assailant then knelt, jabbing a knee into the man's back.

"No. Only frightened." John ran his hand down her back, brushing twigs and leaves from her coat.

"Aubrielle?" The blond-haired man pushed to the front of the spectators.

Aubrielle stiffened in John's arms. Her face remained away from the onlookers, pressed against his shirt.

"Remain here," the officer instructed to John. "Officer Sarchet will require your names and a statement." He handcuffed the man on the ground, gripped the vendor's arm, and pulled him roughly to his feet. "This one comes with me."

As soon as the officer pushed the attacker through the throng of people, Aubrielle's blond friend pushed through the break in the rail, only to be shoved back by Officer Sarchet.

"Stay back, *s'il vous plaît.*" Officer Sarchet blocked his path.

"But I know her."

The officer withdrew a pad and pencil from his pocket, ignoring the man at his back, and addressed John, "Your names."

"I'm John Larson."

"*Un Américain?*" Officer Sarchet made a note at John's nod and looked to Aubrielle. *"Et vous, mademoiselle?*

Aubrielle had turned her head when the officer spoke. Her head and her hand rested against John's chest. "Aubrielle Cohen."

Officer Sarchet took down their addresses and a brief statement of what happened in his notepad. "Is there someone we can contact to verify your information, *Monsieur* Larson?

"My attorney in the States is Monroe James." John gave the officer the telephone number.

"Do you require a doctor?" Officer Sarchet asked Aubrielle as he closed his notepad.

Aubrielle shook her head. "*Non. Merci.*"

"I'll see she gets home." John held Aubrielle's elbow as she passed through the opening in the rail onto the landing.

Most of the crowd had disbursed, but Aubrielle's gentleman friend remained. He reached to take Aubrielle's arm as she stepped onto the walkway.

Aubrielle pulled back, leaning against John. "Henri, I've no wish to argue with you right now."

"I must know if you are uninjured." Henri's survey lifted from Aubrielle's face to John's. "Who is your new friend?"

"I'm an old friend." John gave Henri a hard smile. "I'll make sure Aubrielle gets home safely." John edged between Henri and Aubrielle and supported her as they descended to the arched walkway and her cart.

"I'll stop by your house to check on you," Henri called.

Chapter 10

Aubrielle Cohen

Aubrielle couldn't stop trembling.

What's wrong with me?

She replied to the officer's questions with John Larson's handkerchief tight beneath her nose.

I'm freezing.

Tears slipped from her eyes, and she dabbed them in frustration. In an instant, trust in her self-judgment had been taken from her.

Was this my fault?

The warmth of John's hand beneath her elbow reached through her coat. His touch provided comfort, strength, and support. If she could have huddled inside his jacket—her bruised face tight to his chest until the shudders stopped—she would have.

She recognized Henri as he reached for her arm. Without thought, she leaned back against the solid comfort of the American. "Henri, I've no wish to argue with you right now."

John angled her toward the step, away from the crowd, and Henri slipped from her mind.

"I'm an old friend." The rumble of his deep voice was a pleasure and reassurance against her back. "I'll make sure Aubrielle gets home safely."

Was he an old friend?

The familiar embrace of his arm around her shoulder unsettled and confused her.

Is this déjà vu?

His touch and voice were at odds with her reasoning. She'd never met John Larson before.

I would remember him.

As he helped her onto the pony cart's front seat, Aubrielle couldn't recall the last time she'd sat on the bench behind her pony.

Had Mama still been alive?

John looked at her old pony, checked the straps and breast collar, and then glanced back at her and raised one brow.

"There are no reins, only a lead." She sniffed, shivered, and pulled her coat tight around her throat. "I always walk beside Éclair." Bits of leaves and soil clung to her jacket, and she brushed at the material, only to realize the contact stung her palms. The heels of her hands were scraped raw from her ordeal. For a moment, she couldn't look away from her injuries. His voice brought her head up.

"Éclair?" John chuckled as he patted the small horse's neck and scratched the hair along his crest. "He doesn't mind being named after a pastry?" John grinned at Aubrielle.

A short laugh mixed with a sob escaped, and she pressed her knuckles against her lips. She shook her head. "*Non.* Mama named him."

"Well, then. Come along, Éclair. Let's take our Lady home."

She rested her sight on the width of his shoulders as he led Éclair through the park. Without prompting, he turned along the Seine and crossed the Alma Bridge.

Uneasiness curled in her stomach, and she sat straighter, staring a hole in his back. She had seen the American before, watching her through the fog at the park, and again, standing at the window, outlined by light.

"You followed me," her voice choked out. She cleared her

throat. "Stop!" She rapped her knuckles against the wooden seat. "Is that how you know where I live? You followed me home?" Panic turned to nausea, and she swallowed a bitter lump in her throat.

John eased Éclair to a halt along the side of the road. He stroked the pony's neck, then squinted up at Aubrielle, sunlight bright on his face. "I bought a bouquet of lilies from you yesterday." He shrugged and watched a couple cross the street, arm in arm. "I know no one in Paris. I had hoped to speak to you and ask if you knew of an apartment for rent near the park." John ran his hand across his mouth and faced her. "But you hurried off before I could make your acquaintance."

Aubrielle leaned forward and whispered at him, aware of the people around them. "So you followed me home? Do you think that is acceptable?" Aubrielle blinked. For a split second, an American cowboy stood before her, one hand on his hip, while the other rubbed along his chin. The image so clear, she gasped, and her heart clenched. Her eyes fluttered in time with her heart, and the tall, well-dressed man who saved her in the park stroked Éclair once again.

"It shames me to admit it." John bowed his head. "But I did follow you home." He looked into her eyes and held out his hand in supplication. "I never meant to frighten you." His face and eyes were sincere. "And I would never harm you." He dropped his arm to his side. "I rented an apartment not far from where you live, and I returned to the park today to introduce myself." He shook his head. His eyes pleaded with her to understand. "I didn't even know your name."

Aubrielle pulled her dark hair back from her face. A breeze had picked up, and she crossed her arms across her chest, chilled in the cold sunlight. "Just take us home."

John nodded, and without comment, continued to lead Éclair down the street.

He walked beside her pony until they reached her back gate. He opened it and waited as Éclair pulled the cart into the yard. As she passed, their gazes met.

She looked away. "You don't need to stay. I can take care of Éclair."

"I'll look after your animal," he said as he closed the gate. "But first, I'll see you inside with your feet up and a warm drink in your hand."

Her brows rose at his audacity. "*Non,* you shall not." She scooted to the edge of the high seat and began the short climb to the ground. Her arms felt unaccountably weak and her knees burned when her legs bent. In the short drop from the cart, her ankle caught wrong and twisted. She yelped in surprise and pain, but instead of falling to the ground, strong arms captured her.

"You couldn't wait for my help?" He lifted her and settled her weight against his chest. "You're always so stubborn." He walked past the small horse and mounted the stairs to the residence.

Aubrielle put her arms around his neck and ducked her head. It was too much. She ached from head to toe and continued to tremble. She'd been shoved into the dirt and attacked, and now her savior, her knight, called her stubborn.

Tante Mae opened the door at the top of the stairs. "Saints, what's happened to the lass?"

Her neighbor's voice, so familiar and filled with concern, brought Aubrielle's head up and she pressed her lips to stop them from quivering.

John carried Aubrielle through the door and into the front parlor.

Mae followed them into the room.

"Aubrielle was attacked at the park." He sat her in a well-worn green armchair and pulled the footstool close. "The police arrested the man, but Aubrielle still needs care."

"I don't need your care." Aubrielle's voice splintered. She covered her face and gave in to the tears.

John rose from his crouch beside Aubrielle and held out his

hand to the older woman. "John Larson."

"Mae Moroney." *Tante* Mae grasped his fingers for a moment. "Please, call me Mae." She released John and ran her hand along the back of Aubrielle's head. "Where are you hurt, child?"

"I'm not." Aubrielle turned away and gulped into the handkerchief.

"Her hands and knees are skinned. They need to be cleaned and bandaged. Her nose and chin look scraped as well." John removed his overcoat and tossed it onto the couch. "She twisted her ankle just now, and I thought I saw a scratch on her right thigh."

Aubrielle's watery look jumped to John as he spoke. "What?" she whispered and pulled up her skirt. The three long inflamed scratches from thigh to panty shocked her. Her mouth fell open as she glared at the proof of her violation. *"Non. Non. Non."* The room spun, and her heart fluttered.

Warm hands captured her face. Dark kind eyes, filled with sadness and understanding stared into hers. "Breathe, Aubrielle," his voice, soft and low. Intimate. "Mrs. Moroney will clean your scrapes and bandage your leg." His thumb brushed a tear from her cheekbone. "You are home. You are safe."

Pots clanked in the kitchen as *Tante* Mae filled a pan with water and set it on the stove to heat.

Aubrielle exhaled. She placed her hands over his, relishing the warmth and nodded. *"Oui.* You are right."

"I will stand between you and every terror in the world, but I can't when the terror is inside your mind." He brushed the hair from her forehead. "There is a warrior in you. I've seen her. She's strong and stubborn."

Aubrielle shook her head. "Warriors don't cry."

"That's not true, my dear. Warriors do cry, and they know fear." He offered her a smile as he moved back to let Mae take his place. "But they don't let fear win."

Tante Mae set the tub of soapy water beside the footstool, then helped Aubrielle out of her coat. "Here ye' go, darlin'. Let's clean you up a bit."

The hot water both stung and felt divine on her cold hands. Goosebumps marched up her arms, and she shivered. Whatever magic John's words held had helped. The tight knot of panic inside loosened. Her gaze caught his just as *Tante* Mae took hold of her chin to clean her face.

"What's this? What's happened?" Aubrielle's father tottered into the room. His trousers hung on his thin frame by narrow black suspenders. His sleeveless undershirt stained from breakfast. Her Papa stopped short and stared at John. His mouth fell open, and his eyes widened.

Tante Mae handed Aubrielle the washcloth and stepped around the footstool. "All is well, Lou. Your girl took a tumble in the park, and we're cleaning her up."

"Marguerite?" He blinked red-rimmed eyes at Aubrielle, then lifted his shaking veined hand and pointed at John. "I remember you."

"Papa isn't well," Aubrielle told John.

Tante Mae gripped Lou's shoulders. "Lou, this is Aubrielle's friend, John Larson. He's over from America." She nodded at John. "John, this is Aubrielle's father, Lou Cohen. He isn't feeling his best right now." Mae guided Papa toward the kitchen. "Are you hungry, Lou? It's almost time to eat."

The old man shuffled toward the kitchen staring over his shoulder at John. "I remember you, sir. I haven't forgotten."

Chapter 11

John Larson

"Who does he think I am?" John asked in a hushed voice as Mae Moroney ushered Aubrielle's father into the kitchen. John's gaze dropped to Aubrielle, and the desire to fall to his knees and take the washcloth from her torn hands surged inside his chest.

I wish she remembered me.

Aubrielle dabbed her skinned knee with the wet cloth. "It's hard to tell." Her tangled hair swung as she shook her head, then she looked up at John through long dark strands. "Perhaps an officer he knew in the war?" She glanced toward the kitchen and shrugged. Concern clouded her large dark eyes. "He's getting worse."

John gave up trying to maintain his distance and dropped to his knees beside the chair. He held out his hand for the washcloth. "Let me do that."

"*Non, non.*" Aubrielle hooked a long curl behind her ear. "I made a terrible mistake today, *monsieur*. I trusted." She shook her head and her expressive eyes filled with sadness. "Now you ask for me to trust again. I am unsure—and more so—I am embarrassed by such kindness." She released a deep breath and lowered her chin. The rosy tint in her cheeks confirmed her words.

"Don't be." His hand trembled as he placed her foot on his thigh. "The water has run down your leg and into your stocking."

He untied her shoelace, set the saddle shoe aside, and rolled the ankle-high hosiery over her heel. "You're still too cold." He clasped both hands around her foot and silently caught his breath as her chilled skin touched his. The ache in his chest crawled his throat, and he blinked to clear the moisture from his vision.

Aubrielle shuddered and closed her eyes. "You cannot know how delightful that feels," she whispered as she leaned her head back.

John cleared his throat. "You've had a shock. We need to keep you warm." He lowered her foot into the hot water, stood, and pulled the crocheted blanket from the back of the couch and draped it around Aubrielle's shoulders. "Now the other foot."

"Why do you do this for me?" Her eyes fluttered open, and her gaze followed his movements.

John set her sock and shoe aside and lowered her other foot into the warm water. "Why?" He raised a brow and smiled. "There's a long answer and a short one. The long one is filled with tales of adventure and damsels in distress and should wait for a better time." He picked up the washcloth from the water then glanced up to find her curious gaze following his every move.

"Anyone would have helped you at the park, Miss Cohen. I was simply the closest and heard your cry." He squeezed the water from the cloth and wiped the dirt from her knee. "As for helping you home, and cleaning your legs—what man could say no to this?" He raised his brow at her bare feet and winked.

"Now you play the fool to make me laugh." Aubrielle matched his grin.

Mae set a small bottle of Merthiolate on the side table. "I'll take care of the rest, Mr. Larson. I'm familiar with treating injuries." She took the washcloth from his hands. "I was a nurse during the Great War." She knelt beside the washtub. "Dinner is at seven. We don't dress but try not to be late. Lou likes his meals on time."

"Thank you." John shrugged into his coat. "But there's no need to feel you must repay me."

"Nonsense." Mae held the medicine dauber suspended above Aubrielle's knee. "It's the least we can do. Brie is like a daughter to me."

Aubrielle touched his arm as he passed the chair. "Thank you again, Mr. Larson." Her attention darted back to the red drop of antiseptic above her knee. "I would like you to have dinner with us as well."

"All right. But please, call me John. Both of you."

Mae gave a short nod and turned to Aubrielle. "This will sting, darlin'."

Aubrielle buried her face in the blanket. "I know," came the muffled reply.

John hurried from the room, through the kitchen to the back door.

Aubrielle's father looked up from his lunch as John strode past. "Good to see you again, sir."

John paused at the door and studied Lou Cohen, certain he had never met the man before today.

A wisp of gray hair hung from Lou's balding head and dangled between his eyes. Skin blemishes covered his head and hands. Both trembled as he struggled to lift the utensil to his mouth. His dark eyes shone as he tipped his head and his attention shifted to the soup. The bright light of recognition faded from his face. He stared vacantly at his empty spoon.

Aubrielle's yelp from the front room encouraged John to grip the door handle and hurry from the house.

After he had taken care of Éclair, the afternoon stretched before him, empty time until he could be with the woman who owned his heart again. He made his way down the alleyway and across the street. He strolled through the market and purchased a bottle of wine to gift Mrs. Moroney for tonight's dinner. He passed a flower cart and smiled. Aubrielle would not appreciate a floral present.

He stopped at the tailor and waited to be measured for another shirt. The tailor found three shirts intended for tall men and assured

John the alterations could be completed in an hour.

Down the row, he entered a tanner's shop. Leather wallets and hats filled the wall to his right. Since he already had a belt and wallet, he turned to leave when a display case of women's leather gloves caught his eye.

"*Avez-vous trouvé quelque chose à votre goût?*" The clerk reached into the case and laid several pairs of gloves on the glass top.

"*Oui.*" John tapped the glass above a pair still inside the case. "I would like to see the white ones."

The clerk pursed his lips when John switched to English. "These are size six, ivory-white kid gloves. The reverse seam stitching around the fingers and down the side is exquisite." He laid the gloves on the counter. "As you can see, there is raised wave stitching on the back of the hands, a lovely detail."

John lifted a glove and placed it on his palm. From his wrist, the longest finger of the glove barely brushed the inside of his first knuckle.

The length is perfect.

"Can they be exchanged if the size is wrong?" His regard rose to the young man.

The salesclerk nodded. "But of course." He reached below the case and retrieved a shallow box. "Would you have this wrapped with a bow?"

"*Oui, s'il vous plaît.*" John paid for his purchase, picked up his shirts from the tailor, and returned to his flat.

On the landing outside his door, he rearranged the packages in his arms to search his pocket for the key. Inside his apartment, he looked out the window at the back of Aubrielle's home. The late afternoon sun cast long shadows across the alley and glinted from her back window. He grinned in anticipation of presenting her with her soft new gloves. If she'd worn these this morning, her hands would not have become scratched by twigs and mulch.

He set the packages on the couch, and his cheerful mood

evaporated. Her life, so precious and fragile, would flash by soon enough compared with his. He exhaled through clenched teeth and pressed the heels of his palms into his eyes.

I've missed her so much. To lose her now would be unbearable.

The foreknowledge he had of the coming war did not provide the specific details he needed. Vague dates and a rough outline of the conflict had been miraculous when he received the prophetic information sixty years ago.

I must convince Aubrielle to leave France. To leave Europe altogether and return with me to America.

He glanced across the room at the clock on the dresser. The tick of the second hand caught his attention. He'd gone from having too much time, an eternity of waiting, to an uncertain amount of time to take Aubrielle to safety.

John shook his head as he loosened his tie. He pulled the cloth from beneath his shirt collar and tossed it on the couch beside the packages. For now, for tonight, he need only wash, change his shirt, and be on time for dinner with his love. He had to secure her heart before he could secure her future.

The afternoon's winter sky had darkened into the night as John prepared for dinner with Aubrielle and her family. A bath and one of the new shirts he'd purchased had him feeling like a new man. Anything was possible.

Aubrielle is alive and well and will remain that way as long as I am by her side.

He smoothed back his hair in the mirror and straightened his tie.

Faltering footsteps pounded up the stairs. Instead of a knock, a heavy thump stressed the hinges, then a scrape down the door to the landing.

John opened the door and stared in disbelief as Billy, the British smuggler, fell across the threshold.

A dark stain bled down the left side of Billy's slacks. "They've shot François." He blinked up at John then grimaced as he curled, holding his side and gasped. "We need your help."

* * *

Aubrielle Cohen

Aubrielle stood at the front window long after *Tante* Mae had called her to supper.

He didn't come.

She listened absently to the stilted conversation between Mae and Papa in the kitchen. Beside her, the radio played an orchestral song she recognized, but couldn't name at the moment.

Purple something, I think, or is it blue?

A sudden thought sparked, and she spun from the window and hurried to her room at the back of the house.

Both *Tante* Mae and Papa raised their heads from supper to watch her stalk through the kitchen.

Where could he be?

Aubrielle pushed back the drapes from her window and stared at the darkened apartment across the alleyway. John had rented the vacant apartment above the butcher. He'd acknowledged as much when he admitted to following her this morning.

Had that really been just this morning?

It felt as though a lifetime had passed waiting to see him again.

She let her bedroom curtains fall back into place and retraced her steps into the front room.

Why hasn't he come?

The sharp rap at the door propelled her headlong back through the kitchen, her stomach aflutter. Her rapid pace pulled at the bandages on her knees.

"Qu'est-ce que c'est?" Her father looked up in confusion from his plate.

"My gracious, child. No need to run." *Tante* Mae wiped her lips with her napkin. "Invite Mr. Larson in. His place is set."

Unable to hide the wide grin on her face, Aubrielle pulled open

73

the door and blinked.

Henri Vogl held up a handful of wilted lilies. "I told you I would stop over and check on you." He looked past Aubrielle into the house. "What is that amazing aroma?"

"Don't make him stand out on the porch, Aubrielle, invite him in. His supper is getting cold." *Tante* Mae came to a sudden stop as she entered the cloak room. Her mouth formed an awkward O as she stared at the unexpected guest.

"*Merci beaucoup*." Henri stepped through the door and thrust what appeared to be the last of Aubrielle's flowers into her hands. "These are for you." He removed his hat and nodded at *Tante* Mae. "Supper would be delightful. Thank you."

Chapter 12

John Larson

John pulled the British smuggler across the threshold and closed the door. He dropped to one knee and tried to open Billy's coat.

The smuggler groaned and curled tighter, wrapping his arms around his side.

John gripped the man's arm. "Let me see where you're hurt."

Billy's scrunched eyes barely opened, and he stared at John. "He said we could trust you," he panted through tight lips.

"Who said you could trust me? François?" John glanced at the door then back to Billy. "Is he with you?"

Billy shook his head. "He was, mate." He gasped and rolled to his back with a grimace, opened his arms and let his head loll back against the hardwood floor. "But I couldn't get him out."

"Out of where?" John opened the smuggler's coat and noted the slick red blood that soaked the Brit's clothes. He tore open his shirt and found the small round hole. "You need a doctor."

"Gah!" Billy gasped as he raised his head and winced at the bullet hole in his side. "There's no time. We've got to go back for François."

John left Billy on the floor and searched the kitchen drawers. He returned with a clean but discolored dishtowel and pressed it to the bullet wound. "Hold this tight." He moved Billy's hand to the towel.

The smuggler's head dropped back to the floor, and he bared his teeth, gritting against the pressure on his wound. "I can't leave him. He'll die."

A firm thump from the floor below hushed their conversation.

John opened the paper-wrapped package of his last new shirt and ripped the material into long strips. "Keep your voice down. The butcher lives below me." John cast a brief glance out the window at the light in the house across the alleyway. "Keep the padding tight while I—improvise." John steadied Billy's hand on the towel, then pulled the torn strip of cloth beneath the arch in the smuggler's back. "Tell me what this is about. How did you know where to find me? Start at the beginning."

Billy nodded. "After you got out of the truck by the river, I followed you."

The fog had been thick off the Seine that morning, sounds muted by the moisture. The only way John had found Aubrielle was by the painful magic that pointed toward her. He hadn't suspected the smuggler stalked him. "Why would you—" John held up his hand. "Never mind. Go on."

"I trailed you and the flower girl. Heard you ask the butcher about the flat." He caught his breath as John tightened the binding.

John wrapped a second strip of linen around the smuggler's waist and tied the ends. The bleeding had slowed, but the bullet remained inside and would need to be removed. He helped the smuggler sit against the wall then filled a glass with water from the kitchen sink. "Sorry, but I've nothing stronger." He handed Billy the glass. "Who shot you?"

"That's the rub then, ain't it?" He took a sip, cringed. "There's no reason to have dealt with those blokes. I told François that very thing." His face tightened with pain, but he'd caught his breath, and his words were less halting when he spoke. "We shipped most of the weapons north to François's contact with the army." He studied his bandage then looked up at John. "François held back a dozen maybe. Said he wanted to broker a new deal with a new buyer." He clenched his eyes closed. "I don't know why."

John sat on the couch. "That makes no sense. All of the guns were for the French Army. Why split the shipment?" He shook his head. "And what would make François decide you could trust me?"

Billy took another sip. "As to the weapons—I've asked that same question." He set the glass on the floor and rubbed his mouth. "But that was François's decision." His eyes squinted as he peered at John, and then he shrugged. "As for trusting you, it's because of Keats."

"Master Keats?" John leaned forward and tipped his head. "What does she have to do with this?"

"Not the missus." Billy shook his head. "Her husband, Nigel."

John raised a brow at the smuggler. "I happen to know Master Keats is a widow."

"Aye, she is. But her husband, Nigel, was best mates with François during the Great War." Billy swallowed. "They were all good friends back then; Nigel, François, and Ken Rice." Billy dropped his gaze to the floor. "François said Ken stepped up to watch over Nigel's wife after his best mate disappeared."

John stood and paced to the room. "From what I know, Master Keats doesn't require watching over." He stood silent for a moment, then spoke over his shoulder. "Besides, even if all this is true, it still doesn't explain—"

"You sailed aboard the Giselle-Marie with Nigel's wife. You were armed and set ashore in France by Ken Rice, himself." Billy sat straighter and grunted with the effort. "Recommendations don't come much higher than that to François, mate." He struggled to his feet and leaned heavily against the wall, gasping. "We need to go back for him."

"You have a bullet in your side."

"It will keep. It has too." Billy took a step forward. "I can't leave him there to die."

John nodded and picked up his coat.

"You should take your gun." The smuggler staggered away from the wall and buttoned his jacket over the torn and bloodied shirt.

John dropped his overcoat on the couch. In the bedroom, he removed the weapon and shoulder harness from the dresser drawer. Pulling the holster straps over his shoulder, he adjusted the chest strap, checked the load in the snub-nose, then slipped the gun into the holster. "Where are we going?" John returned to the front room, shrugged on his overcoat and put on his hat.

Billy's face remained pale, but his light-colored eyes were clear. He opened the door, and cold air from the stairwell eased into the room. "An abandoned warehouse along the Marne River, southeast of the city."

John turned off the light and followed Billy onto the landing and locked the door. "How do you propose we get there?"

Billy held tight to the railing as he lowered himself carefully to each new step. "We'll have to hail a cab, mate."

"I'm not your bloody mate, Billy." John pointed toward the alley. "We'll cut through the back way and find a cab on the boulevard." He put his arm around the young smuggler, thankful Billy was both tall and thin. "Let's pick up a bottle of cognac before we hail a taxi."

"I could use a drink."

"I want you to smell drunk, not be drunk." They rounded the building and continued down the ruelle. John looked over Billy's head toward Aubrielle's back door. On the stoop stood the pretty boy from the park, flowers in hand. The house passed from view as the door swung opened.

Damn.

On the boulevard, John stopped outside a tobacco shop. "Lean against the light pole. I'll be back." Once inside, he purchased a half liter of cognac from the merchant. He opened the bottle as he exited the shop and handed the liquor to Billy. "Take a sip and spill some on your coat."

"What a waste." Billy tipped the glass flask to his lips then splashed his jacket. He took another quick taste and handed the bottle back to John. "There's a cab down the way."

John hailed the taxi and Billy gave the driver directions.

The driver sniffed at them suspiciously, but eventually gave a nod and put the car into gear.

Billy laid his head back against the leather seat and exhaled loudly. "I could use another nip."

John met the cabbie's eyes in the mirror. "Maybe you should wait until we get out."

John paid the driver when he pulled to a stop, and then helped Billy from the cab.

The driver sped off down the dark road before John could ask him to wait. "You won't make the walk back to the apartment."

"I won't need to." Billy followed the old building along the road toward the river. He pointed ahead into the darkness. "The truck's still here." His voice was low, gauged for only John's ear.

John nodded and pulled his gun from the holster.

Billy stopped at the edge of the warehouse and peeked around the building. "They're gone." He staggered away from the structure and crossed to the truck, limping as he held his side.

John glanced around the corner into an open area beside the dock. The cold night was quiet with only the sound of the river. He could smell the faintest hint of gunpowder in the still air. "Did they take the guns?"

"They couldn't have. We only brought three weapons."

John crossed the dirt road to the vehicle. "Then this wasn't the meeting for the trade?"

"Aye, it was." Billy leaned against the passenger door. "The first meeting. We brought samples to prove their quality."

John eyed the abandoned work area, then dropped to his haunches and studied the ground. "What went wrong?" He picked up a spent shell casing and dropped it into his pocket. From this angle, he could see several casings scattered near the truck.

"François stayed here while I met in the open with their leader." He brushed the back of his hand against John's jacket. "I could use another taste. It warms the belly."

John handed him the bottle. "Keep it."

Billy took a quick drink. "I should have come back for François, but we were yards apart when the first shots were fired."

"Who fired the shots?"

"I don't know, mate. "He pointed into the darkness. "I met their leader, a man named René. He'd just handed me the francs in exchange for the three weapons when I heard a shout, then gunfire." Billy shifted his gaze to John. "René thought we betrayed them. I saw that much before I was hit."

"You weren't armed?"

"No. The men who make the exchange never are." He pointed toward the clearing. "From where I stood, it sounded like the gunfire came from back here, but it was hard to tell with the echo." He gripped the open window and peered into the cab of the vehicle. "Why would they take François?" He shook his head.

"Maybe they didn't. He may have taken shelter in one of the buildings." John lifted his gun and moved into the open, away from the truck. "Wait here. I'll have a look around."

Chapter 13

Aubrielle Cohen

Aubrielle held the napkin to her lips and watched Henri finish the last of *Tante* Mae's tasty shepherd's pie. Most of her friends, the ones who had stopped associating with her when her father's illness advanced, would have been thrilled to have Henri Vogl seated at their table for dinner.

Foolish girls, for more than one reason.

Henri caught her stare and winked. His confident grin a testament to how wonderful he thought he was.

Aubrielle bristled with annoyance and held firm to good manners. She smiled across the table at *Tante* Mae. "Thank you again for the excellent dinner."

"You're very welcome, my dear." Mae reached over and touched Papa's shoulder as his head dipped toward his plate. "Let's get you to bed, Lou." She helped Aubrielle's father to his feet and guided him toward his room.

"How long does he have left?" Henri asked. He placed his napkin beside his empty plate. "Are you sure he's not contagious?"

Aubrielle pressed her lips into a firm line as her eyebrows rose. "That is certainly a possibility." She rose to her feet. "What a terrible fate that would be for one such as yourself. You should leave now before it's too late."

"Perhaps you're right." Henri nodded and stood, his examination raking Aubrielle as he rose, beginning at the hem of her skirt and lingering on her bruised chin. "It would be almost as bad if his affliction were inborn. I'd hate for my children to suffer that fate."

"It's not an inherited illness," she responded in anger then cooled her tone. "But be assured, even if it were, you wouldn't have to worry."

His grin widened. "I do want children." He trailed her into the front room. "Someday, that is, when I'm ready to settle down." He relaxed on the couch, crossed his legs and extended his arm along the backrest. "Come. Have a seat. You can tell me how handsome you think my children will be. I've found girls like to imagine those sorts of things."

Aubrielle pointed toward the back door. "I'm sorry, Henri. I've had a long and horrible day."

"That's right." Henri leaned forward. "Your little incident in the park." He came to his feet and ran his hands up her arms. "I do hope you're fully recovered. You must be cautious who you flirt with."

Aubrielle blinked in disbelief. "I don't find your jest amusing, Henri." She pushed him away and stalked through the kitchen to the cloak room, Henri close on her heels. Near the door, she shoved his coat into his arms. "Please leave."

Henri shrugged into his coat, a half-amused grin on his face. "I make no jest. I saw your flirtation with the tall American."

"I didn't flirt with John. He helped me home." Aubrielle scowled in exasperation and opened the door. "Henri, just go."

"John, is it?" He turned up his collar and paused beside Aubrielle. "I am glad you are all right, Aubrielle," he said in a softer tone.

"*Merci*, Henri. *Au revoir.*"

Henri hesitated a moment as if he would say something more. Instead, he tipped his head. "*Au revoir,* Aubrielle."

She closed the door behind him and leaned against the frame. Henri was by far the most arrogant man she'd ever met.

Why does he pay attention to me when I've made it clear I'm not interested?

With a shrug, she pushed vain Henri from her thoughts. Curious if John had returned home, she hurried to her room and studied the darkened apartment across the alley. Disappointed, she let the curtain fall and went back to the kitchen.

"Your father is asleep. I'm going home." Mae stood outside Papa's closed door and tied a red scarf around her head. "It's a shame John didn't come to dinner. I wanted to thank him again for his help today."

Aubrielle nodded and cleared the dinner dishes from the table. "I was sure he would come."

"As was I." Mae pulled her coat. "Perhaps we'll hear from him tomorrow and find out what kept him away."

Aubrielle scraped food from the plate into the garbage can and placed the dish in the sink. "Perhaps." She rolled her eyes at the older woman recognizing the amused look on her face. "All right, yes. I hope John provides a good explanation for missing dinner tonight."

"You were disappointed to have the pretty blond lad at your table and not your big Yank."

Aubrielle shrugged one shoulder as she pushed the food from another dinner dish. "Goodnight, *Tante* Mae."

"Goodnight, lass." She grinned as she buttoned the top button on her wool coat and stepped out into the night.

* * *

John Larson

John crossed the open area beside the dock to the nearest warehouse wall and pressed his back against the brick. Away from the shelter of the entrance, the wind blew off the river, and the air was bitter cold. His breath drifted in a plume of steam toward Billy and the truck. The lights from Paris illuminated the low winter clouds, but he was far from the city, along the Marne. Even with his eyesight accustomed to the darkness, only the outlines of the buildings were distinct.

The cluster of warehouses beside the abandoned dock felt empty. Lifeless, except for the scurried movement of a giant river rat.

John moved through the compound, checking each door. All were locked. He surveyed the ground at each intersection for shell casings or footprints but found nothing. After a thorough inspection of the area and buildings, John returned to the truck.

He holstered his weapon and adjusted his coat as he glanced through the truck window at Billy. "No one's here."

Billy spoke from the shadows inside the truck cab, "Why would they take him?" His voice was tight with pain.

John opened the door and settled behind the wheel. "My guess is they want the rest of the weapons. They might think you have more than you do." He took the keys from Billy and started the engine. "And you need medical attention—immediately."

The engine roared to life and John pulled the knob for the headlights. Twin beams cut the darkness, revealing a narrow, paved road to the main thoroughfare.

Billy shook his head. "There would be too many questions."

John put the truck in gear, and they circled toward the main road. "You've got a bullet in your side, kid."

The vehicle bounced onto the higher pavement, and Billy groaned. "The police will detain me and you too, most likely." Billy pulled his hand from inside his coat and stared at his blood-glazed palm. "How do I explain who shot me? They'll arrest us."

John glanced at Billy. "All right. I'll think of something. In the meantime, direct me back to the apartment."

When they reached the butcher shop, John continued to the

corner and turned up the alley. Behind the bakery, he pulled the truck to the side and cut the engine.

"Wait here." John stepped from the car without waiting for Billy's reply. No light came from Aubrielle's home, but that was never his destination, at least not tonight. Without a watch, and beneath a cloudy sky, he could only estimate the time. The light from the bakery window suggested it was early morning. The bakers were already at work.

A light came on in the second-floor residence, and John hurried through the gate and up the back steps. He tapped softly on Mrs. Moroney's back door.

Several moments passed. John was about to knock again when the curtains over the door's glass panel moved.

Mrs. Moroney peered out, her pin curls covered by a sheer night scarf. She blinked and tipped her chin up to view John's face. She disappeared momentarily to unhook the chain then opened the door wide. "My goodness! John Larson. Are you all right?" She clutched her dressing coat tightly to her neck. "Please, come in. It's far too cold to stand outside."

Unwilling to offer explanations from the back stoop, John entered Mae Moroney's warm kitchen.

She closed the door behind him and squinted up at his face. "What's amiss John?"

John pulled the fedora from his head. "Mrs. Moroney—"

"Mae, please."

John smiled at the baker. "Mae. I need your help."

"Anything." She waved towards the table. "Have a seat. I'll put the kettle on."

"It's not your ear I need." He waited until she stopped and looked at him. "It's your nursing skills."

"Whatever is wrong? You look fit as can be."

"It's not me. It's a friend of mine. An acquaintance." He hesitated.

How best to explain Billy?

"Certainly, I'll help. However, I can." She peered past John toward the door. "Where is your friend?"

John glanced at the door, then touched her arm to gain her attention. "His name is Billy. He's been shot."

"Oh my." Mae's hands fluttered to her mouth for a moment, and then her lips thinned. "Is there a reason you didn't take him to the hospital?"

"There is." John spun the brim of his hat in his hands. "Billy was shot while smuggling arms destined for the French Army. Not something the police would view well, even if the cause is just." He studied Mae's face. The decision to help had to be hers. He didn't want his large frame to be an intimidating factor. "There's also a good chance the men who shot Billy are seeking him. A hospital would make him an easy target."

Mae bit her bottom lip between her teeth. Her eyes darted around the kitchen as she slowly lifted her chin and gave a nod. "Aye, bring your friend up. I'll tell the boys downstairs to open without me this mornin'." She reached up to pat her hair and touched the scarf covered pin-curls. "Ack! I'll dress first." She made a shooing motion at John. "Get your friend. I'll leave the door unlocked." She flicked her wrist at the long cook's table in the center of her kitchen. "I'll get this ready. You can put Billy up here." Without waiting for more information, she hurried toward the front of the house.

John rushed out the door and down to the truck. He tossed his hat through the open driver's window, then rounded the vehicle and opened the passenger door. He grasped Billy before he could topple to the ground. "Wake up, Billy. I've found someone to help us."

Billy blinked at John. His brows drew together in confusion. "Where's François?"

John put his shoulder beneath Billy's armpit and stood. The smuggler's toes barely touched the ground. "We'll get to François. Let's take care of you first." John held Billy's wrist with one hand

and gripped the smuggler's belt with the other. He didn't want to put the man over his shoulder for fear he'd drive the bullet deeper. "Stay with me, Billy. We need to go up those stairs."

"I'm going to be sick." Billy's pale skin appeared gray in the light from the back door.

John held Billy around the chest beside the back gate until the heaves stopped, and then again levered Billy's arm over his shoulder and guided him up the back steps.

In the kitchen, Mae had changed into a dark brown dress protected by a full bib apron. The center counter had been cleared, padded with blankets and covered with a shower curtain.

"Take off his coat and help him up there, John. Here's a pillow for his head."

John leaned Billy against the makeshift surgical bed and removed his coat. "He's lost a lot of blood and fortified himself with cognac."

Billy's eyes fluttered, and his knees buckled.

John dropped the jacket and caught Billy as he fainted. Before he fell to the ground, John slipped an arm beneath Billy's knees and lifted the tall, thin Brit to the counter.

Mae waved her hand at Billy's unconscious state. "Just as well to my way of thinking. The lad won't feel a thing."

Beside the stove, next to her cooking utensils, Mae had gathered bandages, gauze wrapping, and a sewing kit. She looked over the items, washed her hands, then faced the young man on her counter. "Let's see what we have now."

She cut away John's temporary bandages and clucked her tongue at the blood-soaked kitchen towel. "I think we can do better than that." She glanced at John. "Do you know if the bullet is still inside the lad?"

John nodded, then spoke when she turned her back to him to examine the wound. "It is. I thought it best to stop the bleeding. I didn't—"

"You did fine, Johnny." Mae closed her eyes as she slipped her finger into Billy's open wound. "Aye, there it is." She withdrew her finger and crossed to the sink to rinse her hand. "He's lucky, this one. That bullet had barely enough oomph to break the skin." She dried her hands on a clean dishtowel, set it on the counter beside the bandages, and picked up a large pair of kitchen tongs. Instead of turning toward Billy, she looked into a big pot on the stove that had just begun to boil. She turned off the burner and fished out a long pair of tweezers.

She placed the steaming utensil on the towel, then removed several small items from the boiling water. When she finished, she prepared the bandages, picked up the cooled tweezers.

"You're not squeamish, are ye?" Mae asked.

"No." John took a step back and bumped into the kitchen wall. "Let me know if you need assistance."

Mae pulled the bullet from Billy's side, held it up to the light for a moment, then metal clinked upon glass as she dropped it into a custard dish.

She released the long tweezers into the hot water on the stove and picked up a hooked needle from the towel. With steady fingers, she threaded the needle with thick black thread.

Mae hooked the needle into Billy's skin, pulled most of the thread through, took another small stitch, then looped the needle underneath and pulled the half-knot tight. "Your friend is not terribly injured—for being shot, mind ye." She performed another looping stitch. "He'll have to be kept quiet for a few days until the skin knits."

"That won't be easy. Billy's anxious to find his friend."

Mae cast a quizzical glance at John. "You have a missing smuggler?"

"Billy thinks the gunmen have him."

"I see. And he'll want to look for his friend." Mae raised an eyebrow at John. "Hand me those small sewing scissors. That's a good lad." She clipped the thread and dropped the needle into the steaming water.

With a hand on her back, she studied at John. "Are ye going to help him?"

John looked into Mae's steady eyes and slowly dipped his head. "Aye."

Mae started to grin then suppressed her smile. "And Aubrielle? What are you going to tell her? She'll be wanting to know why you missed dinner."

"I…" John hesitated. "I don't know how she would react to all this."

"You care for the lass? And I see you do." Mae untied her apron. "Would you like my advice?"

John blinked in surprise and nodded.

"A gun-smuggling patriot is more exciting than a flower peddler, no matter how handsome." Mae felt Billy's forehead and lifted his wrist to take his pulse. "Keep her away from the danger, mind ye, but be honest with her, as much as you can." Mae cocked her eye at John. "And she'll be needing some help to pack and move their personal belongings."

"Move?"

"Aye. Lou and Brie are movin' in with me. They'll need to be out of their building by the end of the year." She patted Billy's cheek, but the young man showed no signs of stirring. "You'll have to carry him out. I need to clean the kitchen and make Lou his breakfast before sunrise." She removed her bib apron and folded it away with her medical kit. "Can you manage him?"

"I can. If you open the doors, I'll carry Billy back to my place."

Chapter 14

Aubrielle Cohen

Aubrielle woke to dull thumping inside the house—a persistent pounding that shook her bed.

Papa?

She hurried from her room pulling on her dressing gown and knotting the sash. Across from the kitchen, the door to her father's room stood ajar. "Papa? Are you ill?" She pushed open the door, and her sight darted from the empty bed to her father, doubled over on the floor.

He raised his face and stared at her, his yarmulke dusty and askew on his head. Angry tears streamed down gaunt cheeks and mingled with blood from the cut on his forehead. "*Dieu tout-puissant, pardonnez-moi.* I do not remember the words…" his voice dissolved into sobs. He collapsed forward as though in prayer and continued to beat his forehead on the wooden floor. "*Seigneur Dieu, pardonnez-moi.*"

"Papa—no!" Aubrielle dropped to her knees beside him and gathered his thin shoulders in her arms. She hugged him to the ache in her chest.

"The words are here, Marguerite." He pounded his knuckles against his temple knocking the skullcap to the floor. "But when I am ready to speak them, they fly away." He covered his face.

"Help me pray, Marguerite."

"It's Aubrielle, Papa."

He pulled away from her arms and studied her face. "Of course, it is. My Aubrielle." He lifted his hand to touch her face then stopped and stared at the blood on his palm. *"Qu'est-ce que c'est?"*

Aubrielle curled her lips between her teeth and struggled against tears.

He won't understand why I cry.

"You've cut your head, Papa. *Ce n'est rien.*"

He touched his forehead. "I did?"

She took his hand and helped him stand. "Come. I'll make us some breakfast and wash your face."

"Attends—I remember now." His face fell as confusion battled with despair. "You must help me pray, Aubrielle."

"I can't, Papa." Her hand touched her mother's silver cross which she wore on a chain around her neck. "I only know Mama's prayers."

His eyes followed her hand to the shiny crucifix. "That's true. I remember now." He crawled to his dark wooden dresser and searched through two drawers, scattering the contents on the floor. "I bought this for your Mama, years ago. Before we wed." His hand trembled as he raised an old velvet jewelry box to Aubrielle. "She wouldn't wear it, of course. Marrying me was a lesser sin than wearing this."

Aubrielle opened the box. A glint of light caught and flashed from the necklace chain. The six-pointed star—the Star of David—must have remained hidden in her father's dresser for years. She reached for the familiar crucifix that dangled above her collarbone and swallowed. "It's lovely, Papa."

"Would you wear it sometime? For me? Like you wear your mother's cross and rings to remember her?"

"Of course, I will." She picked up the black cap from the floor and set it on her father's bed. "Come. Sit at the table, Papa, and talk to me. I'll clean your forehead and make coffee."

* * *

Keys jingled at the back door, and Aubrielle looked up from her coffee.

Tante Mae came into the kitchen. Her head wrapped in a black wool scarf that matched the buttons on her coat. A covered basket over her arm. She stopped when she caught sight of Lou's forehead. "Did he take a fall?" She set the basket on the counter and pulled off her knitted gloves.

"Not exactly." Aubrielle reached over and patted her father's shoulder. "He was frustrated."

"As difficult as his illness is for us, it's much harder for Lou." Mae nodded to the jewelry box on the table. "I didn't know he still had the necklace." She pulled the red cloth from the basket and withdrew a freshly baked baguette. "Does his frustration have anything to do with the pendant?" She set the crusty loaf on a plate in the middle of the table.

"No, I don't think so." Aubrielle tore away a corner of the warm offering and placed it in her father's hand. "He gave it to me." She drew in a breath and lifted one shoulder. "Is it true Mama wouldn't take his gift?"

Mae set a tray of sliced cheese and meat inside the refrigerator. "Marguerite loved your father, you know. She loved him dearly." Mae raised an eyebrow at Aubrielle. "The necklace now, that had more to do with your grandparents than with your mother."

"Mama's parents?"

"Aye," Mae tucked in the red cloth over the basket and put her gloves back on. "Marguerite was an only daughter, like you."

"Mama never spoke of them."

Her father stared vacantly at the bread in his hand.

Mae lifted the basket. "Marguerite told me she was dead to her parents after she married Lou." Mae captured Aubrielle's attention with her steady gaze. "A thing she never regretted, mind ya." Her face softened, a smile curved her lips, and she winked. "I'd expect a visitor today if I were you."

"John?" Aubrielle sat straight. "But how—"

"I spoke with him early this morning, and I'm headed across to his apartment just now to check on his friend." The back door opened and closed.

What friend? Aubrielle brushed at her dressing gown and touched her rolled hair. "Papa, finish your breakfast and let's get you dressed. It sounds as though we'll have company."

* * *

John Larson

John rubbed his dark hair with a soft white bath towel, then wrapped the damp fabric around his waist and went to check on Billy.

Billy had slept on the bed last night while John had attempted to sleep on the couch. After an hour, he resigned himself to the floor. A man with his frame simply didn't fit on regular sized furniture.

Billy peered at John through gummy eyes. "Bloody hell, you're big!" He leaned his head back and stared at the ceiling. "Even when you're near naked. How'd I get back here?"

John crossed his arms and rested his shoulder against the doorframe. "I carried you, and it was no easy task. You're heavier than you look."

Billy chuckled, then moaned and held his side. "I feel worse today, mate." He struggled to sit, barely suppressing a groan and shook his head. "I could use a bit of help."

John gripped Billy's hand and eased him forward, then tucked an extra pillow behind his back. He brought Billy a glass of water and placed it on the bedside table. "Mae Moroney, the woman who removed the bullet and sewed you up, said you'd be on your back for a few days."

"I can't stay in bed. I have to find François." He grimaced as he reached for the water. "I know he'd do the same for me."

"Do you remember who he spoke with? Did he mention any names when he arranged the exchange?"

"Aye, he did." Billy drank from the glass and choked. He gasped and tried to stifle a cough as he replaced the glass on the table, spilling a good portion. "Ah, bloody hell."

"Are you all right?" John wiped the water from the floor and table with a dishcloth from the kitchen.

"Aces." Billy leaned back and closed his eyes. "François did mention a name, but I doubt the man had anything to do with his disappearance or the gunfire last night."

John opened his suitcase and lifted a pair of slacks. He dropped the towel from around his waist and pulled on the trousers. "Go on. I'm listening."

"François said he met with a Maurice Bonet. *Monsieur* Bonet owns a cabaret on the Right Bank, near Montmartre. *La Fleur Chantante*. Ever heard of it?"

"No." John shook his head. "And you don't think Bonet is involved?"

Eyes closed, Billy's pallor remained gray. He rolled his head from side to side. "I don't see why he would. He brokered the sale—"

John paused buttoning his shirt and gaped at Billy. "He what?"

"Bonet knows the buyer we met last night. He knows how to contact them."

John pulled his shoes from under the dresser and sat in the corner chair. "You said the man you dealt with seemed as surprised as you were by the gunfire. He acted as though he thought you were the one who betrayed the exchange."

"That's true, mate—but that René chap—he might have discovered who fired those shots." Billy heaved a sigh and ran his palm along the bandage. "With luck, we might have a line on who has François, and why."

"You say 'we' like you're going somewhere." John pulled the laces on his Oxfords tight then straightened his tie in the mirror and pulled on his suit coat. He opened the dresser drawer and pushed the gun and holster aside. Inside the hand-tooled wooden box, he leafed past his work documents from *The Yankee Dream* and the *Giselle-Marie* and withdrew a cream-colored sheath with an embossed seal. The elegant envelope disappeared into his inside pocket.

A knock at the entrance halted their conversation. The men exchanged a quick glance in the mirror.

John finished his tie then crossed the apartment and opened the front door.

Mae Moroney beamed when she saw John. The short brisk walk left the apples of her cheeks bright red. "G'morning, Johnny. Don't you look grand?" She hurried inside out of the stairwell's morning chill. "How's our patient today?"

"Billy's awake and feels good enough to complain." John picked up a set of keys from the kitchen drawer. "Here. Just in case I'm not in when you check on Billy."

The keys sank into the pocket of Mae's wool jacket. She set her basket on the couch and unbuttoned her coat. "That's good." She indicated her container as she set her coat and scarf beside it. "I've brought a bite for the poor lad, and clean bandages, which he'll enjoy less I'd wager." Mae looked John up and down then nodded. "She's expecting you. I told her I was coming here to see your friend."

"You told her about Billy?" John's brows rose as he retrieved the wrapped package that held Aubrielle's white leather gloves. He closed the coat closet and tucked the flat ribbon-adorned box beneath his arm. "What did she say?"

"Nothing that bears repeating." She pulled a roll of gauze from the basket. "Go on, now. I'll lock up when I've finished. Oh, and I'll expect you for supper this evening at Aubrielle's house." She pointed at the bedroom. "You can bring a portion back for your friend and save me the trip."

Chapter 15

Aubrielle Cohen

Aubrielle eased the door to her father's room shut and stood silent for a moment, eyes closed, and head bowed.

Mon Dieu, give me strength.

Papa had barely eaten and could not be tempted by *Tante* Mae's fresh baked bread. Instead, he claimed it was well past evening prayer and promptly returned to his bed.

At least he knew who I was when he whispered good-night.

In her room, she sat in front of the small vanity that had belonged to her mother and covered her face. As shocking and heart-wrenching as Mama's sudden death, three years ago in a car accident, it felt less brutal than Papa's slow decline. His long illness challenged them both to the limits of their strength. At times, he understood how ill he was, and apologized profusely for adding to her burden. At others, he called her by her mother's name and spoke of having a child one day.

His tears this morning were especially hard to bear. A simple Hebrew prayer was all he asked.

And I couldn't even give him that.

She'd watched Papa practice Judaism her whole life. That she and Mama worshiped differently never mattered to a child beloved by both parents.

In her entire life, she had never accompanied Papa to the *Synagogue de la Victoire* where she would have been separated from him and placed in the womenfolk's prayer room. Instead, Aubrielle attended mass at St. Joseph's near the *Champs-Élysées* with Mama and *Tante* Mae.

Aubrielle straightened her spine as an idea took hold. She turned to her mirror and removed the rollers from her dark hair. The curlers scattered across the vanity, and she pulled her hairpins and brush from the drawer.

I'll speak with the rabbi today.

He may have a suggestion how she could ease her father's spirit. Perhaps he could even teach her a prayer or loan her a prayer book.

And if he did, could Papa read it?

Her mind raced with all she could ask the temple elder as she twined the thick curls on either side of her head around her fingers. Without breaking her train of thought, Aubrielle secured the roll of dark hair to her head with hairpins. The long curls at the back of her head she captured in a large green barrette.

Although she had never been inside the synagogue, she knew its location. As soon as *Tante* Mae returned, she would set out. She dressed in a light green button-up blouse, her full green print skirt, and white, low-heeled Oxford pumps. She laid her warm wool overcoat across her bed and found a soft black scarf to cover her head.

The sudden tap on the back door startled her from her thoughts, and for a moment, she couldn't understand why *Tante* Mae didn't use her key. Then she remembered.

Monsieur Larson.

A tickle of anticipation fluttered in her stomach followed closely by a wedge of anger. She would not forgive his abandonment of her dinner invitation for a night of revelry with friends so quickly.

Aubrielle glanced at her reflection in the mirror and smoothed a curl. After his second knock, she left her room and opened the door.

A gust of cold air ushered in, and she shivered. "*Monsieur* Larson. What a surprise."

"Good morning, *Mademoiselle* Cohen." He touched the brim of his hat, his smile inviting and relaxed. "Mrs. Moroney said you would expect me."

"But who knows if you would show, *monsieur*?" Her thin smile didn't reach her eyes. "After all, you told me yesterday you had no acquaintances in Paris, yet *Tante* Mae said she must tend to your friend this morning."

"I owe you an apology." His smile faded, and he tipped his head. "An unforeseen emergency arose."

"An emergency so dire you could not send regrets?"

"I had thought to stop when I passed your home last night, but you had another guest at your door."

He saw Henri.

Aubrielle blinked as heat spread across her cheeks. "A guest should not have stopped you."

"That's true." His smile reappeared. "If I might come inside and explain?"

"By all means—" She opened the door fully and extended her arm. "I'm sure your excuses will prove entertaining."

She preceded him down the hallway indicating the closed door adjacent to the kitchen. "Papa is resting," she informed him in a soft voice. "We may talk in the front room."

John removed his hat and set the gift box on the center table. "I brought you a gift."

"An apology gift?"

"Not originally. I'd intended to give it to you before dinner last night," John said.

"I see. Then please, offer your explanations, but be brief. I have an errand to run as soon as *Tante* Mae returns."

"Very well. When I told you I knew no one in Paris, it was true.

I wasn't aware these men had remained in the city."

"So, you have more than one friend here?"

"I have two acquaintances. One who is injured, and the other, as of last night, is missing."

"Injured and missing?" Aubrielle sank into the chair. "Please, have a seat."

"Thank you." John removed his coat and sat across the table from Aubrielle. "First, I must explain how I know these men." John ran a hand across the back of his neck.

"There is no commerce between our countries right now. America has declared both Britain and France 'hostile nations' due to your war with Germany. The only ship I could find bound for France intended to smuggle American weaponry to your countrymen to fight the Germans."

Aubrielle nodded.

"After we brought the weapons ashore, they were sold and loaded into a truck. Since the smugglers and I were both headed to Paris, they offered me a ride. Once we had parted company, I hadn't thought to see them again." John's searching gaze never left her face.

"Go on," Aubrielle said.

"Last night, one of the men arrived at my door with a gunshot wound to his side. He told me they'd been betrayed during the arms exchange."

"Betrayed?" Aubrielle shook her head. "Are his injuries serious? Will he recover?"

"Mrs. Moroney believes Billy will recover. I'm still trying to locate his friend, François."

"I had no idea you were involved with assisting the French Army—"

"My part was minimal. I assure you. Had Billy not arrived when he did, I would have been with you last night instead of searching for François. Please, accept my apology."

"*Oui.* Of course."

"*Merci.*" John relaxed back in his chair. "And now, you should open your present."

Aubrielle pressed her lips to stop her grin and reached for the container. "You should not bring me gifts." The ribbon slipped from the box. She opened the package and pushed back the tissue paper. Ivory-white, kid gloves were revealed. She caught her breath. "These are lovely."

"Try them on," John urged.

"I should not. These are costly gloves. Too expensive for me to accept."

"Nonsense. There were far more high-priced gifts I could have chosen. Besides, these gloves suit you, and you need them. If you had worn gloves yesterday, your hands would have been spared."

Reminded of the attack in the park, Aubrielle glanced at the scuffed skin on the heel of her palms and placed the glove into the box. "This is true, but then your fine gift would have been marred by my foolishness."

"What happened yesterday wasn't your fault. Never think that. You trusted someone you thought you knew."

"And I barely know you, *Monsieur* Larson. How can I trust anyone anymore?"

The sadness in John's eyes belied the smile on his face. "*Mademoiselle* Cohen, on my life I swear, I will never betray your trust."

Something moved inside her chest, and her throat tightened. She took his outstretched hand and gave a short chuckle as she wiped away a tear. "You must think I'm daft, *Monsieur* Larson."

"Not at all. And please, call me John."

The sudden rattle at the back door caused Aubrielle to pull back her hand from his and wipe her cheeks as she came to her feet. She looked down the hallway and waved to Mae. "Papa is asleep," she said in a hushed voice.

Mae nodded and removed her coat and scarf before joining the couple in the living room. "Your young friend is mending well," she told John. "Oh, what lovely gloves."

Aubrielle's cheeks grew warm. "They're a gift from John."

"John is it now?" Her teasing smile was warm. "They're beautiful." She gestured down the hall. "Your Papa went back to bed?"

"Yes. He's confused this morning." Aubrielle glanced toward her father's door. "Would you stay with him while I run an errand?"

"Yes, of course, dear." Mae glanced between Aubrielle and John. "Perhaps Mr. Larson would accompany you?"

"It would be my pleasure." John lifted his coat and hat.

"That is kind of you, but I truly don't need an escort."

"You are most capable, I know, but please don't deny me the pleasure of your company." John gave Aubrielle a short bow, then grinned and winked at Mae.

Aubrielle rolled her eyes and paced down the hall to her room.

Why am I so taken with this American?

His playful banter was not unlike Henri's, which only annoyed her. She shrugged on her coat and pulled her long hair from beneath the collar, then tied the scarf around her head. When she stepped from her room, John was waiting in the cloakroom near the back door.

"Don't forget your gloves. It's cold outside." John held out the leather gift with a question in his dark eyes.

Aubrielle took the gloves with a smile. "Thank you, John."

Chapter 16

John Larson

The mist from their breath trailed them down the steps and across the yard.

John eyed the low clouds as he held the gate for Aubrielle. "Must you run this errand today? I believe we may have snow."

"Yes, I must." She tugged the scarf beneath her chin. Her nose had already turned pink from the cold temperature.

"Where are we going?" John followed her down the alleyway and onto the narrow, cobbled street.

"To the *Synagogue de la Victoire.* I must speak to a rabbi about Papa."

"That is too far to walk with snow threatening. I will flag a cab up ahead."

Aubrielle glanced back at John. "I don't take cabs when I can walk."

"Nevertheless." John raised his hand to a passing cabbie, and the vehicle slowed to a stop. "This will make your task much quicker—and warmer."

At the synagogue, Aubrielle opened the car door as soon as the cab stopped.

John paid the driver, then stood on the sidewalk beside Aubrielle, his interest drawn across the street to the magnificent architecture.

"Do you know the rabbi?" John looked at Aubrielle.

She caught the side of her lip between her teeth. A frown line creased her brow. "*Non*. I've never been inside."

Together they crossed the street and stepped beneath the tall arches. John opened the middle door, and they walked in from the cold.

A thin-haired middle-aged gentleman in a dark suit and a yarmulke approached. He greeted them with a short bow. "*Shalom mademoiselle, monsieur.*"

"*Bonjour.*" Aubrielle cast an uncertain glance at John. "Would it be possible to speak with a rabbi?"

"Certainly. How may I help you?" He responded in English, and his smile took in both John and Aubrielle.

Aubrielle blinked. "I'm sorry—I didn't realize—"

"No need to apologize." His welcoming grin grew wide. "You are tourists then?"

"No." Aubrielle swallowed. "I had hoped to speak with you concerning my father."

The rabbi handed John a yarmulke from a wooden case by the door. "In respect for our King." He gestured toward the side of the temple. "Perhaps some privacy is needed. There is a room this way we may use."

John removed his hat, fit the yarmulke on the back of his head, and then followed Aubrielle and the rabbi away from the sanctuary.

In a small meeting room lined with chairs, the rabbi gestured to the seats. "Please, be comfortable. I am Rabbi David. Again, how may I serve you?"

Aubrielle took a seat in the nearest chair." My name is Aubrielle Cohen. My father is Louis Cohen. He comes here to worship, or he did before he became too ill."

"I'm sorry." The rabbi's smiling face grew somber. "I remember Lou Cohen. I didn't know he was sick." He turned to John and offered his hand. "Rabbi David."

"John Larson. I'm a friend of the family."

"A pleasure to meet you, Mr. Larson. American?"

"Yes."

Rabbi David released John's hand and sat across from Aubrielle. "Tell me about your father."

Aubrielle looked down and wrung her gloved hands. "He suffers from Mad Hatter's disease." She shrugged one shoulder. When her gaze rose, tears filled her eyes. "The illness has progressed so rapidly this fall and has taken much of his memory." She shifted in her seat. "I fear he hasn't much time left."

John pulled a handkerchief from his pocket and handed it to her.

She dabbed her eyes. "I apologize."

"It's quite all right. Losing your father this way—" Rabbi David shook his head. "How may I help?"

"He has asked me to help him pray. He can't always remember the words." She paused and took a breath. "But I can't. My mother raised me in the Catholic faith. I don't know any of papa's prayers."

"And your father has no family, other than yourself? Do you not have an uncle or aunt who practices Judaism?"

"*Non.*" Aubrielle held the handkerchief to her nose. "None that I know."

Rabbi David brushed his palms together as he considered his response "Teaching you the prayers, which are learned over a lifetime, would be difficult." He tipped his head and set his palms on his thighs. "Although, perhaps there is another way to give your father comfort." He glanced between Aubrielle and John. "Hanukkah begins in a few days. It may be that the joy of ceremony—lighting the *hanukiah* and celebrating together—will bring your father the peace you wish for him."

Aubrielle sat straight. "When does Hanukkah begin?" Hope blossomed in her face.

"At sunset on the sixth. Are you familiar with the celebration?"

"Somewhat." Aubrielle nodded. "It has been years since we

celebrated Hanukkah. When Mama was alive, we celebrated both Hanukkah and Christmas." She looked at John. "I know where Papa stored his *menorah*, the *hanukiah*, but I'll need to purchase candles."

"We can do that." John's chest tightened as though her smile tugged at his heart.

"Your father may also enjoy a game called *dreidel*. Do you know it?"

"I think so." Aubrielle lips curled in a slow smile. "We played it when I was a child."

"Good. Then I recommend you also purchase an inexpensive toy *dreidel* and perhaps a few chocolate coins—*gelt*. Those are very popular now. Otherwise, use small candies or coins." The rabbi gave John a significant nod.

Rabbi David is giving them something to share. A memory for Aubrielle to hold.

Rabbi David leaned forward and laid his hand over Aubrielle's. "Please remember that we are here for you, as well as your father. When he passes, send a message to the synagogue. We have volunteers that serve the community and will take care of matters necessary to bury your father within his faith."

Aubrielle's eyes widened, and she swallowed. "Yes, of course. *Merci.*"

Rabbi David rose to his feet and shook hands again with John. "Let me know if there is anything else I can do for you." He turned to Aubrielle. "Take all the time you need. You will not be disturbed."

"Thank you, Rabbi," John said.

Rabbi David tipped his head to Aubrielle and John then departed.

John sat beside Aubrielle. "Are you all right?"

"I am." She sniffed into the handkerchief and wiped her eyes. "Rabbi David is a thoughtful man."

"He is." John nodded. "He had good suggestions." John took

the handkerchief Aubrielle offered and put it back into his inside pocket. "Are you ready to go home?"

"I am." She rose and moved to the door. "I need to make a list of things I'll need before Hanukkah and find Papa's *hanukiah*."

John returned the yarmulke to the visitor's box and slid his fedora on his head as he escorted Aubrielle out of the temple.

When their cab stopped in front of the bakery, John asked the cabbie to wait as he followed Aubrielle from the car. "I have an errand of my own to run." As he spoke, his head bent naturally toward her.

Aubrielle leaned forward and tilted her head back. "I'll be waiting." She licked her lips and closed her eyes.

John's stomach clenched with desire. He wanted to taste the mouth she so innocently offered. His arm encircled her waist and tightened as he pulled her close to his side. From the corner of his eye, he glimpsed one of Mae's bakers standing at the window of the *boulangerie*.

Instead of claiming Aubrielle's parted lips, he kissed the apple of both cheeks in quick succession. "I won't be long." He released her. When he glanced at the window, the baker had gone.

Aubrielle backed from his arms. A blush deepened the color on her face. She waved her gloved fingers as he returned to the cab, then walked to the side of the Cohen's Fine Millinery store and disappeared between the buildings. Her frozen breath hung in the still air.

"*Où allez-vous?*" The cab driver inquired as he looked over the front seat at John.

John closed the cab door. "*La Banque de France. Merci.*"

John paused as he entered the bank and raised his index finger to catch the attention of a bank official. He removed his gloves one finger at a time and nodded as he approached the man. "*Bonjour, monsieur.* I would like a word with your head banker, *s'il vous plaît.*" He spoke both English and French with a noticeable British accent.

"Of course, *monsieur*. May I present your name and the nature of your inquiry?"

"*Bien sûr*. Tell him John Locke, Earl of Hawthorn, would like to open an account and withdraw funds." He tossed his hat on the lobby sofa and stared down at the official with a steady smile. "A transfer from my London bank would be the first order of business." He removed his overcoat and laid it alongside his fedora. "I trust the paperwork and authorizations can be accomplished without delay?" From his inside suit pocket, he withdrew the envelope, the Earl of Hawthorn crest embossed on the front. He offered it to the banker.

The bank official hesitated, his eyes round. He took the envelope, nodded, and took a step back.

"There's a good lad. Off you go. I'm in a bit of a rush." John folded himself onto the sofa, crossed his legs and adjusted his cuffs. "I've dinner plans with a young woman this evening and simply cannot be late."

Chapter 17

Aubrielle Cohen

Aubrielle paced the hallway from kitchen to living room for the third time. "If he doesn't come tonight, I don't know what I'll do," she said to Mae over her shoulder.

"He'll be here," Mae called from the kitchen. "The snow may have caused him some delay."

Aubrielle stopped in the passage and closed her eyes.

He meant to kiss me—I know he did.

Her fingers gently played across her parted lips.

What would it be like to have John's mouth touch mine?

She was no wanton. Henri had tried to kiss her at least a dozen times this year. She had always pushed him away or turned her head aside. Her other hand brushed her breast, and her nipple tightened. She gasped softly at the sensation, and her eyes sprang open.

In the kitchen, Mae hummed a cheerful Irish song while she cooked.

Aubrielle rubbed her forearms and continued into the living room. She paused beside her father seated in the living room chair. "Papa?" Thoughts of John fled for the moment, and she touched her father's shoulder.

His hands trembled as they rested on his knees. He sat hunched forward, his back muscles taut, unable to relax and murmured to himself as though in a trance. He didn't acknowledge Aubrielle's touch.

She crossed her arms and retraced her steps to the kitchen. "I'll set the table." The dishes and silver sat ready on the counter across from the stove.

Had John intended to kiss me?

Heat infused her face, and she fumbled the utensils, dropping them onto her mother's fine china. "*Merde!*"

"Here now." Mae turned from the stove. "Settle your nerves, darlin'. I'll set the table."

"*Non, non.* It is fine. Nothing's broken."

A short tap on the back door caused Aubrielle to turn on her heel and bump against Mae.

"Brie!" Mae exclaimed with a chuckle and clutched Aubrielle's arm.

Her face heated again at the knowing look in *Tante* Mae's eyes, but Aubrielle's lips curled into a grin to match Mae's, and she gave a nervous laughed.

"That's better, now take a breath. No need to rush." Mae took the silverware from Aubrielle's hands. "Go on then. Answer the door."

Aubrielle straightened her skirt and touched her curls.

"You look grand." Mae turned back to the stove. "Take him to the living room and talk with your Papa while I finish up."

Although she hurried from the kitchen, Aubrielle rested her hand on the door for a moment before turning the handle.

He wants to kiss me.

Her stomach fluttered.

If he tries again, I will let him.

She struggled to quell her excited smile and opened the door.

"Henri?" *No, no, no.* Her eyes scanned the *ruelle* behind the unexpected arrival and caught a glimpse of John as he rounded the corner. "What a surprise."

"*Bonjour,* Aubrielle." Henri's smile showed a dimple in each cheek. "How are you feeling today?" His eyes narrowed as he studied her. "I hope I haven't arrived at an inopportune time."

"Not at all," Aubrielle muttered as she stretched to look past Henri's shoulder. "I'm feeling much better. *Merci.*"

John slowed to a stop as he entered the back gate. One hand held a bottle of wine. His gaze caught Aubrielle's, and a single brow rose in query.

Henri spied the direction of her interest and turned. His smile faltered, and he muttered, "I see I should not have arrived unannounced."

The aroma of *Tante* Mae's corned beef and cabbage drifted out the door, and Henri's stomach growled loudly.

John followed Henri's footsteps through the dusting of snow and mounted the steps. He extended his free hand to Henri. "It appears we meet again, *monsieur*. I'm John Larson."

"Yes. Aubrielle's friend from the park. Henri Vogl." Henri shook John's hand then turned to Aubrielle. "Perhaps another time would be better."

"Nonsense!" Mae called over Aubrielle's shoulder. "Come in, both of you, and close the door. Dinner is ready, and there's always room for another chair."

Aubrielle couldn't read the look on John's face as she stepped back from the door. "Please, come in."

Henri entered, grinned at Aubrielle then addressed the older woman. "Whatever you're cooking certainly smells wonderful, Mrs. Moroney." He pulled off his cap and trailed Mae into the kitchen.

John placed the bottle of wine in Aubrielle's hands and closed the door. "*Monsieur* Vogl is a frequent guest in your home?"

"Only recently." The light from the kitchen fell along the hallway, leaving the back door and cloakroom in shadow. Aubrielle pulled the bottle to her chest and held tight with both hands.

I need to see his eyes.

"I'm not sure why Henri comes here."

"No?" John leaned close. "I could tell you why." He shrugged his overcoat from his shoulders and removed his hat.

"Is that so?" Aubrielle gripped the bottle and tipped her head back. "I've even less idea why you come here." *Stop talking.* "I've known Henri for many months. He's only a friend."

"A close friend?" John reached behind her and hung his garments on pegs. "Perhaps it is I who should leave." Instead of backing away, he leaned forward to whisper in her hair. "Although I could never leave your side for long."

His hushed breath beside her ear sent a shiver down her neck. She closed her eyes. "John—"

"Come. You have a guest waiting." The weight of the wine bottle lifted from her arms, and her hand was enfolded in his. "Tonight should prove interesting."

When they approached the kitchen's bright light, Aubrielle pulled her hand free of John's and lifted it to the heat in face. *Bon Dieu!*

"If you could put this platter on the trivets, I'd be much obliged." Mae pointed to three crocheted hot pads set in the middle of the table.

Henri placed the large server of steaming corned beef, cabbage, potatoes and sweet carrots where Mae directed. As he straightened, he looked at Aubrielle and winked. "Your *Tante* is a marvelous cook."

Mae chuckled and placed a long loaf of fresh bread on the table beside the butter. "We've little to spare these days, but always enough to share." She caught Aubrielle's stare and grinned in delight. "Go wake your Papa." Her eyes widened as John lifted his gift. "Wine? I'm not sure this simple meal will do it justice."

"The wine is for you, Mae. Open it or not. The decision is yours."

"Oh, we'll open it." She handed John a corkscrew from the drawer. "If you would."

Aubrielle hurried into the quiet living room. John rattled her thoughts.

Does he realize how much?

Papa's head had tipped back, and his mouth sagged open. He emitted a brief snore.

"Papa?" She touched his shoulder, but he remained fast asleep.

Mae's voice reached from the kitchen. "Mr. Vogl, if you would reach into the cabinet behind you, you'll find proper glasses for the wine. Aye, those are the ones. Thank you."

Aubrielle shook her father's shoulder. "Papa? Dinner is ready. Are you hungry?" He had lost a lot of weight in the last few months. His frame felt of skin and bone.

He blinked his dark eyes open with a small snort and stared up at her. "*Non.* I'm not hungry, Aubrielle. Let me rest." He closed his eyes and turned his head away.

* * *

John Larson

John leaned back in his chair and swirled the Merlot in his glass as he studied Aubrielle's other guest.

Across the table, Henri Vogl continued to eat his meal. He paid little attention to the conversation and replied only to direct questions.

He behaves like a man half-starved rather than a hopeful suitor.

Henri's jacket appeared sized for a smaller man—or perhaps a younger one. Though clean, the garment had seen better days.

Aubrielle told of their visit to the synagogue and her plans to celebrate Hanukkah with her father.

"Your Papa's *menorah* is packed away with your mother's Christmas decorations," Mae replied.

"We haven't—I haven't taken those out in years." Aubrielle shook her head. "At first, it hurt too much to look at them and know Mama would never see them again."

Mae nodded. "I understand—and so would your mother." Mae glanced at John. "You should bring those boxes in the house and go through them."

"You're right." Aubrielle traced her finger around the rim of her wineglass. "I need to clean out the storage beside Éclair's stall before we move." She lifted her contemplation from the wine to Mae. "Are you sure you don't mind?"

"I've already made room for you both." Mae laid her napkin beside her plate. "It will be best for all of us to have you close."

"In that case, we shall move after Hanukkah. We can celebrate Christmas at your place and finish with this house and Papa's shop by the New Year."

The conversation paused, and John leaned forward. "So, Mr. Vogl, what type of work do you do?"

Henri waved his fork in the air. "Oh, various things. Most recently, I brokered flowers for the tourist trade. The war and winter put an end to that." He speared a portion of corned beef in his bowl. "And you, sir? What brings you to France?"

John chuckled. "Passion's curse." He raised his glass with a grin. "And a tramp steamer that brought me to these shores. How long I stay remains undetermined."

"You have loved ones in Paris, Mr. Larson?"

John grinned at Henri. "So far, only a few acquaintances and some dear friends." He raised his glass to Aubrielle and Mae."

"And your line of work, if I may inquire?" Henri persisted.

John ran his hand along his neck. "I've been involved with acquisition and trade, but as you said, war and winter have dampened those ventures." He sipped his wine, then set the long-stemmed glass on the table. "We both appear to be at loose ends, Mr. Vogl."

"Please, call me Henri."

"Did no one think to wake me for supper?" Lou Cohen yelled from the hallway. "*Qu'est-ce que ç'est?*" He staggered forward, his arms flailed as he pointed at the table.

John came to his feet, as Aubrielle rounded her chair and reached for her father.

"Papa, I tried to wake you—"

"*Non!*" Lou slapped his daughter's hand away. "*Ne me touche pas!*"

"*Monsieur* Cohen—" John stepped between Lou's raised arm and Aubrielle.

Lou's wild blow glanced across John's shoulder, and he lurched into John's chest.

John steadied the elderly man. "All is well, *Monsieur* Cohen. Try to be calm."

Lou gasped and let his head fell back to look into John's face. "Sir? You've come again?" His eyes filled with tears. "I thought you'd gone."

Who does he think I am?

"I'm still here." John turned slightly and saw Mae had set a clean plate at the table. "Look, Mrs. Moroney has your supper ready."

Distracted, Lou's interest shifted. "Oh yes. *Je vois.*"

John helped him to the table and steadied him as he took his seat.

"Here you are, Lou." Mae placed his dinner in front of him and handed him a spoon. "I'm glad to see you've got your appetite back."

Aubrielle released a small sob. She covered her mouth with both hands to silence her distress. The big brown eyes that watched her father brimmed with tears.

"Come." John wrapped his arm around her shoulders and walked toward the living room. "He'll be all right." John stopped and faced Aubrielle. "Your father was only confused."

She nodded and leaned against him as she wiped her tears. "I know. He became confused when he woke and heard strange voices." She blinked up at John and half sobbed a chuckle. "I wonder who he thinks you are."

John inhaled slowly to calm his pulse. The length of her body pressed against his in a familiar manner, and his body reacted. *Oh, my love.* He brushed a stray curl caught in the moisture on her cheek.

Her head tipped back to see his face. "Thank you," she whispered. Her attention dropped to his mouth, and her lips parted.

Desire flooded John, and he fought the impulse to lower his head and capture her mouth with his. Aubrielle wanted to be kissed, and he desperately wanted to claim her lips for his own, but not here. Not now.

"I think I should be going." Henri's voice reached them from the kitchen.

"I need to go as well," John's deep voice was filled with regret.

Aubrielle straightened and turned aside. "Whatever must you think of me?" Her face darkened in a heated blush.

He clasped her hand to keep her close and bent to whisper in her hair. "Only that you and I want the same."

Her gaze sought his.

He lifted her hand to his lips. "As I said, I'll never be away from you for long."

Chapter 18

John Larson

John looked up at the sky and blinked a snowflake from his eyelash. Sometime during the evening, the snow had picked up again. He carried Billy's supper in the bag Mae packed for him as he trailed Henri down the steps to the back walk. Near the stable, he brushed snow off the nearby stool, set the bag down, and opened the stable door to check on the little horse.

Éclair's ears perked with interest as he moved forward to beg for attention.

Fresh straw covered the floor, and Éclair's water and food trough were full. *Aubrielle must have taken care of Éclair while I was at the bank.* John scratched between Éclair's ears and rubbed his neck. "Good boy."

"What are you doing?" Henri stood in the doorway.

"Checking on Aubrielle's pony." John gave Éclair one last pat on his neck. He closed the door behind him, picked up Billy's supper, and walked with Henri toward the *ruelle*. "She has a lot on her mind. Checking on her pony is the least I can do."

Henri nodded and opened the back gate. "Where are you staying while you're in the city?"

John pointed across the alleyway. "Third floor—where you see the light."

Henri turned his collar up. "That's rather close for coincidence."

"Yes." John chuckled as he latched the gate behind them. "What about you?"

Henri shrugged. "I find myself displaced at the moment." He removed himself from the bitter wind as he paused between John's building and the next one. "I was staying with my uncle, but there arose—a complication."

John studied the young man. To a stranger, he and Henri would appear much the same age, their mid-twenties. How long had it been since he felt that young? *A millennium at least.* "Can you not reconcile the complication?"

"I doubt it." Henri looked down at the snow, then back along the narrow passage. "The issue is tied up with the war. My family is Austrian, you see, but *Onkel Hersch* has lived in France for forty years." Henri shrugged. "I came here during Austria's civil war, about five years ago." He shivered visibly and shoved his hands deeper into his pockets. "Since the *Anschluss*—Austria's agreement to be annexed by Germany—*Onkel Hersch* has been afraid my presence will remind his associates of our heritage—Austrian—the same as Hitler." He shuffled his feet and glanced at John. "Once France declared war, the welcome at my *Onkel's* home was withdrawn."

"I see." John stared over Henri's head at Aubrielle's back door. Her room remained dark. "Where are you staying now?" When Henri didn't answer, John focused on the young Austrian. "Henri?"

"I thought you saw my bag." Henri studied John. "When you checked on her horse."

"You—" John shook his head and ran a hand along the back of his neck. "You're sleeping in the Cohen's barn? In Éclair's stall?"

"Not in the stall." Henri's face had flushed dark red. "Near the back, by the grain and storage closet. It's not bad. The barn is warm at least. Better than sleeping on the street."

"You're the one who cleaned the stall." John shook his head. "No. Get your bag. You can't stay there."

"What?" Henri staggered back as though John had struck him with his fist. "Do you think I want to sleep there? I've no place else to go."

"Did you not hear the talk at dinner?" John leaned in to see Henri's face. "The Cohen's are moving in with Mae Moroney. Aubrielle will be in the stable tomorrow looking for her father's *menorah*. You have to leave."

Henri ran a hand over his face. His eyes searched the darkness as though the falling snow held some secret answer. "There's no other place." He sniffed and cleared his throat, then nodded and straightened his shoulders. "One last night and I'll find a new location tomorrow. In the daylight."

"Another garage?" John shook his head. "No. You'll sleep on my couch." *I'm going to regret this.* "You can stay with me until you get back on your feet." *I hope he and Billy get along.*

"You'd do that for me?" Henri's head tipped to the side, and his eyes narrowed. "Why?"

"Hell, I don't know. Perhaps because you're Aubrielle's friend. Or maybe because I've slept in the rough before and I know what it's like to need a hand up." John lifted his hat and scratched his forehead. "Get your bag. I still have errands to run tonight and Billy needs his supper."

Henri called back from the Cohen's gate, a grateful smile on his face. "Is Billy your cat?"

John ran his hand over his face and laughed.

* * *

John considered Billy's reflection in the mirror. White bandages wrapped his thin chest and side above a pair of clean brown slacks Mae had provided the smuggler. "It's only been a day," John reminded him. "You need to stay in bed and heal."

"But what if something happens?" Billy pushed the dirty blond hair out of his eyes. "What if you need me?"

Henri leaned his shoulder against the door frame. "I'll go with you," he offered John.

John and Billy exchanged a brief glance in the mirror as John slipped the leather straps of his shoulder holster over his shirt. He slid the revolver into its sheath then turned to Billy. "If something does happen, I won't have to worry about you slowing me down." John opened the bedside table drawer and withdrew the stacks of banknotes from the arms sale. One by one, he shoved the bundled notes into the inside pocket of his overcoat.

Billy watched and pressed his lips. "Remember to ask for Maurice Bonet. He knows François." Billy flinched as he shifted in the bed. "Make Bonet tell you how to contact that René chap."

"I'll speak with *Monsieur* Bonet and ask about both François and the seller." John slipped his jacket over his shoulders, covering the holster, then turned back to the mirror to adjust his tie. "I won't be gone too long."

"Will you take the truck?" Billy asked.

Henri raised a brow. "You have a truck?" His glance went from Billy to John.

John had moved the truck from the alley to the street across from Mae's *boulangerie* the night before. "No. I'll hail a cab." He stopped at the foot of the bed and stared down at Billy. "Your supper is on the kitchen counter. You should eat it before it gets cold."

"Right." Billy nodded and sat up. "Gah! The stitches pull when I move."

"If you can't walk from here to the next room how much help would you be tonight?" John shooed Henri out of the way.

Henri backed down the short hall and into the kitchen. "What's wrong with him?"

"He took a bullet in his side the other night. Mae stitched him up." John put on his overcoat. "No, this is too dangerous. You shouldn't get involved." He settled his fedora on his head and reached for the door. "There's no shame in staying here with Billy."

"I don't care." Henri's eyes were wide as he snatched his cap and jacket from the couch. "I'll go with you." He pulled on his coat and glanced back as Billy wobbled into the kitchen. "Better than staying with a cranky Brit."

"I heard that," Billy called.

John held the door while Henri walked out and hurried down the stairs. "It's possible Bonet has heard something about François. If not, I'll ask him to arrange a meeting with René. I'd like to know what he saw that night."

Billy nodded as he lowered himself into the chair and opened Mae's bag.

John closed the door and caught up with Henri at the bottom of the stairs.

Large white flakes floated down through the glow of the streetlamp. Glistening cold and white, it covered the cars parked along the street.

"Who shot him?" Henri asked with a quiet voice.

John rolled his shoulders. The holster and gun were an unfamiliar weight across his back and beneath his left arm. "We don't know." They moved into the street, away from bushes and winter plants weighted with snow. "But whoever shot Billy took François."

"For what purpose?"

They turned at the cross street and continued toward the broader avenue.

"Billy thinks they hope to exchange François for the remaining American weapons."

Henri slowed his pace and stared at John. "Acquisition and trade, was it?" He hurried to catch up with John's long stride. "Who is Maurice Bonet, and why do you think he knows who has François?"

John stopped on the broad avenue and looked both ways.

Traffic was sparse on the snow-covered boulevard with no cab in sight. "Bonet owns a musical club—*La Fleur Chantante*—on the north side. Do you know of it?"

"Actually, yes." Henri tucked his chin as he and John headed north, into the slight breeze. "I've been there. It's high class. You think the owner, this Bonet, snatched Billy's friend?"

"We don't know." An icy breeze snaked down John's collar, and he buttoned his coat's top clasp. He glanced back, hoping to spot a cab. "Bonet set up the meeting for the arms sale—he's the broker. He'll know how to contact the buyer. Billy hopes one of them will have information about François—perhaps a ransom demand."

John threw up his hand and waved at a passing cab.

The driver slowed to a stop and rolled down his window. *"Où allez-vous?"*

John bent to the window. *"La Fleur Chantante."*

"Entendu. Montez." The driver cranked up his window.

Henri opened the back door and slid across the seat.

The cabbie started the meter as soon as John sat down and closed the door.

Chapter 19

John Larson

The cab slid to a stop across from the club. John paid the fare, then paused to observe the club's exterior. The narrow front, between two adjacent businesses, had been cast in rough-cut gray stone. Whimsical painted flowers decorated the transom above the double doors. Beside the entrance, a billboard promised a special New Year's Eve Extravaganza for the price of a ticket.

John's arm brushed the hidden weapon beneath his jacket.

Had Bonet engineered the betrayal from the beginning?

He straightened his coat and studied Henri. *An arrogant young man with a rapidly changing view of life. I hope I don't get him killed*

"There's usually an attendant outside the entrance," Henri commented.

John leaned into the door, and it swung opened.

Henri followed John inside.

An accordion provided a soft musical background enhancing the intimate setting. The depth and grandeur of the club must have cost the owner a small fortune. Besides *La Fleur Chantante,* and smuggling arms, what else lined Bonet's pockets? Double-dealing?

A raised stage with a short walkway stood center along the long wall. Around the platform, a sea of table lights glowed pink, a reflection of the blood red tablecloths. The small dance floor next to the stage and musician's area would allow patrons to enjoy their bal musette.

"Puis-je vous aider?" A big man in a dark suit waited beside a small reception podium. The tall, muscular man, who except for his height, reminded John of his former shipmate Taylor—short hair, thick neck, and broad shoulders.

"Bonjour," John replied, removing his hat. *"Monsieur Bonet, s'il vous plaît."*

The doorman's brow furrowed, and he glanced over his shoulder.

John followed the guard's gaze past the wrought-iron rail that edged the elevated seating area. Several men and women occupied a curved red leather booth. The club's only occupants tonight.

The big man turned back to John. *"Je suis désolé. Nous sommes fermés."*

Henri scoffed. "Clearly, you're neither sorry nor closed. If you were closed, the door would have been locked."

The doorman scowled at Henri, jutting his chin and rotating one shoulder.

John stepped between them and pointed to the group of people beyond the doorman. "Is that *Monsieur* Bonet? We'd like to speak with him."

The doorman clenched his fists and popped his knuckles.

John ignored the man's threatening demeanor and called across the club. *"Monsieur Bonet? Un moment, s'il vous plaît"*

The small group seated at the booth fell silent and observed John. "I would speak with you about François Belliard."

The doorman craned his neck to see the reaction from the table.

John moved forward.

The guard stopped John with a hand to the middle of his chest.

"I'll only take a moment of your time," John called to the table.

A man in the center of the group spoke briefly to his companions then waved John forward.

"*Votre arme.*" The guard narrowed his eyes and held out his hand.

John raised a brow at the guard, unbuttoned his overcoat, and pulled his revolver from beneath his jacket. "How did you know?" He placed the gun in the man's open hand.

The impassive doorman stowed the gun beneath the podium. "You may retrieve your weapon when you leave," he advised in heavily accented English.

"Perhaps you should lock the door," Henri whispered to the doorman when they walked past.

As John approached the stairs, two females fled the table. Dressed in identical shimmering dresses, the women sparkled. Small tufts of colorful feathers, connected to their headbands, swayed in the air as they scurried away.

Three men remained seated. One man, with a red birthmark or dark scar along his jaw and down his neck, waited beside the booth.

John dismissed the men dressed in the same dark suit as the doorman and focused on the smug-faced gentleman seated at the back of the curved bench.

Heavy-set, with an olive complexion and a thin mustache along his upper lip, the club owner lounged between his companions. *Maurice Bonet.* The older man's body language, paired with his costly, cream-colored silk, proclaimed his elevated status. Full red lips pouted beneath a broad nose, thick brows, and dark, greased-back hair. Heavy lidded eyes studied John as he approached. "Have you come to beg forgiveness for your friend?" He picked up his half-smoked cigar and crushed the damp end between his teeth. "I do not deal gladly with fools. Where is François? Afraid to face me?"

John allowed the women to pass down the steps before he mounted the short stair. He hadn't considered the possibility Bonet would hold François responsible. His hope of a positive meeting sank into the reality of an angry confrontation.

So be it.

John let his disgust at the situation flare, and he ground his teeth.

Perhaps Bonet has something to hide.

"Beg your forgiveness?" John stalked toward the table. "On the contrary."

The men seated on either side of the owner came to their feet at John's rapid approach.

John ignored them. He narrowed his eyes and glared at Bonet. "I'm here to determine what role you played in this disaster."

"Explain yourself." Bonet removed the cigar from his lips, never breaking eye contact with John. "Who are you and what do you mean by my role?"

John inhaled slowly through his nose. "My name is John Larson. My companion is Henri Vogl." John glanced at the men standing beside the booth, then concentrated on Bonet. "To my knowledge, only the seller, the buyer, and you, had foreknowledge of where and when the exchange would take place." John's anger sparked again, and he tamped down his fury and impatience. "Is that correct?" he said through clenched teeth.

"So?" Bonet sat forward. "François betrayed my trust and attempted murder to cover his duplicity." His thick lip curled. "I should have you shot as an example of how I repay such dishonesty." His face colored with anger, and a string of spittle quivered from his lower lip.

"John?" Henri whispered in alarm.

John leaned forward and rested his knuckles on the table in front of Bonet. "If what you say is true, then why did François gun down his partner? The man who held both the cash from the trade and the keys to the vehicle hauling the merchandise?" John straightened, reached in his coat and tossed down several short stacks of 1000-franc notes in front of Bonet. "Keep the weapons. Keep the buyer's money for all I care. I want my man back." He hit the table with his fist. "Give me François."

The club owner blinked at the notes on the table. "You think I—" His wide-eyed stare lifted from the franc notes to John as his high color bled pale. He waved his hands at his men. "Bruce, Marcel, leave us. Karl, bring fresh wine."

"*Oui, monsieur*," the man with the dark scar said with a short bow.

The suited men moved away. One crossed to speak with the doorman while the other two slipped out through a passage near the stage.

When they were alone, Bonet muttered, "I've been misinformed about certain critical aspects of this—disaster."

John tossed his fedora to the tabletop behind him. "Convince me of your sincerity. From where I stand, you are the one with the most to gain."

"I've gained nothing! Because of this embarrassment, my reputation as a broker is tarnished. In the end, that's all you have in this line of work. The trust of your associates."

"*Monsieur* Bonet, I have one man recovering from a gunshot wound, and one who remains missing." John held tight to his temper, but his voice rose despite his best effort to stay calm. "Your reputation means nothing to me in light of everything your brokerage has cost."

"*Monsieur,* I assure you, I had nothing to do with this." Bonet shoved the stacks of cash to the far side of the table. "I am appalled."

From the door near the stage, the marked manservant came back carrying three long-stemmed glasses and a bottle of wine.

Henri leaned forward, his voice low. "If not you, then who? The buyer lost their cash, which we have generously returned. We've lost both men and merchandise. It seems, if you are indeed as innocent as you claim, there is but one remaining possibility."

Bonet's steady gaze switched from John to Henri. "What do you mean?"

"How well do you know the people who work for you?" Henri

leaned in and whispered, "How much do they overhear?"

The manservant approached the booth and set the glasses on the edge of the table. "*Votre vin, monsieur.*" He held the unopened bottle to Bonet to inspect.

Bonet read the label. "*Merci, Karl. C'est très bien.*"

Karl uncorked the bottle, poured a sample in one of the glasses and stepped back.

Bonet tasted the vintage, gave a single nod of acceptance, then set his glass back on the table.

Karl folded a napkin around the bottle and poured wine into Bonet's glass. He paused and looked at John. "For you, *monsieur*?"

"No, thank you. We're leaving."

Karl nodded, set the bottle in a wine-stand near the booth and stood back, hands folded in front. He looked from John to Henri, and then with increasing alarm, at his employer's stare. "*Ai-je offensé, monsieur?*"

Bonet shook his head. "*Non, ce sera tout.*"

Karl gave Bonet a short bow, turned and walked away.

"Do you intend to return the francs to the buyer?" John asked.

"*Bien entendu,*" Bonet responded.

"Then if you would," John said as he reached for his hat, "ask them if they remember seeing anyone that night. François's partner spoke to a man named René. Perhaps he may know something." John straightened the hat's brim. "Put out the word that we are willing to ransom our associate, if that's what it takes to guarantee his safe return."

"Certainly." Bonet picked up his wine, swirled the vintage, and then studied the liquid in the glass. "How shall I contact you?"

"You don't. Either Henri or I will contact you tomorrow." John buttoned his coat as he walked away. "I hope you have good news."

"Yes, of course," Bonet agreed. "I have but one last question, if I may."

John paused and looked back. "Yes?"

"What is your role concerning François and the arms sale?"

"How am I involved with the American weapons?" John asked. "*Oui.*"

"I'm the American." John put his hat on, retrieved his gun from the doorman, and followed Henri from the club.

There were no cabs outside. Henri buttoned his jacket as he looked both ways along the parkway. "That was invigorating."

"What made you ask about Bonet's employees?"

"I'm Austrian." Henri shrugged. "And by how Karl pronounces certain words, he's German.

Chapter 20

Aubrielle Cohen

Chanted Hebrew prayers woke Aubrielle from a sound sleep.

He's remembered.

For half a breath, she was a child again, with Papa at prayer before going downstairs to work, and Mama preparing breakfast in the kitchen. She held onto that illusion for as long as she could, but the silence from the kitchen tore at her heart.

"Marguerite?" Papa called from his room.

Aubrielle opened her eyes. The reality of another sunrise slanted through her curtains.

Perhaps Tante Mae can stay with Papa today while I shop for candles and candies.

She'd hoped to have purchased the Hanukkah items by now but hadn't been unable to leave the house for almost a week.

Mae had knocked on the door four days ago, apologetic and rushed. Antoine, her head baker, had become seriously ill. Mae would be busy at the bakery and unable to sit with Lou until Antoine returned to work.

John had come to her house each morning, willing to escort her to the market.

She had turned him away each time.

He'd even offered to stay all afternoon and help take care of

Papa, but she'd declined that offer as well.

John had enough on his mind.

Besides, were I to add my burdens and heartache to his, our potted mix would grow a sour relationship of thorns instead of the perfect bloom I desire.

She made a face at her poetic whimsy. If she were honest, she also wanted to bathe and look her best for John.

Flowers grow best in a well-tended garden. Her mother's voice scolded in her memory.

"Marguerite?"

"*Un moment, Papa.*" Out from beneath her covers, the room chilled her skin, and she pulled on her housecoat.

Her father stood in the hall, shirtless and shivering—a skeleton of the man she remembered. He pointed a trembling finger toward his room. "Someone poured ice water on my bed. *Pourquoi?*"

"Oh no," Aubrielle murmured as she fought back tears he wouldn't understand. *Poor Papa.* "Let me run a warm bath for you."

"Aubrielle?"

"Yes, Papa?" She wrapped a bath towel around his naked shoulders, switched on the bathroom light and knelt to prepare a bath.

He followed her and stood in the doorway. "I had a dream," he said above the sound of the water. "I was a young man who served a knight." He shivered, and his voice grew reminiscent. "I took care of his horse, and I polished his armor until it shone like the sun."

Warm water spilled over Aubrielle's wrist, and she closed the drain and stood. "What a pleasant dream."

"It seemed real." His unfocused gaze changed, and he looked at her. "Where's your Mama?"

Aubrielle took a deep breath. She had no answer he could accept at this moment. To speak the truth would break his heart. "I'll find you something to wear."

She pulled clean clothes from his drawers.

His bedding will need to be laundered.

The wringer-washer was downstairs in the shop. If Mae could watch Papa, Aubrielle would be able to wash their bedding and clothes, hang them to dry in the sun, and then iron the clothes. A full day's work.

So much for shopping.

And time was running out. Hanukkah would begin at sunset the day after tomorrow.

At least, I found Papa's special menorah.

In the bathroom, her father hadn't moved. She set his clothes on the counter beside the sink and turned off the tub faucet. "I'll be down the hall if you need me."

His eyes shifted to her, then away.

"Papa? Take off your wet clothes and get into the warm bath. It will feel good."

"I'm sorry, *ma belle* Aubrielle." His lips trembled.

"Sorry?" She leaned forward to see his face. "For what?"

"*Ma belle fille*, so like your sweet mama. I know she's gone. I know that, but I forget sometimes." He looked into her eyes. "My child shouldn't be trapped caring for a sick old man. I can't—I know I can't—remember things. I try—" A single tear slid down his cheek. "*Pardonne-moi, s'il te plaît.*" He held a trembling hand beside her face.

Aubrielle took his hand. "*Je t'aime, Papa.*"

His bent and trembling fingers stroked her hair. "*Je t'aime, ma fille.*"

Aubrielle sniffed and wiped her face. "You should get in your bath. The water will grow cold."

He bobbed his head once and laid the bath towel from his shoulders on the counter. "*Merci.*"

"I'll be in the kitchen if you need me." Aubrielle closed the door and covered her mouth. As swiftly as she could, she walked down the hall to her room, threw herself on her bed, and cried.

How cruel for Papa to know, in moments of clarity, how much he had lost. She gulped air and buried her face in her pillow to hide the sound of her tears.

When the rush of emotion had passed, she stood and inspected her reflection in the vanity. "*Merde!*"

Once in the kitchen, she could hear the occasional splash from the washroom. She dampened a dish towel with cool water, tipped her head back and laid the cloth across her eyes.

The jingle of keys against the back door caused her to lower her chin and open her eyes. The towel dropped into her hands.

Mae came in with a bag of groceries. She set the foodstuffs, along with her keys, on the counter and looked with concern at Aubrielle. "What's amiss, lass?"

Aubrielle shook her head. "Nothing." She shrugged. "Papa." She wiped her face and summoned a smile for Mae. "I'm surprised to see you this morning."

"Ah well." Mae unloaded her bag. "Antoine is back and feeling much better." She handed Aubrielle a brick of cheese and a wrapped package of sliced meat from the butcher. "Slice a bit of the cheese and put the rest in the box, would you dear?"

When the groceries were put away, Mae folded the bag and examined Aubrielle. "I can see you need a break." She set a loaf of bread on the cutting board and pulled the bread knife from the drawer.

"I can't." A heavy sigh escaped her throat. "Both Papa and I have laundry."

Mae made angled cuts in the loaf. "I have a laundry woman coming on Wednesday. She can do both."

"No, *Tante* Mae—"

"I won't hear an argument." Mae placed a piece of cheese on the bread and handed it to Aubrielle. "You've been inside for four straight days. You need to get out. Even when I'm here every day, I go home at night." She stacked cheese on a slice of bread for herself. "You need a break, and the snow has melted. Take a walk in the park."

"I need to shop for Hanukkah," Aubrielle admitted. "I have a bit of money set aside. I hope it will be enough." She took a bite of Mae's treat.

"Don't worry about money for your candles and such. I'm looking forward to your Hanukkah holiday, and besides, you'll be working for me soon enough, selling in the park."

"You'd do that for me?"

"For both you and your Papa. When Lou finishes, wash up and get ready." She winked at Aubrielle. "Perhaps one of your young men would like to go with you."

"My young men?" Aubrielle's face warmed at Mae's teasing. "I've turned John away every day this week. He's bound to have given up on me." She picked up a piece of cheese. "And Henri only comes to the house when he knows you'll be cooking."

Mae raised an eyebrow. "Somehow, I doubt that."

Aubrielle covered her grin with her fingers and hurried to her room. Her limited wardrobe left her few choices, but she settled on a warm wool blue dress. When her clothes and undergarments lay ready on her bed, she turned to her vanity. Unbidden, her attention fell on the small box her father had given her. The Star of David— the necklace her mother had never worn. With sure hands, she removed the silver cross from her neck and withdrew the delicate golden chain from the small red box. The six-pointed star of gold caught the light and shimmered at her throat.

I'll wear it for Papa.

* * *

John Larson

John slid the straight razor down his chin one last time then turned his head to view the other side of his face in the mirror. *Done.* He rinsed the blade and removed the remaining soap from his face with the towel as he walked to the kitchen.

Henri lounged at the table eating croissants with Billy. "There you are," Henri lifted his chin to John. "I brought a bit of breakfast back with me."

John tossed the end of the towel over his shoulder and picked up one of the flaky pastries. "Did you learn anything new from Bonet last night?"

Henri swallowed and nodded. "Bonet spoke to that René fellow you asked about." He waved his bread toward Billy. "René saw two men struggle near your truck just before the gunfire. Afterward, he had the impression there were several men involved in the attack, but he didn't stick around to find out." Henri took a sip of his coffee. "René said he didn't know you'd been hit." He raised his gaze to John. "And he was very pleased to get his money back."

"I'm sure he was." John leaned against the counter and bit into the buttery pastry.

"But we're no closer to finding François." Billy tossed his half-eaten croissant onto the table. "I fear it's been too long."

"If they want the rest of the weapons, they'll keep him alive," John reassured Billy.

"Then why no demands? Why haven't we heard anything?" Billy set his elbows on the table and slid his fingers into the thick hair on both sides of his head.

"We will—or we'll find him on our own." John addressed Henri, "Did you learn anything else about your friend, Karl, or Bonet's other employees?"

"Not my friend, but yes." Henri nodded. "Karl's employment includes a room behind the stage area. Since Bonet has an apartment above his club, Karl must stay close and remain at Bonet's beck and call." Henri lowered his voice. "Recently, Karl has left the building as soon as the club closes and often doesn't return until mid-afternoon."

"How did you learn that?" Billy's eyes were wide.

"Bonet is inconvenienced. He complains loudly."

"Where does Karl go?" John narrowed his eyes at Henri with interest.

"Bonet doesn't know, but it might pay to find out." Henri picked up another croissant.

"I agree." John left Billy and Henri to discuss Karl and finished dressing. He unwrapped one of several new shirts he had ordered from the garment maker.

Mae had come by earlier that morning and told him she would stay with Lou today so Aubrielle could get away from the house for a few hours. He grinned at himself in the mirror as he adjusted his tie.

I'll see Aubrielle today.

All the women she had been faded in light of the person John had come to know. All the similarities and differences combined into the girl he had always loved.

Aubrielle.

Henri and Billy looked up as John passed through the kitchen. He picked up his coat and hat and spoke over his shoulder. "Maybe we can discover where Bonet's manservant goes after club hours." At the door, he turned and looked at Billy and Henri. "In the meantime, I'd appreciate it if you would see to Éclair's stall. It no doubt needs cleaning."

* * *

John tucked Aubrielle's gloved hand inside his arm as they crossed the street. The blue sky and bright sunshine belied the hint of a chill in the breeze. Winter was not done with them yet.

"What is the name of the shop again?" John asked.

"Asher's Market. It's a Jewish store and will have everything I need to purchase." She looked up at him and shielded the late morning sunlight with her palm. "I hope you'll be able to join us each evening when we light the candles."

A fist of emotion clenched his heart.

Was it always like this?

"I would be honored." The witch who had cursed them so long ago—Nescato—had been mistaken. She swore he would love only one woman for all eternity, yet in every life, Agaria was unique, even though she retained the same beloved essence in her soul.

And I fall in love each time, just as I did the first time.

The neighborhood around Asher's Market boasted a café, a greengrocer and a handful of clothing and shoe stores. Locals congregated along the street between Asher's and the eatery.

"Perhaps we could dine at the *Café Jardin de Lune* after you finish shopping." John pointed to the small restaurant as they passed.

"Perhaps." Aubrielle pulled a folded slip of paper from her purse. "If you would wait for me out here. The aisles inside are narrow, and the crowd will be more than usual because of the holiday."

At the front of Asher's, he pulled her hand free of his arm and kissed the back of her glove. "I'll watch for you from here."

Aubrielle's eyes widened, and she raised her hand to her blushed face. "Yes," she whispered. "I'll return shortly." She took a step back, still gazing into his eyes, then turned and entered the store.

Although the café's outdoor tables remained empty, beyond the windows, the seats inside were filled with diners. Several people waited at the entrance to give the *maître d'* their name.

John crossed the street and added his name to the list. As he walked back to the market, he saw a face he recognized.

Karl stood beside the entrance to Asher's Market. With a pencil and journal in hand, he spoke briefly to each shopper who approached the Jewish store. He made notations in his book, and then would move on to the next customer.

John leaned his shoulder against the storefront stone facade and watched with interest.

Curious.

Aubrielle walked out the door, her purchases boxed and wrapped in brown paper.

Karl approached her, tipped his head and spoke for several moments.

Aubrielle nodded. As she listened, she reached up and touched her necklace. She replied to several questions, nodded to Karl, and then looked over and caught John's gaze. Her smile brightened. She edged sideways to avoid two women going into Asher's and made her way to John's side.

John took her package. "What was that about?" he asked, with a nod toward Karl.

Bonet's manservant had stopped the two women, making note of their answers. He opened the door for them to enter, then made another quick note in his book.

"The man asking questions?" Aubrielle glanced over her shoulder. "He works for Asher's Market." She grinned at John. "They'll have a drawing on the last day of Hanukkah to give away a prize. He asked my name, address, and the names of everyone in my family. Papa has a chance to win too." Aubrielle raised her eyebrows at John. "We're lucky to have our names on the list."

Chapter 21

John Larson

Could Bonet's valet have taken a second job?

"I put our name on the seating list at the *Jardin de Lune.*" John took Aubrielle's elbow.

I'll have Henri check with Asher's Market.

John ground his teeth as uneasiness crawled between his shoulder blades.

"I'm sorry, John. I wish I could. Another time would be better." Aubrielle paused with John in front of the café. "The restaurant is too busy, and I can't be gone very long. *Tante* Mae is with Papa, but if her other baker becomes ill…" She shrugged one shoulder. Her dark eyes pleaded with him to understand.

"A brief stroll in the park, then. The fresh air and sunshine will do you good." He held out his arm. "We'll purchase pies from a vendor and still have you home in half the time."

The path to the park led them toward the river and put the wind to their backs. John's attention returned to the woman at his side, and he struggled with disbelief.

She chose to be here—with me. His heart soared.

Sunlight sparkled across her necklace, and he blinked. A sudden foreboding curled low in his gut, and his mood darkened. Foreknowledge, a terrible gift given to him long ago, had seemed a distant fairy tale. Splendid with human advancement—flying machines and automobiles. Unbelievable in its horror.

And now here—with this woman—at this time and place. Terrifying.

They waited at the streetlight then crossed the bridge over the Seine.

We'll have to leave France, leave Europe altogether.

Those distant words had painted an ugly picture of a genocidal maniac.

London bombed and burned and trains leaving Paris bound for camps in Poland.

"You are quiet today," Aubrielle observed. She pointed at a puddle of melted snow. They avoided the water and passed beneath the Eiffel Tower.

"I know." He forced a smile and clamped down hard on his panic. "I'm sorry."

I still have time.

Not far from the entrance, a food vendor sold warm meat pierogies to several servicemen. John and Aubrielle waited in line. When they held their meat pastry, they strolled to the closest bench and sat facing the sun.

"What's on your mind?" Aubrielle bit into her pie and warm gravy ran down her chin. She giggled and held a napkin to her mouth. "Careful."

Even her playful smile couldn't lift his anxious mood. "I was reminded today of Hitler's publication and how filled with hate the man is." He shook his head.

I must carry this burden of knowledge in silence—or be thought insane.

"Don't think of him." She caught a drop of meat sauce on her tongue, then took another small bite. "He won't get into France," she assured, the napkin covering her lips.

Is it her youth or her trusting nature?

He bit into his pie, and it tasted like ash in his mouth.

I've lived too long, despite my appearance. Jaded and fearful.

He took another small bite, then tossed the pie and wrapper into the trash receptacle.

"Are you not hungry?" She narrowed her eyes and tilted her head. "You're upset with me after all."

"Not in the least." John set back and rested his arm along the back of the bench. "But I am a fool to waste a precious day with you on fears of an uncertain future."

Uncertain to some.

He took a deep breath and exhaled through pressed lips as he studied the blue winter sky.

I have an old man's soul in a young man's body.

He took the empty pastry wrapper she offered and tossed it into the trash.

And I ache with a young man's need.

"Every moment with you is far too valuable to squander with worry." He brushed her cheek with his knuckles.

She leaned into his touch and smiled. "Then don't worry."

"Hmm," he chuckled and gestured with his other hand. "Over there, across the way. Do you know what happened there?"

She shook her head. "No. What do you mean?"

"That's where you stood the first time I saw you." He turned toward her and searched her eyes. "I swear—I've never seen anything or anyone, more beautiful." He leaned forward and tasted her lips with a gentle brush of his mouth then drew back to gauge her reaction.

Her eyes opened and stared into his. She lifted her hand and touched the fingertips of her gloves to her lips. Then she reached out and caressed the side of his face, pulling it toward hers. "Again." Her eyelashes fluttered closed, and she raised her face.

John ran his fingers through her hair behind her ear and listened for the small intake of breath he knew would follow.

Youth's passion coupled with a legacy of loving memories.

"I know you." He spoke too soft for her to hear, then lowered his mouth to hers.

Her lips parted beneath his, and she met his declaration with one of her own—without words, the tilt of her head spoke to him. The soft white gloved hand slipped behind his neck and held him close.

A pulse of desire spread downward from John's gut.

And she knows me.

Thankful for the box of candles resting on his thighs, he broke the kiss and raised his head. In an instant, he memorized her face, her lips, soft and moist—her long lashes fanned beneath delicately arched brows, the same color as her dark hair.

Lashes lifted from her cheeks, and her eyes searched his. Her russet-brown irises sprinkled with flecks of gold, caught the winter sun and reflected its light. She returned his stare, her pupils large and inviting. Her lashes lowered. With small deliberate movements, she dropped her hand from his neck and clasped them together in her lap. "I thought…that was—" Her face infused with color, and she turned her head away.

"A kiss. Heartfelt and sincere. The first of many I hope we share, only with you." He positioned the package on his lap to shield the embarrassment of his ardor.

We shall require more privacy.

She looked at him from the corner of her eye. "The first of many?" A gentle smile spread across her face. She lifted her chin and gazed across the parkway. "I'd like that. Perhaps more than I should." She remained silent for several moments, staring at the place she used to sell flowers in the morning, then she brushed her hands down her thighs. "But for now, I must return to Papa." She stood and held out a hand to John. "Ready to walk me home?"

"Of course." John adjusted his overcoat as he stood to conceal the evidence of his desire. He tucked her package under his arm and took her hand.

He declined Aubrielle's invitation to stay for dinner, as well as Mae's offer to send food home with him for Billy and Henri.

I'll speak to the butcher tomorrow and have meat delivered to Mae.

The generous woman continued to offer help to everyone during difficult times. The least he could do was help her feed those she loved. Besides, he intended to share many dinners with Mae's adopted family.

John paused to check on Éclair before he crossed the alley to his building. Watching Karl write down names, and remembering the horrors that had been foretold, firmed his resolve to discover the truth about the scarred valet. John opened the door to his apartment and cast a quick look around. "Where's Henri?" He walked to the kitchen and poured himself a glass of water.

Billy lay on the couch cleaning his nails with his pocket knife. "He went to *La Fleur Chantante* again." He looked up at John. "Did you bring dinner?"

John shook his head as he tipped the glass back and swallowed the last bit of water. "No. We've enough left over for a meal, plus Mae's bread and meat from the butcher." He rinsed the cup and set it on the drainboard. "If you're hungry, find something to eat then get cleaned up. We're going to find Henri."

Billy swung his bare feet to the floor. "You have news of François?" A pained expression flashed across his face, and he pressed his hand against his side.

"No news, just an ugly feeling. I'm going to play a hunch." John rested the heels of his palms on the counter and stretched his back.

"Must be some hunch, mate." Billy stood with deliberate effort and crossed to the lavatory. "I'll be put to rights in a jiff."

"We have a stop to make along the way."

John drove the truck to Asher's. There were few cars on the road after sunset. "I watched Bonet's valet stop and speak with the market's customers today. He wrote down their names and addresses." John parked across from the store.

"Why would he do that?"

"I didn't have the opportunity to speak with him. He told Aubrielle he worked for Asher's." John opened the door. "I intend to go to the market and ask."

"Not you." Billy pulled the lever to his door and eased from the truck with a groan. "The valet saw you the night you went to the club. Lord knows, you're hard to forget. I'll talk with the owner just in case this Karl is still in there." He shut the door and hurried across the street.

John strummed his fingers on the cold steering wheel. Across the diagonal, the *Café Jardin de Lune* had begun to empty its dinner crowd. Couples stood along the walkway huddled in their coats.

After several long moments, Billy emerged from the shop. He paused to let a cab pass, then crossed the street and opened the door. "I spoke with the owner." His lips drew back, and he hissed through his teeth as he climbed into the truck. "Gah."

"What did he say?"

"The owner chased the man from the storefront after several customers complained." Billy pulled the door closed. "Whatever he was doing here, he doesn't work for Asher's Market, and there is no prize to be given away."

"Aubrielle gave him her name and address." Urgency rose in John's chest.

"Let's find him and ask him what he was doing, mate."

John put the vehicle into gear and pulled into traffic. They had to park two blocks from *La Fleur Chantante*. "Busy night." John handed Billy the keys and slid his revolver beneath the driver's seat.

The doorman stood outside tonight. He nodded a greeting to John as they approached. *"Votre arme?"*

"Je n'en ai pas." John opened his coat to display his empty holster.

"Merci." The guard opened the door. *"Bonne soirée."*

Inside, the crowd made the small venue feel tight and alive with motion. Servers moved between the tables, delivering food and drink orders while couples danced near the band. A dark-skinned woman with a sultry voice sang on stage.

John checked his hat and coat and turned to survey the crowd while Billy flirted with the coat girl. Bonet wasn't on the upper level where he had been nearly a week ago.

"John." Henri stood and waved from a table across the long room.

"This way," John said to Billy then wove through the crowd to Henri's table.

"You're a surprise." Henri resumed his seat and gestured to the empty chairs. "I haven't seen Bonet yet, although I doubt there is anything new. He would have sent someone out to find me."

John sat and signaled to a waitress. "Have you seen Karl?"

Henri shook his head. "No, but they're usually together." He pointed to an empty booth in the elevated section behind them. "The reserved table is for Bonet and his men."

"*Bonjour.*" The waitress said to John and Billy. She picked up Henri's empty glass and placed it on her tray. "*Un autre?*"

"*Oui,*" Henri replied. "*Merci.*"

"*Et pour vous?*" She looked at Billy and John.

"What he's having." John gave a nod toward Henri.

"*Ah, un Américain.*" The server smiled. "We see not many." She smiled at Billy. "*Et vous?*"

"Same." Billy grinned at the woman.

The waitress noted their order and turned away without looking up from her pad.

"I tell you, Bill—if you're not in uniform, the women want nothing to do with you," Henri laughed. "Our server, Lisette, has a *petit ami* in the army."

"You know her name?" Billy's brows rose in apparent disbelief.

"I've been here every night for a week." Henri shrugged and cocked back his head. "I know everyone's name."

Lisette wove through the crowd. Her tray held high above her head. She set the platter on the table and served the men their drinks.

John dropped several coins on her tray. "*Merci.*"

She winked at John, lifted her serving platter and swirled away between tables.

Henri tasted his drink, then set it down and leaned back to look beyond John's shoulders. "Bonet just came in."

The reserved seats were to John's back. John nodded and continued to watch the woman on stage. "Is Karl with them?"

Henri nodded. "Karl, Bruce, and Marcel. His usual associates." Henri studied John. "What do you want to do?"

John tasted his drink, then looked at both Billy and Henri. "I want to ask Karl what he was doing at Asher's. I want to know why he asked for Aubrielle's name and address."

"Bonet doesn't like to be interrupted. Club guests are supposed to request an invitation to meet with Bonet from the waitress."

John shrugged and shook his head. "I don't give a damn about his rules." He turned as he stood and stared across the railing at Bonet.

"John, you should sit down," Henri stated and cast a nervous glance at John, then toward Bonet. "We don't want to cause a scene."

"I don't intend to cause a scene, but I do mean to ask Karl a few questions." John spoke to Billy, "If you hear anything other than polite conversation, get the truck." He looked over his shoulder at Henri. "Is there a back exit to the club?"

"Yes." Henri took a quick gulp of his drink. "Through the stage door and past the kitchen." He rose to stand beside John. "It opens onto a delivery *ruelle*. I don't know if it has a name."

"I'll find the alley," Billy said. "I'll either sit here and finish my drink or meet you at the back door with the truck." He glanced over his shoulder at the elevated seats.

Maurice Bonet had seen John stand. His stare never wavered as he spoke to the man seated beside him. Tonight, Bonet wore a rust-colored silk suit and tie, making his olive complexion look green in the subdued club light.

Bonet's man nodded and buttoned his jacket as he rose. He walked to the railing near John's table. "*Monsieur* Bonet has no additional information for you, Mister Larson."

John took a step to the rail and looked up at Bonet's bodyguard. *This one is Bruce.* "I understand. I would still like to speak to him."

"Regarding what, may I ask?"

John shook his head and followed the elevated rail to the short flight of stairs near the back wall, with Henri close on his heels.

Bruce kept pace with the men along the banister. "Gentlemen, I insist you return to your seats."

Chapter 22

John Larson

John mounted the steps and stared down at the security man. "I'm not here to disturb *Monsieur* Bonet, but I do intend to speak with him." He looked beyond Bruce and met Maurice Bonet's curious stare. "And whether he knows it or not, *Monsieur* Bonet wants to hear what I have to say."

Bruce took a step forward. "No."

"Bruce," Maurice Bonet called. *"Laisse-les passer."* He lifted his hand in a familiar gesture and beckoned John forward.

Bruce stood aside and folded his arms.

John and Henri approached the booth, with Bruce close behind them.

"Mister Larson, I spoke with *votre ami,* Henri, yesterday." Bonet nodded to Henri and replaced his arm around the attractive redhead. On Bonet's left, a brunette sipped her drink and raised an arched brow at John. "If I had any information about our mutual friend, François, I would have told him."

"This isn't about François." John shifted his stare from Bonet to the valet, Karl, who stood beside the curved end of the booth. "Or at least, not *only* about François."

Karl lifted his chin and stared down his crooked nose at John. His jaw clamped shut.

Bonet looked between the two men then spoke sharply to John. "Speak plainly, *monsieur*. You interrupt my evening."

"Henri said your valet is often unavailable to you during the day—his whereabouts unaccounted for." John's lips curled into a phony smile. "Ask him where he was today, around noon."

Bonet set forward in his seat and turned toward his valet. "Karl?"

Karl rolled his shoulders and lowered his head. *"Monsieur?"*

The club owner heaved an exasperated sigh. *"Ne la joue pas stupide. Réponds."*

"He was outside Asher's Market, writing down the customers' names and addresses." John took another step closer. "What I don't know is why."

With a sudden movement, Karl lunged forward and flipped the small table in front of Bonet into John's path. Then he turned and ran toward the stage.

Women screamed, and glass shattered as the table crashed to the floor.

John rounded the fallen table and raced after Karl.

Karl ran down the short flight of stairs and jumped onto the stage. He glanced over his shoulder then grabbed the singer by the arm and threw her to the ground.

The club erupted into chaos. Musicians crouched beside the stage. People came to their feet shouting. Couples on the dance floor turned and stared.

John hopped over the elevated rail, wove through the panicked crowd, and vaulted onto the stage. "Are you all right?" He helped the singer to her feet.

At her quick nod, John chased Karl through the backstage door. To his left, a short set of steps led to the shallow backstage area. A crash ahead spurred John past the dressing area and through the kitchen door.

Two cooks looked from Karl, near the rear exit, to John. *"Qui êtes-vous? Qu'est-ce que cette merde?"* The cook on the far side lifted a hatchet.

John pointed at Karl *"Attrapez-le pour Monsieur Bonet."*

Karl fled out the back door just as the hatchet embedded in the door frame beside his head.

John rushed past the cooks who had burst into laughter and yelled vulgarities after Karl.

Karl is not well-liked.

He followed Karl into the alley.

The winter air chilled the perspiration on his forehead as he exhaled plumes into the night and listened. To his right, a garbage can crashed to the ground and rolled, spilling garbage across the pavement. The tap of shoes and a shadow fled down the alley.

Henri burst from the door and ran into John's back. The impact knocked Henri to the ground. As he regained his feet, he pointed down the alley. "There!"

Karl had reached the cross street and rushed into traffic. Tires squealed, accompanied by horns and yelling.

John raced forward.

We can't lose him, not now.

Karl would never return to the club, and John had questions he needed Karl to answer. As John rounded the corner onto the street, the rattle of Billy's truck caught his attention. "Henri—tell Billy to follow." John crossed in front of the angry motorist and scanned down the block.

Karl made it to the next cross street. He glanced back at John, then turned and disappeared around the corner.

John raced down the sidewalk after Karl.

Midway down the block headlights came on. An older model Renault pulled away from the curb, gaining speed as it careened toward John.

At the last moment, John jumped out of its path.

Karl glared from behind the wheel. His lips pulled back in a snarl, the dark mark on his face and neck visible in the glow from the dashboard.

The wheels squealed as Karl turned the corner, barely missing Billy's vehicle.

John hurried to the truck and jumped into the bed. "Don't let him get away."

Billy ground the gears, and they lurched into motion. They picked up speed after they followed Karl onto the boulevard heading south.

John crouched behind the cab to get out of the frigid wind.

Inside the cab, Henri pulled John's revolver from beneath the bench seat. He checked the rounds, then looked back at John.

"Just don't shoot yourself," John muttered.

Traffic south of town thinned, and soon the only car ahead of them was Karl's. *He's leading us back to the warehouse along the Marne.*

The old Citroën truck could not keep up with the Renault, and Karl's headlights became a distant glow disappearing at each dip in the road. With a final flicker, the light died out altogether.

Billy punched the dashboard.

John clenched his teeth. *No.* Karl must have turned off the main road. He pounded on the cab and Billy rolled down the driver's window. "He turned," John yelled. "Watch for a side street."

Billy nodded.

Past the warehouse district, the run-down neighborhood became low-income apartment buildings along both sides of the road.

The truck slowed, and Billy turned into the first complex. Headlights off, he eased up on the gas and rolled down the street. The windows in most of the apartments were dark.

Henri pointed.

John stood and looked over the cab. The Renault set at the curb up ahead.

Billy turned down the adjacent street and parked. When the engine stopped, both he and Henri got out.

John stood in the truck bed and watched the windows in the apartment nearest Karl's Renault. *Where did you run?*

Henri pointed as a light came on in the third-floor window.

John hopped out of the truck bed and landed on the walk beside Henri. "My gun," he whispered. The weapon in hand, he dashed toward the building entrance.

Billy and Henri followed close behind.

Inside, a hallway led to the first-floor apartments and a staircase led up. John mounted the steps and stopped on the third-floor landing. Light shone beneath the first apartment, and muffled voices came from behind the door.

Henri stepped to the far side of the doorway and nodded.

John glanced at Billy then knocked. The voices inside went silent. *What if this is the wrong apartment?* He gripped his revolver.

The door eased open, and an older woman with gray ratted hair, smudged makeup, and a silk housecoat stared up at him. *"Qu'est-ce que vous voulez?"* She puffed on her cigarette and blew smoke into the hallway.

"Karl," John yelled over the woman's head. "I know you're in there." His glare dropped to the slattern in the doorway. "Move aside, *madame.*"

The woman's eyes widened momentarily, then looked to the side of the door without turning her head. *"Pas parler anglais."*

"I think you do speak English." Movement behind the woman caught John's eye.

"John, watch out!" Henri ducked low and slammed into the door just as gunfire exploded inside the apartment. He and the woman fell to the floor, where he grappled for her arms.

John brought up his weapon and entered the apartment, stepping over Henri and the screaming woman. "Karl, let's talk. No one needs to get hurt."

Karl dodged out from behind the kitchen wall, pointed his gun at John's head, and pulled the trigger. The hammer fell on an empty chamber.

John turned and stared into Karl's astonished eyes. "Don't—"

Karl pulled the trigger again, but the gun refused to fire. His mouth dropped open, and he shook his head. "No, this can't be true."

John knocked Karl's gun aside and punched his fist into the man's face.

The sharp crack of Karl's weapon echoed in the apartment as he fell to the floor and dropped the gun. Blood flowed from his broken nose onto his white shirt. "She didn't lie. It's true. You live."

John holstered his gun and grabbed the valet's jacket, lifting him by the lapels. "The names you collected at Asher's Market." He rammed Karl into the wall. "What are they for?"

"The Jews?" Karl gripped John's wrists, his eyes blinked in confusion. "Those names have been sent to *Einsatzgruppen.* Why do you care?"

"What's *Einsatzgruppen*?" John shook Karl.

"It's German. It translates to Task Force." Henri stood beside John, Karl's gun in his hand. "It's part of the Nazi *Schutzstaffel* or SS. If they have Aubrielle's name and address, they will come for her."

"The woman—*your* woman—is a Jew?" Karl's brows rose, and he laughed with delight.

John fought his urge to snap the German's neck. Instead, he glanced at Henri. "What happened to the dragon lady who opened the door?"

"She bit me." He flushed and pointed toward the open door. "Then fled down the hall."

"Where's Billy?"

"I'm in here," his voice came from the back of the apartment. "There's a locked door."

John looked at Karl. "Give us the key."

"I don't have the key," he smirked. "Stella had it. She takes care of…" Karl's voice faded.

"Takes care of what?" John demanded.

"Of him." Karl startled at the sound of the door being kicked.

"Help Billy," John said to Henri.

Two more loud thumps then a single loud crack rang sharply through the apartment.

"It's François," Billy yelled. "He's alive."

"You might live through the day after all," John muttered at Karl.

The marked man tipped his head back and glared into John's eyes. "I don't fear you or the French police." He spat blood against the wall and lowered his chin. "*Mein Führer* doesn't frighten me as much as the baroness." His lips pulled back in a grimace. Blood from his nose stained his teeth.

"Who's this baroness?" John asked, his voice quiet and filled with menace.

"The Baroness Nescato," Karl whispered. "She searches for you."

Chapter 23

John Larson

"Nescato?" John's gut tightened.

Impossible.

His vision blurred, and he struggled to take a breath. To hear the sorceress's name after two millennia— He inhaled through his nose.

She had to be dead.

"Where did you hear that name?" he demanded.

"Where? From the baroness herself." Karl sneered. "She gave instruction on how to identify you."

"You lie." His jaw clenched as blood pounded in his ears. "The witch, Nescato, is dead."

"The baroness is indeed a witch, although a living one," the valet whispered. "And as impossible to kill as you." He spat another mouthful of blood between John's feet. "*Mein Führer* is fascinated with how her proximity bends—probability."

Billy and Henri emerged from the back room supporting François between them.

The old smuggler attempted to regain his feet. His face was beaten and bloody. He blinked swollen, bloodstained eyes at the two men in the kitchen. "*Tuez-le, mon ami.* Kill that *salopard.*"

The clatter of boots on the metal stair and a woman's shrill shout gave a small warning. Machine-gun fire erupted through the open door, and a man followed the barrage into the room.

John knocked Karl to the ground, pulled his revolver, and shot at the shadowed figure in the doorway.

Their attacker grunted and spun sideways, his back against the door frame. His cap fell to the ground as he lurched upright. He bared his teeth and raised the machine-gun at John.

Henri fired Karl's weapon twice from behind the sofa. Both rounds pierced his target in the chest.

The armed man squeezed the trigger as he fell, firing a burst into the floor.

Cries of terror and running sounded from the hall, but for the moment, the exit stood clear.

John yanked Karl from the floor, wrapped his arm around the valet's neck, and shoved him toward the door. "We need to get to the truck." Near the room's entrance, he nudged the Thompson with his toe. "Billy, take this."

"*Non.*" François bent and grasped the strap. "*C'est pour moi.*"

John eyed the Frenchman. "Suit yourself." He tipped his head toward Karl. "But I still have questions for this one. I need him alive."

A spray of bullets forestalled François's reply and drove them from the opening.

Henri spun out of the line of fire and crouched beside the entrance. He stole a brief glance toward the staircase, looking both up and down. He rested his head against the wall and held up one finger and pointed up. Then wiggled his fingers like running legs and pointed down and out toward the stairs.

François lunged into the doorway with a raw scream. Bullets from his weapon pinged from the metal stairs as spent casings littered the floor. When he released the trigger, he swayed backward into the room.

Billy steadied him. "We need to get you to the hospital, mate."

Blood dripped from the electrical wire hanging from François's wrists. Although he'd been cut free, the remaining wire dug deep into his flesh. He peered at his friend through slits in his swollen eyes. *"Oui, je sais."*

"First, we have to get out of here." John swung Karl forward, lifting the Nazi off his feet.

Karl held onto John's forearm with both hands as he gasped for breath.

Henri eased into the hall. His gun trained on the stairs leading to the top floor. Satisfied, he glanced at John as he walked around the body. "Here's another of your automatics."

"Take it," John responded.

Henri slipped Karl's revolver beneath his belt and picked up the machine-gun. He headed down the stairs, the weapon snug against his shoulder.

"You've got François?" John asked Billy as he hauled Karl out the door. Without waiting for a reply, the big man stepped over the dead shooter and backed toward the stairs. His head swiveled back and forth as the building's occupants sprang to life.

In the absence of gunfire, curious residents peeked from their doors. The terrified ones scurried through the hallway in their nightclothes seeking a safe exit. Doors were thrown open and slammed shut. The sharp sound ricocheted down the hall like gunfire. A shout of anger, followed by rushing footsteps, echoed down from the corridor above.

John hurried down the steps. Below him, he saw Henri make the turn on the second landing headed to the ground floor.

A man wearing a blue nightshirt yelled profanities in French as he shook his finger at the stairs.

At the bottom, Henri held the door. "Hurry."

John pushed Karl through the doorway and put his back to the building. His arm tight around the German's neck.

Billy pulled the keys from his pocket with one hand as he and François left the stairwell into the night air. His other arm supported François.

Above them, glass shattered.

John spun away from the falling shards, carrying Karl with him.

The *rat-tat-tat* of automatic fire punctuated sparks on the pavement and nipped at Henri's heels. He dove into the street behind the line of parked vehicles.

Past the cars, Billy and François hurried toward the truck.

"Damn—" An elbow rammed into John's stomach just as his shoulder exploded in pain, knocking him to his knees.

Karl spun from John's grip and dashed away.

John picked up the gun with his off hand and stumbled between the cars to the relative safety of the street. He sat down hard on the pavement and looked over at Henri.

Henri shot a short burst toward the window then crouched down and glanced at John. "You've been shot." He fired off another half-dozen rounds.

"I'll live," John replied. *I always do.* "Where did Karl go? Was he hit?"

"No. He made it back inside." Henri ducked as muzzle flash sparked in the window. A spray of bullets punctured tires and shattered car windows.

John rotated his shoulder. The round had pierced the meat of his right deltoid. Blood flowed freely down his arm. He looked up the side street toward the truck. He expected to see Billy and François dead on the street, but both men were missing. "Billy has the keys," he said to Henri.

"I don't know how much ammunition is left," Henri replied. "But I have Karl's revolver. Go to the truck. I'll cover you."

John waited until Henri fired at the window, then he staggered to his feet and ran up the street. He dodged onto the walkway, using the cars as a shield.

Ahead, beside the truck, lay François and Billy.

François cradled Billy in his arms. When he saw John, he raised his head. "Billy's been shot. I pulled him out of the street, but—"

John touched Billy's neck. *He has a pulse.* "He's alive. Were you hit?"

"Yes." François closed his eyes. "I'm too weak to get him in the truck."

Behind them, the gunfire from the window increased, then discontinued. John looked back at the building and caught sight of Henri, dodging between parked cars. "They're coming for us. We have to go."

Henri ran up behind John and slung the Thompson into the truck bed. "Billy?"

"He's alive. Help me get him in the bed." John pulled the keys from Billy's fist and shoved them in his pocket. He lifted Billy's shoulders while Henri guided his feet.

"I'll hold him." Henri climbed in the back and sat beside Billy. "Let's go."

John rounded the truck and slid behind the wheel as François pulled the passenger door closed. The engine cranked twice then roared to life. John dropped it into first and pulled onto the street. "Where's the nearest hospital?" he asked François.

"That would be the *Hôpital de la Pitié,* straight ahead. Head back to town. It's not far."

"Why did Karl take you?" John asked the smuggler. "What did he want?"

"Our German friend wanted the rest of the arms shipment." François lifted his hand from his stomach and stared at it. "He wasn't satisfied with only three weapons." The fresh blood on his hand mixed with that from his wrist.

"How badly are you hurt?" John turned onto the main boulevard into Paris.

"Not as badly as Billy." He exhaled a ragged breath. "But if I pass out, give the doctor my full name, François Belliard and tell them to contact the *Sûreté nationale.*" He grunted as the truck bounced over a bump in the road. "They'll wonder where I've been."

"I will," John assured him.

Sûreté nationale? Why would the French Police be concerned about a smuggler?

He tapped the steering wheel and checked the review mirror.

Henri huddled behind the cab. His hair tossed by the wind.

Henri and Billy must be freezing. Their coats remained at *La Fleur*—left behind when they chased the German valet. John blinked, then looked at the smuggler from the corner of his eye. "François, do you work for the French Internal Security?"

"*Oui. Contre-espionnage.*" François pressed his hand to his side. "Some of the weapons purchased from the *Giselle-Marie* were used to expose Nazi agents believed to be in Paris." His forehead furrowed and he shook his head. "I thought Ken Rice would have told you."

John rested his right hand in his lap to keep from moving his shoulder. "The first mate on the *Giselle-Marie* knows you're an intelligence agent?"

"He knows." François spat a piece of wire he had chewed from his wrist. "So was he, during the Great War, except on the side of the damned British." He huffed a short chuckle. "His partner, Nigel Keats, gave me the first handgun I ever owned, then married my sister, Giselle."

John watched the road for several moments in silence. Reality continued to fall in and out of place. Facts shifted like sand beneath his feet.

François is who Master Keats meant by family.

"Does Billy work for British Intelligence?"

François laughed then groaned. "*Non.* Billy offered me a way into the smuggling ring—and his friendship." His swollen gaze met John's. "The young man was blissfully unaware of such dangerous intrigue. Until he met me."

"The German who held you—Karl—what do you know about him?"

"Karl Reimer is a Nazi agent and a heinous animal, eager to advance within the Third Reich."

They had reached the city, and streetlights reflected on François's swollen face.

"Turn left up ahead, then your first right. You will see the *Hôpital de la Pitié.*"

"Those names Karl collected... How were they sent and to where?"

"He has a radio hidden somewhere in Paris. He sends encrypted intelligence into Germany." François gnawed another bit of wire from his flesh. He grunted and spat as the truck stopped in front of the hospital. "The only thing their leader hates more than Frenchmen are Jews." His voice dropped, and he leaned toward John. "Hitler prepares for an invasion. He and his generals are always three steps ahead."

The vehicle rocked as Henri vaulted over the side of the bed and ran into the hospital.

"Billy—" François attempted to turn, but instead, he cringed in pain. Fresh blood oozed between his fingers.

"Sit still. Henri will bring help." John turned off the ignition.

Henri hurried from the hospital entrance with two hospital workers in white. "— one is in the back, and the other is in the cab." Henri pointed toward François as he moved to the back of the truck.

John hurried around and opened the passenger door. He put a hand on François's shoulder. "Sit still until they tell you otherwise."

"We need a stretcher," the man in the truck bed called to the assistant by the door.

"Make that two," the woman beside François called out. "And we'll need a surgeon."

They carried Billy in first, still unconscious, then came back for François.

"Keep the keys to the truck," François ground out between his teeth as the medical staff transferred him from the truck to a stretcher. "Billy won't need it for a while."

John leaned close as they lifted François. "Karl mentioned a Baroness Nescato. What do you know about her?"

François shook his head. "I've never heard that name."

"*Ça suffit, le temps presse.*" The orderly held his hand up to stop John, then followed François into the hospital.

Chapter 24

Aubrielle Cohen

Aubrielle struck a match and lit the *shamash* candle. She'd placed Papa's bronzed Hanukkah candelabra on a little table, positioned to display through the front window of the living room. Outside, the sun had set, and the first stars had appeared in the clear winter sky. She blew out the match, caught the sharp scent of sulfur, then faced her audience.

John watched from the hallway. His suit creased at the shoulder where it pressed against the wall. Arms and legs both crossed, he rested one foot on the toe of his shoe. He wore a new brown suit that accentuated the gray circles beneath his eyes. His gaze caught hers and his lips turned up ever-so-slightly on each side.

He looks exhausted.

She tore her attention from John and looked to Henri and Mae, seated beside her father on the couch. "For those of you who aren't Jewish, which is everyone except Papa." She swallowed as heat infused her face. "This candle, set apart from the rest, is called the *shamash,* or servant candle. Only a *hanukiah* has the offset *shamash.*"

"A what?" Henri asked. "John called your candle holder a *menorah.*"

"John's right. A *menorah* is a Jewish candelabra." Aubrielle opened the drawer on the table and withdrew another candle—a twin to the *shamash* taper. "But there are two types. The most common—the *hanukiah*—holds nine candles. It's used to celebrate the Hanukkah festival." She inserted the new candle into the empty socket on the far right. "The other *menorah* is employed in the Temple and holds only seven candles."

She removed the lighted *shamash* candle from its raised stem and turned to her father. "I know there are prayers we should say before I light today's candle, but I don't remember them."

Her father stared at the floor, as though he hadn't heard. His skeletal, spotted hands trembled as they rested on his knees. The bones in his face stood in sharp contrast to his dark, depressed eyes.

"Papa, do you remember the Hanukkah prayers?"

"Maybe we could all say the Lord's Prayer instead," Mae offered. She rested her hand on Lou's shoulder but received no response.

Aubrielle lowered her head. "No." Blinking disappointment from her eyes, she turned toward the window, her voice just above a whisper. "I don't think that would be appropriate."

"Blessed are—blessed..." Lou's voice, low and rough with phlegm, splintered into silence.

"That's right, Papa," Aubrielle said. "Do you remember more?"

Lou coughed, and air wheezed through his sunken chest. A drop of moisture beaded beneath the tip of his nose, and a single tear slid down his cheek. He never looked up or said another word.

Aubrielle held a hand to her chest as sadness tightened her throat. She turned back to the *hanukiah* and dashed a droplet from her eye. A breath of resignation filled her lungs as she lit the first night's candle. Returning the *shamash* taper to its holder, she stared at her somber reflection in the window. "Thank you, Papa. Amen."

Mae put her arm around Lou's shoulders. "It's all right, Lou— shh." Her sad eyes sought Aubrielle's. "Now comes the fun part."

"That's right." Aubrielle forced a smile for her father. "Until the candles burn down, we shall eat *latkes* and play *dreidel* here in the living room."

"The potato bread and sour cream are in the kitchen." Mae moved to stand.

Aubrielle held out her hand to Mae. "Stay with Papa. I'll get them." She glanced at John as she passed him in the hall. "I have the candy and *dreidel* in my room."

"I'll bring another chair," John offered and followed her into the kitchen. "I want to apologize for not coming to see you yesterday."

"There's no need." Aubrielle went into her room and reappeared with a brown bag. "Henri came by. He said you were tracking something down." She set the package on a tray beside the *latkes* and sour cream. "Did you find it?"

"No." He ran a hand across his eyes. "They've disappeared."

"They?" She lifted the tray. *More troubled John than mere exhaustion.*

John nodded and released a long exhale. "It's something we need to discuss, but the explanations will take some time." He rested both hands on the back of the kitchen chair and leaned forward. His shoulders slumped with fatigue. "For now, I'd like you to consider leaving France—with me."

"What?" The weight of the platter was suddenly more than she could hold. It dropped back to the table with a clang.

"The sooner, the better," John urged.

"Do you need my help in there?" Mae's voice reached into the kitchen.

"No." Both John and Aubrielle called out then stared at each other.

"Do you not see how sick my father is?" Aubrielle hissed. Surprise changed her tone into an angry accusation. She pointed toward the front room, then balled her hand into a fist and rested it on her hip.

John hadn't shaved in a few days, and the short growth of dark hair along his cheekbone accentuated the angle of his jaw. He appeared drained as he blinked at her words and ran a hand through his hair. "Of course, I see." He didn't respond in kind to her anger. Instead, his tone held both resignation and urgency. "And I do understand, however—"

"There is no *however*. Not tonight." She picked up the tray. "We can discuss your inappropriate invitation at a more suitable time." With a warning glare, she carried her tray down the hall.

"Our discussion will require privacy," he whispered at her back just before they entered the living room.

Aubrielle set the tray on the coffee table. John's whispered comment sent her pulse racing, despite her annoyance.

My face must be on fire.

"The potato bread looks delicious *Tante* Mae." She took a seat in the cushioned green chair and held a chilled hand to her cheek.

John placed the kitchen chair across from the couch, unbuttoned his suit coat and sat, pulling the chair closer to the table.

"The bread turned out better than I'd hoped." The scent of fresh baked bread drifted around the room. Mae put a slice on one of the small plates along with a scoop of sour cream. She looked sharply at both John and Aubrielle before holding the bread up for Lou to taste.

Aubrielle ignored Mae's look. Instead, she opened the bag of candy and withdrew the *dreidel*, setting it on her lap. She handed Henri the bag of treats. "If you would divide the candy between us, we'll play a game of *dreidel*."

"Five players?" Henri looked over Lou's head to Mae.

"Four," Mae said. "Lou and I will be a team."

"Four it is." Henri separated the small wrapped candy pieces and nuts into piles then held up the netted bag of coin-shaped chocolate. "These too?"

"Yes." Aubrielle picked up the *dreidel* and turned it in her hand. "I used to play this by myself for hours." She scanned her father's face. "Do you remember, Papa?"

Her father stared glassy-eyed at the pile of candy and nuts on the table before him.

"Of course, he does," Mae said and took his hand. "But I'll need a reminder on how to play this game."

"It's easy." Aubrielle pushed one piece of candy from her pile to the center of the table. "Everyone puts in a nut or a bit of candy."

"Ante up." John nudged a nut from his pile into the middle.

"Gambling?" Henri picked up his golden chocolate coin. "With this?" He flipped the coin off his finger with his thumb. It spun into the air. He caught it before it touched the table.

"A game of chance," John replied.

Aubrielle looked at John from the corner of her eye. "You've played before?"

"Only once," he offered with hesitation. "A very long time ago."

Aubrielle raised a brow at John's cryptic answer, then lifted the Jewish toy to show Henri. "The spinner, or *dreidel*, has four sides. Each side is painted with a different symbol—each symbol tells you what move to make." She turned the painted toy until a wiggly W was on top. "The symbol with three prongs tells you to put another piece of candy into the pot." She turned to the next side. "This backward C means you get nothing, and the turn passes. The upside-down Y is the good one. When this side lands face up, you win all the candy in the pot.

"The last side has a broken symbol. With this one, you split the pot. Half is yours and the other half you leave on the table." She spun the handle between her fingers, whirling the painted colors into streaks. "After each turn, everyone puts in another piece of candy. When you're out of candy, you're out of the game." She snapped the fingers of her other hand and held out the *dreidel*. "It's very simple."

"So, besides all the candy, what does the winner get?" Henri took the spinner from Aubrielle and studied each painted symbol.

"The winner gets to eat a piece of candy." Aubrielle laughed. "The rest we save for our game tomorrow."

Mae put a chocolate coin in the middle of the table. "Lou and I are in."

Henri spun the top and cheered when the broken symbol landed up. "Half a win. I'll take it." He pulled in two pieces and pushed one back into the pot. "Ante up." He handed the toy to Aubrielle's father.

Lou lifted the toy up and laughed.

Aubrielle bit her lip as she watched her father. *This is what I hoped for.*

"Can you spin the top on the table, Lou?" Mae paid their ante.

He held the toy toward the table, but it slipped from his hand and clattered to the floor.

Mae snatched it up. "Do you want to try again?"

Lou shook his head and waved his trembling hand toward the table. "You. You do it."

"If you're sure." Mae spun the top. The toy fell with the backward C facing up. They won nothing, and the turn passed.

Papa watched with interest as the top moved around the table. He laughed every time the *dreidel* spun.

The candle had become a wax puddle by the time Henri won all the candy.

Papa's head dropped with weariness. The game and the company had been too tiring for him.

Mae helped Lou to his feet. "It's time for bed, isn't it Lou?"

Aubrielle's father staggered past her chair—his fist wound tight into Mae's sleeve for balance. His gaze skimmed over Aubrielle's but held no recognition. Only confusion and exhaustion.

He won't see the new year. Why did that thought come? Aubrielle shut it away and stood to follow *Tante* Mae down the hall, but John touched her arm.

"Let me." John stepped past Aubrielle just as Lou's legs buckled. He caught her father and eased him to the floor. "I'll carry you, *Monsieur* Cohen. If that's all right?"

Her father stared at John, his rheumy, watering eyes wider than they'd been all evening. His mouth gaped, and he nodded his head.

John slipped his arms beneath Lou's legs and lifted him to his chest with ease, all the while murmuring soft words. "I've got you, *Monsieur* Cohen. Let's get you into bed." He followed Mae into Lou's room. "It's been quite a night, hasn't it?"

Aubrielle trailed them down the hall.

In her father's room, John lowered Lou's legs but kept his arm as support around Lou's back.

"I've got him, John. Thanks for your help." Mae eased Lou to his mattress, then knelt to untie his shoes.

"I'm sorry, sir," Lou whispered, his focus locked on John's face. "I can't seem to find my strength today."

Aubrielle held tight to John's arm and stared at her father. "He's gotten so much worse, in just a few days."

"Tell John and Aubrielle good-night, Lou." Mae pulled a nightshirt from his dresser. "Let's get you to bed."

"Do you want me to—" Aubrielle began.

Mae shook her head as she guided Lou's arm into his nightshirt. "No. Lou and I have this dance down pat." She smiled at Aubrielle. "And besides, you have guests."

"Are we still going to *La Fleur* tonight?" Henri asked from the hall.

"Yes. I want to see if Bonet has heard anything new," John replied. He accompanied Henri into the kitchen. "If you could give Aubrielle and me a moment. I'll meet you outside, and we can go."

Henri nodded to John and stepped around the corner into the cloakroom.

"I thought you said we would talk?" Aubrielle crossed her arms and looked up at John. "Now would be a good time."

John ran his palms down her arms and took her hands. "It would. But there is someone I must find. It's most urgent."

"Your smuggler friend?" Aubrielle pulled her hands away from

John. "Mae told me he no longer stays at your apartment."

"That's true. Billy left with François." He lowered his voice. "The man I seek recently worked at *La Fleur*. If he returns to the club or contacts someone there, I may find a clue to where he's gone." He tried to pull her into his arms.

Aubrielle stopped him with a hand to his chest. She smiled to soften the rebuke. "We should talk first."

John nodded. Exhaustion and disappointment etched his face. "I'll check on you tomorrow afternoon, well before sunset, and then we can have our talk."

"Brie darlin', I could use a bit of help," Mae called.

Aubrielle took a step back. "You'll see yourself out?"

John nodded. "I'll be back late, but if you need me—"

"We'll be fine. *Au revoir*, John."

Chapter 25

John Larson

John pulled the back door shut. He adjusted his fedora then buttoned his overcoat as he glanced up at the cloudless Paris sky. It would be another cold night. A familiar ache he recognized as bone-weary fatigue clung to the back of his neck. He rubbed his palm over the pain even though he knew there was only one cure.

I need sleep.

But there had been little time to rest and his eyes drooped from exhaustion.

After he and Henri had left the hospital, they'd returned to the building where they had rescued François, but Karl and his Nazi allies had fled, leaving no clues. Back at the apartment, Henri helped bandage the bullet wound in John's shoulder—a minor injury that had already stopped bleeding

As the sun rose, John had walked the streets of *Le Marais* district, past the *Café Jardin de Lune* and Asher's Market, hoping to catch a glimpse of the bastard's discolored face.

When those efforts failed, he had made his way home to rest. Instead, every time John closed his eyes he saw Nescato, wrapped in a blood-smeared Nazi flag instead of her animal skins. Sleep had never come.

And again tonight, he hunted the German spy.

Nescato is alive.

Resurrected from his long dead past in an instant, her evil specter, once consigned to bitter memory, again walked the earth. Corrupt with malice. Hunting him.

Karl had said the witch possessed the same immortality she had cursed on John.

Is she bound to love only one, as I am?

His breath stuttered. He blinked the cold, clear skies from his watering eyes.

And if so, is she bound to me?

John's stomach convulsed, scalding his throat with burning bile. He swallowed back the bitterness with clenched teeth.

Impossible.

Nescato should have found him centuries ago, called to John in the same way he'd been magically called to Aubrielle. He halted in mid-step, hand on the rail, as his world careened out of focus.

Except, by her own words—her own monstrous curse—there could never be a threat to his life.

His immortality would leave her forever blind to John's location. Their location.

Blind until now.

Movement in the yard caught his attention as Henri stepped out of Éclair's enclosure. He brushed his hands on his thighs while he waited for John to descend the steps. "Her gelding is fed and watered for the night, but he needs a long walk."

"I agree." John nodded. "But not tonight." He passed Henri and continued out the back gate. "Hopefully, I'll learn something so I can get my hands on Karl Reimer." He crossed the street and continued toward the avenue.

"You're not going to drive the truck?" Henri asked.

"No. A cab is quicker and will draw less attention."

"What did you learn at the hospital?" Henri ran to keep pace as John rounded the corner.

John glanced at Henri and slowed his stride. "François and Billy are no longer there, or they were admitted under different names." He raised his hand for a cab. "The staff told me they had no record of attending to either man."

A cab changed lanes and pulled to the curb where they stood.

Henri rounded the vehicle, shaking his head. "That's odd." He dropped into the seat. "No, ridiculous. What could have happened to them?"

The back doors of the cab shut in unison and the cabbie looked over his shoulder. *"Où allez-vous?"*

"La Fleur Chantante, s'il vous plaît." John lowered his voice, "The *Sûreté nationale* must have moved them. It's the only explanation I can muster."

"Will we ever know if they survived?"

"I don't know, Henri." John stared through the window at the lights on the tower. "I hope so."

They lapsed into silence. Just before the last turn, Henri looked at John. "Aubrielle's father doesn't have long."

"No. He doesn't."

The cab stopped in front of the club. John paid the cabbie then shook his head in dismay at the line. "We might not get in."

"We'll get in." Henri held out his hand to slow traffic, and both men hurried across the street.

The new doorman nodded as Henri approached. *"Bonsoir, Vogl. De retour à nouveau?"*

Henri grinned. *"Bonsoir,* Webber. Is *Monsieur* Bonet here tonight?"

"Of course." Webber passed them through the line. "He told me to keep an eye out for you."

Henri raised a brow at Webber as they passed the doorman and entered the club. They checked their overcoats and hats, then surveyed the cozy club.

There were a few empty chairs, but beverages on the table held the seats for the dancers. An accordion player led the house band in a musette as couples twirled in each other's arms near the empty stage.

"This way." Henri nudged John's arm and stepped into the crowd heading for the owner's booth.

Bonet spoke briefly to the men at his booth, his scrutiny on John and Henri.

The men rose from their seats and disbursed into the club.

"*Mes amis.*" The large man's arms swung wide to indicate the open seats to either side of him. "How are you this evening?" Bonet's red suit matched the leather booth and cast his skin the color of green olives.

John released his suit button and folded himself into the booth. "*Bonsoir, Monsieur* Bonet."

"Bébé." Bonet signaled a waitress. "Bring my friends some refreshment."

"Coffee." John gave the busy waitress a weary smile. "Black."

"And you, *monsieur*?" She looked at Henri and grinned.

"A glass of the house wine, *s'il vous plaît.*"

The waitress winked at Henri and swished her skirt as she disappeared with her tray into the crowd below.

"My Bébé, she likes you." Bonet flicked his cigarette ash toward the tray and chuckled. "I like you too, Henri Vogl." He puffed and blew smoke toward the ceiling. "I like you both." His smile widened, and he included John in his glance. "As it happens, because of recent unfortunate events, I have an opening in my staff for a personal valet." He crushed the cigarette out and picked up his glass. "Would either of you be interested?"

Henri sat forward. "I would be."

Bonet rolled the edge of his napkin beneath his thumb. "That position includes room and board since you will need to be available to me for certain periods outside of business hours."

"You've not heard from Karl?" John asked.

"*Non.* He never returned after you chased him through my kitchen." Bonet withdrew another cigarette from his silver case and tapped the end on the table. "Although I have come to know, through certain sources, that Karl remains in Paris." He raised a thick brow at Henri. "You'll have to empty the room of his things." His lighter flared, and he inhaled. "A Nazi in my employ." He shook his head, chuckled, and blew a smoke ring at the table lamp. "Next thing you know, I will have dealings with the *Sûreté nationale.*"

"Karl left personal items?" John exchanged a quick glance with Henri. "Could we see the room?"

Bébé stopped beside Henri and rested part of the tray on the edge of their table. She delivered the coffee and wine along with the bill.

Bonet picked up the tab up and stuffed it in his pocket. "If Henri takes the job, the room and all its contents would be his." Bonet laughed in delight at his wit. "You'd have to ask him."

John shifted his attention to Henri.

Eyes bright, Henri picked up his glass and swirled the wine. "I think we'll be able to come to an agreement. When would I start?"

Bonet's grin widened. "Tomorrow afternoon would be soon enough although you are welcome to the room immediately. Bébé can show you where it is when she returns." He pulled a leather string with a key attached from his vest pocket. "This opens the new lock on the back door." Bonet raised his brow and leaned forward as he handed Henri the key. "Do not lose it."

Face flushed, Henri jammed the key into his jacket pocket and took a small sip of wine.

Bonet switched his attention to John. "And you, *mon ami?*"

"You have a job offer for me as well?" John tasted the hot coffee.

"Not as prestigious as my offer to your friend, but you would have access to certain privileged information as one of my security escorts." He sniffed. "Karl was not the only individual to leave my employ recently."

"Really?" John studied the club owner. His name and accent declared him a native of France, but visually, he appeared to be

Persian or perhaps Greek.

"How many openings do you have?"

"Originally two, not counting my personal valet. I've hired Webber for the door, but Bruce has also failed to return to work."

Neither of those men had been killed at the apartment. *How many men accompanied Karl Reimer?"*

"Shouldn't you require references?" John asked. "Considering Karl and his associates."

"You are two of the most honest men I have ever dealt with." Bonet looked from John to Henri. "I have no doubt and no need of another opinion."

"You'll allow me time to consider your offer?" John asked.

Bonet grinned wide, exposing wine and tobacco stained teeth. "For a time—say, two days?" He tapped out his cigarette. "Ah, I almost forgot." He reached into his vest pocket and brought out several colorful tickets. He handed two to each man. "Passes for the New Year's Eve Extravaganza. Henri, you may have that night off, and it would make me happy if you both would bring a guest."

When Bébé returned to their table, Bonet held up his hand. "Leave your tray here and show Henri to Karl's old room."

John slid from the booth when Henri stood. "I must be going as well."

"*Adieu,* John Larson. Let me know by this weekend if you will accept my offer of employment."

"Thank you, *monsieur.*" John followed Bébé and Henri down the steps and along the dance floor to the door on the far side of the stage.

In the back room, Bébé turned left and continued past the raised backstage to the dressing rooms. She passed two curtain enclosures on her right, then opened the door at the end of the hall.

The small room contained a single bed, a nightstand, and dresser, as well as a cushioned chair beside a door. She turned the knob and held out her hand. "*Les toilettes et la salle de bain.*"

"*Merci,* Bébé. " Henri grinned at the attractive waitress.

She returned his regard, assessing him up and down before she walked from the room. *"De rien."*

Both men watched her hips sway as she sauntered down the hallway.

When she paused beside the backstage stair, she waved long slim fingers at the men.

"Bonet is right. She likes you," John said. He opened the dresser drawer and searched Karl's clothes.

"Women always do." Henri opened the nightstand drawer. "A pretty face is all they see. They make up the rest in their heads."

John finished with the third drawer, then turned and considered Henri. "That's why you liked Aubrielle. She isn't impressed with how you look."

Henri shrugged. "She spoke to me as a person and put me in my place more than once. I hoped she would look deeper than my hair or my eyes and find value." He clenched his fist and held it to his chest. "Here."

"She values you as a friend. As do I." John raised a brow. "And so might Bébé if you give her a chance."

Henri closed the nightstand and turned out the pockets of the suits hanging in the open closet. "I'll stay here tonight and finish going through Karl's things." He pulled out a used handkerchief and made a face as he tossed it into a trash can beside the bed. "Give my apologies to Aubrielle. I'm afraid I'll need to miss the rest of her Hanukkah celebration."

John scanned over the dresser top and peered behind a cheap painting of the Paris tower. Too tired to think. "I'll tell her. She'll understand and be happy for you." John called over his shoulder as he walked down the hall. "And you let me know if you uncover anything that will allow us to find Karl."

Chapter 26

John Larson

John closed the door to his apartment. This small space held a different volume somehow, with both Billy and Henri absent. No sound rose from the butcher's family in the flat below. At the window overlooking Aubrielle and Mae's homes, the sleeping city lay silent.

Somewhere in those lights, Karl and his companions hid. The Nazi spy had boasted his group communicated with their command by radio. He'd already sent Aubrielle's name to the SS, and there was every possibility the witch Nescato knew where they were.

He pulled the curtain shut and switched on the table lamp. Henri's things lay scattered around the couch. The bedroom was an equal disaster. Tomorrow he would clean the apartment and return to his bed, but for tonight, the pallet in the corner offered the quickest solution.

He rubbed at the ache in his neck, shed his coat and jacket on the chair. His usual tidy self must have already fallen asleep. Stripped down to his undershirt and skivvies, he switched off the table lamp and rested his head on the canvas sea bag he used as his pillow.

Exhaustion pulled him down into a dreamless slumber.

Tap tap tap.

The long end of Nescato's staff sparked hard against a stone. *"For eternity..."*

Tap tap tap.

Nails hammered into a coffin sealed his immortal body into a six-foot-five-inch box.

For eternity.

Tap tap tap.

John blinked his eyes and for a moment, the absolute darkness caused his chest to tighten. He flung his arm out, tossing the blanket across the room.

Tap tap tap. "John?" Aubrielle's voice pitched to a tight whisper.

Tap tap tap.

"Coming." John struggled to his feet, body stiff and slowed with slumber. He found the light switch on the table lamp then opened the door.

Aubrielle peered up at him from the landing. Her worn coat covered her nightgown, her father's winter boots on her feet. Tears scored her cheeks. Her brown eyes were red-rimmed and swollen. "It's Papa." She covered her mouth and uttered a short sob.

The cold stairwell chilled John's skin. He wrapped an arm around Aubrielle and urged her into his apartment. "Tell me." From his coat beside the door, he pulled a folded handkerchief and placed it in her hand.

She wiped her face, averting her eyes. "I'm sorry to wake you at this hour—"

"No, it's all right." John found his trousers draped across the couch and stepped into them. "What's happened?"

Aubrielle opened her mouth then closed it. She clenched her teeth and inhaled through her nose. Spiky lashes released more tears down her cheek. "John, he's dying." She looked at him, and her lips drew back from her teeth then pressed into a quivering line. "And he wants to speak with you."

John pulled on his shirt, slipped his feet into unlaced shoes and grabbed his overcoat from the chair. "Did you tell Mae?"

Aubrielle shook her head. "He was insistent." She shrugged one shoulder. "He didn't say your name, not exactly, but he made it clear he wants you." She swallowed. Her eyes glistened with tears. "John, he said some very odd things."

John ushered her into the stairwell. "Is your back door unlocked?"

"Yes."

He pulled his door shut and followed her down the stairs, onto the sidewalk, and between the buildings. "Get Mae—I'll go to your father."

Aubrielle nodded and ran to the back gate of the bakery.

John's long legs took him through the backyard, past Éclair's barn, and up the back steps. In the house, he hurried down the hall to her father's room.

Lou lay on his bed. His chest barely moved as watering eyes stared at the ceiling.

"Lou?" John went to his knee and took the old man's hand.

A tremor ran down Lou's arm, and he turned his head, slowed by spasms in his neck until his rheumy eyes met John's. Lou inhaled through his mouth, sucking air into his lungs one small gasp at a time until he could speak. "I waited for you, sir."

John nodded. "Aubrielle's gone to get Mae. They'll be back in a moment."

Lou stared at him. "I can't remember things—but you—you, I know."

"Of course, you do." John squeezed his hand. "Aubrielle said you wanted to speak with me."

Lou's exhale gurgled in his chest. He closed his eyes, brows drawn together in pain, then coughed before his lungs struggled to fill again. "Is it time, sir?" his thin, raspy voice begged the question.

"Time?" *Who does he think I am?* "Lou, I don't know what you mean."

"You told me to wait until—until you—returned." The long rattle and a painful draw of breath.

"No—I don't—" A memory came to John of a medieval battlefield. Separated by the turn of the fighting, the bulk of the opposing army trampled through his camp. John had ridden the white gelding, Zeus, through the encampment after the invaders were driven off. Their tents had been dashed to the ground and set aflame.

In what remained of his father-in-law's pavilion, he'd found his squire, a young man, nearly ready for his own spurs, speared through the chest with a javelin. As he slid from Zeus and knelt beside his young friend, Maury had asked him with the last breath in his body, "Sir, is it time?"

John, known during that age as Sir Jurian Locke, had held his squire's head and nodded. "Yes, Maury. It's time." As though the lad had waited to hear those words, to gain permission from his master, Maury had closed his eyes and exhaled his last breath.

Lou continued to stare at John. "Don't you remember me, sir?"

"Maury?" John whispered in disbelief. "I do remember—but I don't understand."

Lou coughed wetly and inhaled in short, painful bursts. "My Aubrielle—is she your girl?"

John wiped the sputum from Lou's chin with the bed sheet. "Aye Lou, she is. She's our girl."

"Then keep her safe for me." He clenched his teeth, his shrunken frame tensed. His eyes pleaded when they opened. "Is it time, sir?"

"Aye, Lou. It's time." John ran his hand across his face and wiped the tears on his slacks.

Lou squeezed his other hand and nodded. "Thank you, sir."

The reverberation of the back door intruded on their silence.

Aubrielle rushed into the room and knelt beside John at the head of the bed. "Papa?"

Lou's attention shifted by degrees from John to Aubrielle. "My girl—" The rest of his words were taken by the rattle in his chest. His eyes continued to stare at his daughter. His mouth opened to inhale, but his chest didn't rise.

"What's happening? Why can't he breathe?" Aubrielle ran her hand along his face. "Papa?"

"His lungs," John whispered, "have collapsed." Sorrow filled his heart.

Good-bye, old friend.

Lou's body jerked. His mouth opened and closed, an involuntary attempt at a breath, then his eyes lost focus and the slight color in his cheeks bled away. The trembling grip he'd maintained on John's hand released.

John lowered Lou's arm to the covers. In John's extraordinarily long life, filled with bizarre events and inexplicable magic, this last conversation with Lou had been unprecedented.

Aubrielle lowered her head onto her father's chest and cried, murmuring apologies.

John stood beside Mae in the doorway.

"I should have known his time was near," Mae whispered to John behind her hand. "There was something off about him tonight."

John left Aubrielle to mourn and accompanied Mae into the kitchen. He rubbed the sleep from his eyes. "But Lou enjoyed himself. His daughter gave him one last night with his family."

Mae set a tea kettle on the stove. "That poor girl. She's lost so much."

They fell silent and listened to the kettle warm over the flame. After a few moments, the tea kettle whistled.

Aubrielle paused near the kitchen, her eyes downcast. She sniffed and looked up at John. "Were you able to speak to him?"

"I did. For a moment." John wiped a tear from her cheek with his thumb. "He wanted to know you would be all right."

Aubrielle pulled away from John's hand. "He talked to you about me?"

Mae poured boiling water into the teapot. "I'll make us some warm tea, dear."

"He asked if you and I—" John dropped his hand. "If I would watch out for you."

Aubrielle stared at John. "He didn't know what he was saying." She passed by him and seated herself at the table.

Mae set the teapot, and two cups on the table then raised a brow at John. "A cup for you, John?"

"Yes." He sat across from Aubrielle. "Thank you."

Aubrielle dabbed her nose with his handkerchief. "*Merci.*" The white cloth disappeared up her coat sleeve, and she cradled the warm porcelain cup with both hands. "What do I do now?" She gazed into her tea as if the hot liquid knew the answer.

"We'll find his best suit and brush it clean," Mae said.

"I'll go to the synagogue and let Rabbi David know about Lou this morning," John added. "He told us they would help when the time came."

"The only thing I know about death and Judaism is the dead can't be left alone." Aubrielle glanced over her shoulder at her father's room and her lips trembled. "But I'm unsure if that means alone in the house, or alone in his room." Her face contorted with grief. She pulled John's hanky from her coat sleeve and covered her face as her shoulders shook with sobs.

Mae rose and rounded the table. She gathered Aubrielle in her arms. "Shh. It doesn't matter. He knows you're here with him."

* * *

John waited until morning prayers concluded to speak with Rabbi David.

Dressed in a black wool suit, the rabbi entered the small meeting room and extended his hand to John. "I'm afraid I know why you're here."

John nodded. "Lou Cohen passed this morning."

"I'm sorry. My condolences to you and his daughter. I'll speak with the *chevra kadisha*. They're volunteers who care for the dead. They'll take *Monsieur* Cohen's body from his home today and prepare it for burial."

"Thank you, Rabbi."

Rabbi David walked with John from the small meeting room toward the tall exit doors. "Tell his daughter not to worry. By the Eternal Covenant with God, her father awaits *Olam Ha-Ba*, Life Everlasting, in the afterlife. Some scholars believe the dead may be born again, to mend the world or when the soul has left unfinished business in this world."

The rabbi laid a comforting hand on John's shoulder. "Whatever awaits us, death is a natural part of life, as is our grief at losing those we love most. The volunteers of the holy society help families show respect for their dead by faithful observance of our traditions."

At the door, John returned the borrowed yarmulke. "Will there be a funeral service?"

Rabbi David nodded. "Prayers will be spoken by a community elder at *Monsieur* Cohen's grave tomorrow. The Temple maintains an area at the *cimetière du Père-Lachaise*. The Temple will provide both the grave and the marker."

"Is there anything we should do?"

"You should check with the *cimetière* tomorrow morning. They will have a list of burial times. If you like, you may leave a short eulogy with them. His daughter is welcome to read it herself of course, but there is no obligation to do so. The cantor will be happy to include it in the service to honor her father.

"Aubrielle should grieve for her father as dictated by her love for him and by her faith. There are no other requirements."

"Thank you, Rabbi."

John left the synagogue and crossed the street, his thoughts on Lou Cohen, as well as a boy John knew several hundred years ago,

Maury. John still couldn't properly connect the two individuals in his mind. Maury, his young squire, so eager to please the knights he served. Anxious to win his spurs and become a knight—a dream never fulfilled. Maury's life was so different from Lou Cohen's life, that of a father and a husband and a warrior from the Great War.

Would memories of his life as Maury have surfaced had Lou never set eyes on me? Was it his illness, or a face he recognized from a life long ago?

Deep in thought, John continued to walk instead of hailing a cab. He turned north down a narrow, cobbled side street. Women, with scarves around their heads, enjoyed the unusually warm temperature after the cold spell, chatting together as they walked to the market.

This neighborhood would be perfect for Karl to gather names for his Führer.

John searched for a familiar discoloration in the faces of the people he passed.

Children dressed in school uniforms and carrying books rushed down the block to class. The smell of freshly brewed coffee from a sidewalk café had enticed several gentlemen who laughed and talked on the patio.

John's inspection touched upon every adult face, in particular those who lingered near a shadowed doorway or street corner. Today would be a perfect day to search for the Nazi spy, but John had other business to attend.

He waved at a passing taxi, and it pulled to the curb. His search for Karl would have to wait.

Chapter 27

Aubrielle Cohen

Inside the main entrance of the *cimetière du Père-Lachaise*, an assistant at the visitors' pavilion gave Aubrielle a map and pointed out the best route to her father's burial site.

Dark clouds covered the sky as Aubrielle climbed the cobblestone path between grand mausoleums and granite headstones. Papa's modest grave would be along the far side of the cemetery.

As they approached the newer section, the cobblestone walkway gave way to a worn dirt trail. The scent of freshly turned soil overrode the cold smell of molded stone.

Aubrielle held tight to Mae's hand. Her frayed emotions careened from heartbroken loss and guilt-ridden relief to the unreasonable anger of betrayal. She prayed her face did not portray every aspect of her shattered heart.

John and Henri followed behind the women, respectfully silent.

A horse-drawn wagon with a plain wooden casket in its open bed blocked the trail at the top of the rise. A short distance away, several mourners stood at an open grave.

One of the women who had come to Aubrielle's home for her father waited at the edge of the path. She had introduced herself yesterday as Rachel, one of the volunteers who care for the dead.

A black scarf covered Rachel's gray hair, and her back crooked with age. She welcomed the small group as they approached and withdrew a three-inch wide black ribbon from her bag. "This is for you, dear child, for the *Keriah*—the tearing." She pinned the long cloth to Aubrielle's coat. "May you have a long life and find your father's memory a blessing."

Rachel's clear gray eyes regarded Mae. "Are you family to the departed as well?"

Mae shook her head. "Aubrielle is Lou's daughter." She gestured to John and Henri. "We were Lou's friends."

Rachel gave them each a black ribbon. "The graveside service is brief." She took Aubrielle's hand in her icy fingers. "Our cantor has offered to read the eulogy if you feel it would be too difficult."

Aubrielle held a handkerchief to her nose. "Thank you, but Papa would want me to speak for him."

"I'm sure he would." Rachel led the group to a short row of folding chairs. "After the cantor leads us in prayer, it will be your turn to stand and speak."

"Thank you." Aubrielle held Mae's hand as they sat.

I'm strong enough to do this for Papa.

At Rachel's signal, the men who waited beside the wagon lifted Lou Cohen's coffin and walked very slowly toward his grave.

Rachel folded her ancient frame into the chair beside Aubrielle. Her attention remained on the slow procession as she spoke, "I understand from Rabbi David that you do not share your father's faith." Her voice was soft. The tone warm and friendly.

"That's true," Aubrielle replied. "I was raised in the Catholic faith by my mother."

"Then allow me to explain a few of our burial traditions." Rachel trailed her small, wrinkled finger down Aubrielle's black ribbon. "We rip this, or our clothing, to expresses our grief. It represents the tearing of the family and the separation in life from your loved one. As you rend the cloth, you may recite this passage from the Book of Job.

"God has given. God has taken away. Blessed be the name of God."

Aubrielle tore her ribbon, and her gaze met Mae's. Together they recited the passage.

Behind her, John and Henri spoke the words as well.

The pallbearers placed the casket on ropes drawn across the grave then moved back to stand with the other mourners.

One of the older men came forward and faced the casket. He bowed his head and recited Psalm 23—a prayer Aubrielle knew by heart.

"The Lord is my Shepherd. I shall not want."

Aubrielle bowed her head and listened to the cantor's deep melodic voice recite the familiar words of comfort.

I could have said this prayer with you, Papa. Tears scalded her eyes. *I'm sorry, I didn't know.*

When the cantor finished, he asked for a silent prayer. After several moments, he raised his head and stepped back with the gathered mourners.

"You may tell your father's story now," Rachel said.

Aubrielle removed two tear-stained sheets of paper from her clutch and stood. Her stare stayed on the plain wood coffin as she struggled to maintain her composure. *I love you, Papa.*

"You can do this, Brie," Mae whispered.

Aubrielle held the handkerchief to her nose then cleared her throat and read from her notes. "Louis Cohen was born to Joseph and Evelyn Cohen on the first of June,1890. His parents raised Lou, their only child, in Paris.

"In 1915, Lou joined the French Army to fight Germany in Belgium and Northern France." She wiped a tear and looked up from her paper, addressing the small group across the open grave. "Papa told me once that getting shot in the leg was the best thing to happen to him because he met my mother. He always said she was the most beautiful nurse he'd ever seen." Aubrielle covered her mouth with the handkerchief as tears streamed down her cheeks.

Oh, Papa!

Mae rose and stood beside Aubrielle. "Do you want me to finish?"

"No." Aubrielle shook her head and gave Mae an unsteady smile. "I can do this." Her throat tightened, and she swallowed twice before she could continue. She blinked her eyes clear and looked to her notes.

"After the war, Lou and Marguerite returned to Paris and wed. The next year, Marguerite gave birth to their only child, a daughter they named Aubrielle." She squeezed her eyes to clear them of tears and struggled for breath.

"Lou followed his father's trade of millinery and owned a shop where he made fashionable headwear for both men and women. Like his father, Lou became ill from the solvents they used to shape the hats."

A beam of sunlight escaped from a break in the clouds and shone across the city. Aubrielle raised her head and swallowed, her attention drawn to the beautiful ray of light as she continued to speak.

"Papa loved his family. He was devoted to mama and me and provided for our every need." She drew a trembling breath and sniffed even as a soft smile touched her lips. "He purchased a small horse for mother and me. Against his better judgment, he'd said. Mama named the pony Éclair. Papa hated that." She chuckled as memories of her parents pretend arguments over Éclair's name played through her mind. Her voice softened, no longer speaking to the mourners, only to herself and her father. "Then Mama asked you to build a cart so she could sell flowers in the park on the days when you worked long hours. And of course, you did.

"You could never argue with her, not really. I remember you laughed when Mama told us that a hat might keep a man's head warm, but flowers would warm a woman's heart." A tear streamed across Aubrielle' s smiling lips, but she refused to give in to her tears. "So you gave her the flowers her heart desired."

Aubrielle blinked and cleared her throat. She shuffled the pages to read the second sheet. "After his wife passed in a car accident three years ago, Lou's illness grew worse." She looked over her shoulder at Mae. "I could never have cared for him without the help of my mother's devoted friend, Mae Moroney. You've been both the angel God sent from heaven, and the ground that's kept me standing. I know my parents are together now, and they smile down with thanks for you, Mae. They loved you, almost as much as I do."

Mae nodded, holding her handkerchief to her face with both hands. Her chest shook with the force of her emotion.

Aubrielle crumpled the papers in her hand. "Papa's long illness ended yesterday, and I will miss him in my heart forever." She stumbled to her seat beside Mae and embraced her friend.

The pallbearers came forward and lowered the casket into the grave.

Rachel leaned close and whispered in Aubrielle's ear. "The cantor will recite the *Eil Malei Rachamim.* You'll need to stand. When he has finished, you may sprinkle earth onto the casket." She indicated the shovels in the freshly dug soil.

Aubrielle nodded at Rachel then whispered to Mae, "We need to stand." Her eyes and sinuses burned, but the tears had dried. She helped Mae to her feet and held her arm.

The cantor chanted in Hebrew. When he finished, the five people who stood beside him, as well as the pallbearers and Rachel, formed two lines that led away from the grave toward the path.

Aubrielle dug the shovel into the pile of dirt and sprinkled the soil onto the coffin. The sound of dirt on wood echoed in her soul. She pressed her lips and handed the shovel to Mae.

Mae shoveled dirt onto the casket and followed Aubrielle.

As they walked between the congregation lines, each person offered condolences to Aubrielle and wished her a long life.

She stopped at the end of the path to look back. Several of the volunteers shoveled dirt to finish filling the grave.

This doesn't seem real.

She half expected Papa to be home when she returned. With *Tante* Mae at her side, she foolishly felt anxious that Papa would be there alone.

And yet, I know better.

John and Henri spoke together as they approached the women.

When they reached Aubrielle and Mae, Henri stepped forward. "I'm not going back to your home. John may have already told you, but I've moved from his apartment and have a new employer near Montmartre."

"Is that so?" Aubrielle glanced at John, then smiled at Henri. "Congratulations."

Henri took her hand, leaned forward, and kissed her cheeks. "Unfortunately, I won't be able to attend your candle lighting tonight."

"I understand. Come by whenever you can."

Henri touched his hat, then hurried down the cobblestone path toward the cemetery's north entrance.

"I'm glad for him," Aubrielle said.

"Aye," Mae agreed. "I wish the lad well."

"Will you return home with us, Mr. Larson?" Aubrielle glanced at John.

"Yes. I intended to see you back home."

"Fine, then let's be off." Aubrielle turned away from Mae's wide-eyed stare, putting her back to both John and Mae. She retraced their way along the cobblestone path leaving John to escort Mae.

What is wrong with me?

She clenched her teeth. An angry tirade burned on the tip of her tongue.

John sat beside the cabbie and directed him to Aubrielle's home.

Mae reached over and touched Aubrielle's hand. "Are you sure you're all right, dear?"

Aubrielle balled her fists. A burst of rage, so strong it brought tears blurred her vision. "Yes." She shook her head. "No." Anger punctuated her words, "I'm grieved, angry, and perfectly fine."

"I could come in and make some tea," Mae offered.

"No." Aubrielle dabbed at her eyes. "I need some time." Her gaze touched John's as he looked over the back of the seat. She turned away, firmed her lips and stared from the window.

The cab stopped in front of the closed millinery and the busy *boulangerie*.

Aubrielle exited the cab and hurried between the buildings toward her backyard. She could have easily gone with Mae into the bakery and received condolences from Antoine and Paul. But she couldn't have been cordial. Not today.

Not right now.

She rounded the side fence into the *ruelle* and let herself through the back gate. She had every intention of running up the steps, going into her house and locking the door behind her. Anything to get away from everyone and sort out her careening emotions. Instead, she turned into the converted garage, unlatched Éclair's stall and wrapped her arms around the old pony.

Éclair huffed into her hair, then leaned into her as he lowered his head to her pocket.

"No treats *mon cher cheval*—not today.*"* She sniffed and rested her head against Éclair's solid neck.

"Mind if I join you?"

The soft tone of John's voice sent a thrill through her stomach in spite of her anger and misgivings about him. What did she know of John Larson?

Had he spoken to Papa behind my back?

How else could she account for the things her father had said? She rolled her head against Éclair's neck and looked at John from the corner of her eye.

He stood outside the entrance. His large familiar frame cast in shadow, outlined by the gray winter light.

"I'm going inside." She stroked her pony's neck and kissed his soft nose, then locked the stall and walked past John.

The sound of his footsteps followed her up the steps. She unlocked the bolt, entered the door, and then faced him. Accusations of some undefined treachery burned her tongue, and she fought her desire to crawl inside his coat, press her cheek to his chest and weep. The struggle to find the right words failed her, and she simply stared into his eyes.

"May I come in?" His brow rose, and he almost smiled.

Unable to make even this basic decision—to respond with reason to his simple request—she hesitated. In the end, she sighed in exasperation at herself and shook her head. "I don't know if you should."

"I'll mind my manners. I promise." His hand came close to her hair, then lowered to his side. "I think we need to talk."

She stared at him, willing her gaze not to drop to his lips, and when they did, she closed her eyes and turned away. "Yes, all right. Please, come in."

She hung her scarf on a hook, then her coat. Her hands halted as she caught sight of her father's jacket.

John hung his overcoat on the peg beside hers.

"I'll put on a kettle for tea unless you want something stronger." She left the cloakroom without waiting for John.

"I'll have tea." He trailed her into the kitchen and leaned against the wall, watching her as she worked. "You—appear upset with me. Have I done something to make you angry?"

Aubrielle filled the tea kettle then set it on the burner and adjusted the flame. "It's something Papa said."

"Tell me."

She ran a hand over her face. "First, let me ask, had you ever met my father before?"

"I met Lou Cohen for the first time the night I brought you home from the park and cleaned your knees."

"Did you speak to him behind my back? Tell him things

without my knowledge?"

"No, of course not. What is this about?"

Aubrielle shook her head. Her dark eyes swam with unshed tears. "Early yesterday morning, the sound of his labored breathing woke me. It was—I've never heard anything like it."

"It's called a death rattle. An appropriate name for a chilling sound."

"When I got to his room, he recognized me—called me by name, and then asked if Sir Jurian had returned. When I asked him if he meant John, he said, yes. Sir John."

"He was very sick, Aubrielle. His mind—"

"Don't patronize me. I know how ill he was, how confused he could be. I know that what he said makes no sense. I know it. And yet, Papa believed the things he told me." She removed the kettle from the flame and turned off the burner.

"Things about me?"

"Yes." From a jar on the counter, she added measured scoops of loose tea to the porcelain teapot and filled it with hot water.

"What did he say?"

"Mostly that he wanted to speak with you—most urgently—but he also reminisced about holding your magnificent white steed at your wedding."

John looked away.

"Does that mean something to you? Papa also said you had come for me—that I belonged to you." The teacups rattled as she set them on the table.

What are you hiding from me, John?

"Aubrielle—"

"Do you have an explanation? Did you tell him these things? He believed them. He recognized you from the very first time you met him. He—."

"Aubrielle." He raised his voice and pushed away from the wall. "Before I answer you, tell me, do you believe in magic?"

"Magic? I don't believe what I'm hearing. Are you claiming

Papa was under a spell?

"Not at all. But you were raised in the Catholic faith. You must believe in miracles. Miraculous happenings. Unexplainable events."

"Only those sent by God."

"And that is the only magic you believe?"

"Of course."

John nodded. "Then the things your father said to you the night he died must have been visions sent to comfort him, or half-remembered dreams. I know he worried for your safety." John paced away. "I'm a strong and resourceful man. My size alone can impose authority on some individuals. Your papa knew I could protect you."

"Would your answer have been different if I had said yes? If I believed in magic?"

John looked at her for several long seconds before he answered. "Perhaps."

"Why?"

"Because magic opens up new realms of possibility."

Anger flared, and she shook her head. "And again, you patronize me."

Why do I need to listen to this? Today of all days?

"Aubrielle, I never meant—"

"I'm sorry, John. I would like you to go."

He hesitated, as though he would argue, then gave a single nod and left the kitchen.

Aubrielle covered her mouth with her hand and resisted the urge to call him back. The sound of him slipping on his overcoat and the back door opening tore at her heart. Unable to hold herself back, she hurried down the hall. But the door had already closed.

John disappeared down the steps.

She stood at the window and watched him leave.

He never looked back.

Loss and mistrust tugged her heart away from affection and

desire. She hung her head and wiped a tear, turning her back to the window. She paused at her father's room, but couldn't go in. *Not yet.* His room would need to be emptied. The whole house would need emptied and cleaned before she could move in with Mae.

I'll be gone from my home by Christmas.

She wandered across the living room to her father's *hanukiah*. The candles from the first night lay pooled in hard puddles in their cups. She pulled the storage box from beneath the table and packed the *menorah* and candles away. Her heart could find no reason for celebration.

Chapter 28

John Larson

John leaned his shoulder against the wall outside *La Fleur Chantante's* entrance. He wore one of the dark suits Maurice Bonet provided. All male employees dressed alike. Tonight, the club filled early, and a small crowd waited in the cold for their chance to pass through the door. Waited for John to let them in.

He'd taken over the doorman position from Webber, who sat warm in the booth with the owner right now. A cold breeze picked up, and John stood away from the wall, turning his collar against the chill.

Inside the club, Henri would be warm, standing beside *Monsieur* Bonet as his personal valet.

Perhaps I should have held out for an inside position.

The prospective patrons huddled in small groups along the wall.

No one tried to talk their way past John. No one spoke to him at all. Standing guard at the entrance proved a lonely occupation and gave him far too much time to think.

Two weeks ago, Aubrielle had asked him to leave her home. And for two weeks John had stayed away from the woman who bound his heart. He'd watched from his window as Mae's bakers and Henri moved Aubrielle's things to the apartment above the *boulangerie*. He wanted to help her but could not.

Henri had brought a message from Aubrielle. She needed time to grieve and had asked him to stay away.

He could only do what she had asked, although it hadn't been easy. Work helped. Besides the welcome income, it kept him away from her door each night. By the time he got back to his apartment, in the early hours of the morning, Aubrielle was safely tucked into bed.

John found it much harder to leave her alone during the day.

Aubrielle had resumed her daily treks to the park with Éclair and her wagon, this time selling Mae's baked goods.

I'd know if she were in danger. I'd know, and I'd be too far away for it to matter.

John rolled his shoulders. Aubrielle wasn't his only worry.

Karl Reimer continued to evade him. Bonet had pulled favors to find his former employee but to no avail. Reimer and his Nazi infiltrators had vanished like the fog into the city.

A laughing couple exited the club.

John held open the door and raised two fingers. He allowed a woman to enter but held up his hand to the next party of four.

They nodded and resumed their discussion.

As the woman cleared the entrance, Henri stepped outside. "Bonet asked me to check the line." Dressed identical to John, his blue-eyed inspection took stock of the people waiting to enter the club. "There are more in line than I thought."

At the far end of the line, a group argued. Their heated discussion ended when all five walked away from the entrance.

"That makes things easier. As soon as that group is gone, let in the rest. Tell them there is standing room only at the tables along the rail."

"Understood."

"Oh, and Aubrielle and Mae would like us to join them for Christmas Eve dinner."

John stared at Henri. "You've seen her?"

"Aubrielle?" Henri grinned. "I have. Bonet has developed a

fondness for Mae's flaky croissants. I pick up a *demi-douzaine* for his breakfast every day."

John nodded, then grasped Henri's arm. "Will *La Fleur* be closed on Christmas Eve?"

"Yes." Henri pulled his arm from John's grasp and laughed. "Come inside John. The cold up there has seeped between your ears."

* * *

Aubrielle Cohen

Mae took the goose from the oven and rested the pan on a trivet beside the large cutting board. "We'll let this rest for a moment before we carve."

Aubrielle untied her apron and hung it in the pantry. "The table is set. We need only light the candles."

"Good." Mae crossed to the sink full of dishes. "I'll take care of a few of these before our guests arrive."

The apartment layout above Mae's bakery was similar to her house above Papa's shop. Both buildings were two stories with the living space above the stores. Mae had emptied the back bedroom for Aubrielle's use. The same room she'd grown up in at her house. Mae's kindness knew no bounds.

Aubrielle slipped into the washroom and switched on the light. Leaning close to the mirror she studied her face. She pinched her cheeks for color and smoothed a fat curl above her forehead. Her efforts didn't calm her nerves. John would arrive at any moment. Her stomach tensed and rolled at the thought.

I've missed him.

She hadn't seen or spoken to him in over two weeks. How many mornings had she waited in her dark room for the light in his apartment to go out? When she knew he slept, she'd watch a moment longer, then begin her day.

I can't allow him to speak to me like a child.

He'd made her so furious the day of her father's funeral, but she'd been angry at everyone. Angry at the world. Angry at Papa.

It had been good to take the time to grieve and go through her parents' things. To remember them. She'd kept personal nicknacks and trinkets that reminded her of each of them. The rest had been sold at the auction to pay back rent. Finally free of the millinery and debt, she hoped to begin again.

Perhaps with John as well.

A knock sounded at the back door, and she gripped the washroom counter. One last check of her teeth and she hurried past Mae to greet their guest.

John stood at the back door, visible through the glass panel.

Aubrielle dried nervous palms on her green holiday skirt and opened the door. "*Bonjour.*"

"*Bonjour.* Merry Christmas."

"Please, come in."

John wiped his feet on the doormat and handed Aubrielle two bottles. "I didn't know what to bring for dinner, so I brought the wine."

"Always a good choice." She read the labels. "One dinner wine and one desert. Perfect. But Mae said you had provided the goose."

"Ah well, Mae should keep some things to herself." John chuckled as he hung his coat.

Another knock at the door and Henri stepped inside. *"Joyeux Noël."* Henri carried a pillowcase filled with boxes. He handed the bag to John as he removed his coat.

"Are you the *Père Noël* now?" Aubrielle asked over her shoulder as she walked toward the kitchen.

"Not I." Henri laughed. "I bring only a few gifts for dear friends."

"Put them in the front room beneath the tree," Aubrielle directed. "We can open them after we eat."

After the meal had been finished, and the dishes stacked in the sink, Aubrielle and Mae led their guests to the front room.

In the corner stood a small spruce fir tree decorated with Mae's festive handmade ornaments. The living area had only two chairs that faced the front window.

Aubrielle turned the radio on low and tuned to a station playing Christmas music. She sat on the floor beside the tree, curling her legs beneath her skirt.

John opened the bottle of Champagne and poured the bubbly liquid into the tall fluted glasses Mae had supplied. He handed each person a drink.

Mae settled into one of the chairs and set her glass on the side table. "I want to thank you all for sharing Christmas with me."

John lowered himself to the floor between the radio and the tree. "I feel the same way. Without each of you, this Christmas would have been a lonely holiday."

Henri raised his glass. "To the friends who have become my family."

"To friends," Aubrielle echoed and sipped the sparkling wine. Bubbles tickled their way down her throat, as dry acidic liquid assaulted her mouth. She set the glass down and shivered with distaste.

"You prefer the Sauvignon Blanc?" John asked.

"*Oui,*" she replied. Her face warmed beneath his regard. Eager to change the subject from herself, she reached for the gifts. "And now, without further delay, let's open our presents." She handed a wrapped box to John and one to Henri. "These are from Mae and me."

"Cookies!" Henri exclaimed and smiled his thanks to both Mae and Aubrielle. "And sweetbread. This is wonderful. Thank you."

"Thank you." John held the piece of sweet bread beneath his nose and inhaled. "Mmm, it even smells sweet." His smile crinkled the corner of his eyes.

"Hand out my gifts." Henri took the seat beside Mae. "The red is for Aubrielle, blue for Mae, and the brown package is for John."

"Henri, we discussed this." John narrowed his eyes at Henri as he took the package from Aubrielle.

Aubrielle laughed with pleasure at the happy banter between her friends.

Mae pulled out a knitted blue scarf and looked wide-eyed at Henri. "Don't tell me you made this yourself."

Henri grinned. "A woman who works at *La Fleur* makes them."

Aubrielle pushed back the tissue paper and touched the soft red wool. "Henri, this is beautiful." She lifted the large square scarf, folded it in half and pulled it around her shoulders. "It's so warm. Thank you."

John's scarf was brown with beige stripes. He folded it and laid it around his neck. "Thank you, Henri."

"I thought you needed one since you stand out in the cold every night."

"Why are you outside?" Aubrielle moved her gaze from Henri to John.

"I've taken a job at the musical club where Henri works, *La Fleur Chantante.*" John reached into his suit pocket and pulled out an envelope. "Speaking of which, Henri and I would like to invite you both to the New Year's Eve celebration at *La Fleur.*"

Aubrielle took the envelope from John's hand and withdrew four colorful passes. "Will you work that night?" She glanced up at John and caught an unguarded look of affection on his face.

"*Monsieur* Bonet assured me that the evening would be my own."

"This is only a week away." Aubrielle looked to Mae. "What will we wear?"

Mae waved her hand, clearly delighted. "I'm sure we'll find something. It's been so long since I listened to music that wasn't on the radio." She reached over and grasped Henri's hand. Her face flushed with excitement. "Thank you both."

Chapter 29

Aubrielle Cohen

Aubrielle sat on the edge of her bed in the dark. All of her belongings—her vanity, her chair, her bed—now occupied the back room of Mae's home. Similar enough to be a strange blend of comfort and longing. Familiar enough to break her heart.

Her gratitude to *Tante* Mae could not be measured.

What would I have done without her charity? Her trust?

What will she do when I betray that trust?

Mae had gone to bed an hour ago after they finished washing the dishes. She'd been excited at the prospect of going to a musical club and swore she would not sleep a wink. Now her soft snores told a different tale and gave Aubrielle her opportunity.

What magic did John want her to believe?

Did it have anything to do with her sense of absolute safety when she stood beside him?

That's not magic. That's his strength and kindness.

Was it the soft pulse between her legs, or the breathless abandon that scattered her thoughts when he kissed her and ran his hand behind her ear?

That's not magic. That's my affection and desire.

Then what possible explanation required a story steeped in sorcery for her to understand? How did any of these things tie to her father's delusional dreams?

Before good judgment regained control, Aubrielle pulled on her coat and tied her new red scarf around her head. With a last silent survey down the hall, she slipped out the back door and down the stairs.

Nearby, a church bell tolled the hour of midnight, calling the faithful to celebrate Christmas Mass.

John would be awake. His regular work hours stretched far into the morning.

She stopped in the *ruelle* as a shadow passed before his third-floor window. A dark silhouette blocked the light, but only for a moment. Her stomach tightened and tingled with nervousness. She glanced back at her darkened bedroom window, then looked ahead.

I have to know.

Her quick pace took her between the buildings, through the stairwell door, and up the steps toward John. Outside his door she hesitated, fist raised to knock.

Must I believe in magic, or can I simply believe in John?

She rapped her knuckles against the wood and exhaled through pressed lips. Even in the enclosed stairwell, it was cold enough to condense the vapor of her breath.

The door opened, and John blinked at her while he ran a hand through his hair to push it back from his forehead. His chest and feet were bare, as though he'd pulled on his slacks to answer the knock. "Aubrielle. What's happened?" He looked down the stairs behind her, then studied her face. "Is Mae all right?"

"Yes, she's fine." Aubrielle's throat tightened, and moisture fled her mouth. "I'm sorry to alarm you."

John reached out and steadied her. "Are you ill?"

Her inspection traveled up his arm and across the dark curly hair on his chest. She dry-swallowed and lifted her admiration to his eyes. "I wanted to ask you about the things you said." Heat infused her face, and she lowered her lashes.

What I'm feeling isn't magic. It's base and carnal and

intoxicating.

"Come in." John tugged Aubrielle's arm.

Her eyes opened, and she inhaled. John's scent enveloped her as she moved past him into his apartment. He exuded a trace of cologne mixed with a fragrance all his own.

Familiar. Stimulating. Mine.

"The coat closet is beside the door. Let me find a shirt and we can talk." He released her arm, crossed the small apartment and went into the back room.

Aubrielle unbuttoned her jacket and let it slide down her arms. She hung it and her scarf in the closet beside John's overcoat. Except for the furniture, which she suspected had come with the apartment, there were no personal items. No knickknacks on the tables. No photos on the wall.

A temporary home.

His box of Christmas cookies sat open on the kitchen counter. A radio voice, perhaps in the back room, detailed the latest news. The distant announcer droned on about the delicate state of the financial market.

"Would you like me to make some tea?" John had slipped on a wrinkled shirt and fumbled with the button on the cuff.

The white shirt hung open and drew her eyes to his abdomen and the dark hair that trailed down to his trousers. "John, it's the middle of the night. You don't have to dress."

His head came up, and his eyes narrowed. "Tea?"

"No tea."

He ran his hand through his hair again. It had grown since Aubrielle had first met him. Stubble shadowed his jawline as he shook his head. "What time is it?"

"Just after midnight. The bells were ringing when I left Mae's. *Joyeux Noël.*"

He nodded and tipped his head to the side. "Aubrielle, why are you here?" His scrutiny took in every facet of her appearance, then returned to her eyes, as though he hoped to see inside her mind.

"The magic." She moved closer. "I need to know what you meant when you asked if I believed."

His brows rose, and he took a breath. "I can't tell you and hope you'll understand. It's a power you have to witness to believe." As though drawn, he moved a pace closer, and his voice softened. "It's something you have to feel for yourself."

"John, there is something. I feel something." She raised her hand and laid her palm in the middle of his chest. Her fingers trembled against the heat of his body, the springy texture of the dark hair against her hand. "Is this the magic?"

John reached up and ran his hand along her scalp behind her ear, lifting her hair.

Her entire being trembled. Goosebumps rose on her arms and down her spine. The tightness between her legs pulsed. "Ah."

"Brought about by magic, maybe. All the things I know of you. How you like to be touched. How your soul has matured over these many years." His other hand mirrored the first, cradling the weight of her skull. He tipped her head back and lowered his mouth to hers. "The spark between us has always been here. Even in the beginning. You're part of me. *That* is the magic."

Not the gentle kiss from the park, his lips pressed onto hers, opening her mouth, tasting her tongue. Inhaling her essence.

Aubrielle rose on her toes and ran her palms beneath the loose shirt and across the warm, smooth skin of his back. This close was not close enough.

Pulse.

He turned her head and kissed the other side of her mouth. His lips demanded a response. Then his tongue traced fire along her cheek to her ear, and he whispered, "God, how I've missed you."

Her knees buckled as his words tickled her ear.

As if he knew her legs would give way, one muscular arm lifted behind her knees, and he cradled her to his chest. His lips and tongue tasted her neck as her head fell back against his arm. The ceiling moved as he carried her through his apartment. The radio

206

volume increased, and the scent of his cologne filled her senses as he entered his bedroom. She closed her eyes.

John laid her on his bed, and the mattress sank with his weight as he joined her.

Aubrielle opened her eyes, but there was no light in the room. She put her hand out and found John's chest.

He'd removed his shirt and rested on one elbow, above her. "You're always a surprise and delight to me." His free hand ran up her leg, past her knee and caressed her thigh. "You asked about the magic, and I must confess, in this regard, I have an advantage."

"Your years of experience?"

"No, *mon amour*. My knowledge of you. What you like. What you love. What drives you to the very edge—and keeps you there, begging for release."

"How do you know these things when I don't know them myself?

"If you're sure this is what you want, I will show you."

"I want you to tell me first."

"Tell you? Tell you what I'll do?"

"*Oui.*"

His weight on the mattress disappeared. "All right." His hand cradled her foot. "First, I'd take your shoes off. Then your stockings." He unclasped the garter from the silk and rolled them down her legs. His fingers trailing warmth against her chilled skin.

He lifted her ankles and set her feet apart, knees bent, and ran his hands down the inside of her thighs, relaxing them.

Pulse.

"You always liked that." His fingers traced along the edge of her undergarment, slipping inside the silky material for a brief caress.

Pulse.

Aubrielle groaned low in her throat and closed her eyes, abandoning her senses to the sound of his voice and his hands.

"Then I would take off your panties. Raise your hips. Yes, like that." His fingers pulled her lingerie slowly down her legs and over her feet. "You always like me to kiss the inside of your legs, from the back of your knees to—well, I'll show you." He spread her legs again, wider this time, her knees still bent. He lifted her right leg and laid it over his shoulder as he licked behind her knee and trailed his tongue and kisses along her inner thigh.

Pulse.

"Mon Dieu!" she whispered. Her pelvis raised towards his approaching lips.

Pulse.

His fingers separated her folds and his mouth sucked for a brief second on her clitoris.

Pulse.

"Both of your beautiful legs always demand my attention." His mouth paid homage to her left leg. When he reached her center again, he lifted her bottom with both hands, her legs splayed and dangled down his back. "You like this part the best I think." His breath tickled the hair between her legs as his thumbs opened her cleft. "I must have a taste."

The warm wet pressure of his tongue slid up her vulva, licking her like a child would lick an ice cream cone. At the top, his lips found her clitoris again, and he swirled his tongue around it until a warm sensation spread from her center.

Pulse. Pulse. Pulse. "John—"

With a soft kiss, John lowered her hips to the mattress, pulled her skirt down, and sat back. "But first, I need to undress you."

"Sainte Mère de Dieu, John." The warmth faded, and the pulsing sensation slowed. "You cannot tell me I'm the only woman who would like that."

He was silent for a moment in the dark. Aubrielle felt more than saw his shrug. "I don't know. I imagine they might, but I've never been with anyone but you."

"What—"

"Shh. It's knotted in the magic. I can love no woman except

you."

The news broadcast had stopped at some point, and an orchestra played a Christmas melody. Aubrielle stayed silent, listening to John's breath.

"I know I'll never be able to explain to your satisfaction, but I have loved you for what feels like forever. The love I have for you will never die. Never fade. I will always come to you, wait for you, cherish you."

"John—"

"Sit up. I'm going to undress you now."

He helped her to her feet, unbuttoned her skirt and let it slide over her hips to the floor. Hooking his fingers beneath the elastic on her slip he slid the silken material down her legs as his tongue paid homage to the soft skin between her belly button and dark pubic hair.

"John, I can't." Her knees trembled.

His hands and mouth paused. "You want me to stop?"

"*Non, mon amour,* but when your lips touch me, my strength fails."

John chuckled low in his throat and ran his hands up her waist. He loosened the buttons on her blouse, pushing the material away from her shoulder. He kissed her tender neck. "Then I will hurry." He tugged her shirt from her arms, then kissed the mounds of her breast as he released her bra.

When her brassiere followed the blouse into the darkness, his mouth fastened to her nipple, and her knees failed.

As before, John anticipated her response and lifted her to the bed.

The heat of his body settled against her chilled skin.

His lips paid momentary homage to her throat before he rose on one elbow. His free hand caressed each breast, teasing her nipples into hard pebbles.

Pulse.

His hand trailed down her body, and his fingers brushed the heat between her legs. "Open for me."

She parted her legs as his tongue circled her sensitive nipple.

He touched the damp hair between her legs, moving his fingers close to her skin. "Wider."

Pulse.

When the muscles of her legs relaxed, he slipped a finger inside her then trailed the wet tip to her sensitive nub and circled gently.

Pulse. Pulse.

Aubrielle ran her hand down his chest to his cock, but he grabbed her wrist. "Next time you can touch me. This time, I'm already too close."

"Too close?"

His fingers returned to their circling caress. "Too close to this."

Her breath caught on the inhale as the warmth expanded from between her legs into her abdomen and her toes curled.

Pulse. Pulse Pulse.

Her body jerked as the sensation exploded beneath his fingers. His touch softened as wave after wave moved from her center outward, pulsing slower until she lay still in the afterglow.

John moved between her open legs. His torso braced above her. He entered her slightly and withdrew. His arms trembled, and he lowered his forehead to hers. "I'm too close."

"Then don't stop." She pushed her hips toward him, pulling him inside her. "I want to know, John, Show me."

He braced one hand beside her head and wrapped his arm beneath her hips as he eased into her. Deeper that time, far enough to stretch her.

Pain mixed with pleasure, and she raised her hips up to meet his thrust.

His body jerked once then he held himself above her. Motionless. "Jesus. I can't. It's been too long."

"Can't what?" she whispered.

He withdrew and slid home again, then shuddered and groaned. In his stillness, she could feel him pulse inside her and understood. "Don't try to hold back," she breathed.

He buried his face beside her neck and thrust three times, then pressed hard. "I love you," he said into her shoulder as he convulsed one last time. "Only you."

Chapter 30

John Larson

John pulled the bedcover across their naked bodies as their perspiration cooled. He held Aubrielle close to his heart in the dark, her head tucked against his shoulder.

His pulse slowed, although there remained some tightness in his chest. A wellspring of emotion that constricted his throat and seeped from his eye.

Have I ever loved her this much? I don't think so. How deep must this well of emotion be, that I can return again and again, yet lower myself deeper each time into its warm embrace?

Her fingers played idly across the hair on his chest. "What time is it?" Her voice was soft and shy in the dark.

John glanced out the window. Few stars could complete with the city light, but the moon had already set. Christmas morning would soon dawn. "Early. Two-thirty. Maybe three."

She rolled away from his embrace, pushed the cover back and sat up. "Mae will wake early. I need to go." She rose from his bed and in a moment the light in the bathroom came on. The door closed.

John sat and ran a hand over his face. The scent of their lovemaking clung to his body and permeated the room. His shy girl wouldn't like that. He stood and opened the sash on the window an inch. Cold air fluttered the curtain and circled the room with its fresh, clean scent.

John found his trousers and pulled them on in the dark. He picked his shirt from the floor and shook it out.

"John?"

"Yes?" He stepped into the short hallway.

"Could you hand me my clothes?" She peered around the edge of the bathroom door, her blush dark red.

"Of course." Knowing better than to laugh, he gathered her garments with a grin on his face, then sobered as he searched for her second stocking.

Does she regret our lovemaking already?

He placed the bedroom chair in the hall with her clothes on the seat. "Your clothes are out here. I'll be in the front room."

He stood at the window and watched the dark sky and city lights through his reflection. The image of her movement reflected in the window and caught his eye.

She swallowed, glanced at him, then averted her eyes. "I have to go."

In a step, he crossed the room and wrapped his arms around her, pulling her close to his chest. "Listen. Do you hear that?"

"Hear what?" She looked up.

"The sound of my heart."

She rested her head against his chest and wrapped her arms around his waist.

"Do you hear it?"

She nodded. "I do."

"Remember the sound, my love. It beats for you."

Her head tipped back, and dark eyes studied him. "I..." Her face darkened with a blush, and she looked down. "I love you, John."

"And I love you, my lady—my Viking princess—my sorceress."

"All of that?"

"And more."

She pushed away shaking her head and retrieved her coat. "I don't know what I'll tell Mae."

"You owe explanations to no one."

"Hmm."

She gave him a look he knew so well, he threw back his head and laughed. "A kiss before you go, then."

Although her cheeks blushed, she rose on her toes and guided his mouth to hers with her hands.

John intended a chaste kiss, but her soft lips offered so readily inflamed his senses. He pulled her to his chest and tasted her lips sweetly, but thoroughly. With a final brush, he released her.

* * *

Aubrielle Cohen

"John's here," Mae called from the front room.

Aubrielle turned her head from side to side and studied her reflection in the bathroom mirror. Mae had left makeup out for her to use. Mascara for her lashes, a darkening pencil to line her eyes and shape her brows, and lipstick. She put a piece of tissue paper between her lips and pressed like her mother used to when Aubrielle was a little girl. She dropped the tissue in the waste receptacle and stared at the outline of her lips on the soft paper.

John was outside.

Although she hadn't seen him since Christmas morning, he had sent her flowers and had two letters delivered. The notes told of how he looked forward to tonight, of how work and preparations for this evening had kept him away, and of how much he loved her.

He loves me.

"Aubrielle!"

"Coming." She switched off the light and hurried into the front room. They would exit through the bakery to the *rue* tonight, per

John's instructions.

"He sent a limousine." Mae stared out the front window.

Aubrielle hurried to the window and pulled the curtain to the side.

On the street in front of the *boulangerie* idled a large black car. Steam circled a shiny bumper.

"No wonder he wanted us to go out the front. That vehicle wouldn't fit down the *ruelle*."

Mae handed Aubrielle her coat before putting hers over her dark violet tweed skirt and matching jacket.

Aubrielle wore her rose-colored dress with a black belt and black T-strap shoes. She followed Mae down the stairs into the back room of the closed bakery. They walked past the empty racks that would display tomorrow's fresh baked goods.

John stood beside the entrance. Visible through the glass windows, his tailored black suit, and black silk tie looked striking.

Aubrielle's pace slowed to a stop. *His height. The width of his shoulders. His easy smile and expressive brown eyes. His gentle touch.* Without a doubt, John was the most magnificent man she'd ever known.

Mae looked back and paused. "Come along. John's waiting."

John peered through the glass and caught her gaze.

She stared at him while Mae unlocked the shop door. Her pulse sped up, and her face felt hot. She smiled tentatively at first, then broke into a grin.

"Here we go." Mae walked outside and held the door, locking it once Aubrielle stood on the sidewalk.

"Ladies," John kissed Aubrielle's hand, then held his arm toward the black sedan with a uniformed driver behind the wheel. John opened the back door of the limousine. "Henri will meet us at *La Fleur.*"

The spacious backseat could comfortably seat four.

Aubrielle entered and sat in the middle of the bench seat.

John helped Mae into the limousine, then he rounded the

vehicle, taking his place beside Aubrielle.

As soon as John's door closed, the driver pulled into the street.

"Very fancy, I must say." Mae chuckled. "I had no idea what you lads were up to."

"Renting a limousine for the night is only slightly more expensive than taking a cab. My employer gets a good rate and he let me use his name."

"I'd like to meet him," Mae said. She relaxed back against the padded seat and looked out the window.

"You will meet *Monsieur* Bonet tonight." He took Aubrielle's hand. "Are you cold?"

"No." Her heart performed a curious flutter. "Only my hands."

When they arrived, John helped both women from the car, then spoke to the driver for a few moments. He tapped the back of the vehicle as he passed behind it and onto the curb.

Webber stood outside collecting tickets from a group of four. When the ticket holders went inside, he looked at John. "How did you get tonight off?"

"Friend of the management."

Webber laughed and opened the door. He bowed to Mae and Aubrielle. "Ladies. Have a wonderful evening. Happy New Year."

"Oh my," Mae muttered as she gaped at the small club.

"Let's check your coats first. Then we can find our table." John held out his hand toward the young lady behind the half-door.

Aubrielle nodded but couldn't tear her sight from the room. She had no idea such a magical place existed.

On stage, a statuesque black woman dressed in a shimmering gold gown leaned into the microphone. Her voice captured Aubrielle with a song she knew from the radio.

Candle lamps at each table flickered in the semi-darkness. A smoke haze hung near the ceiling along with netting which held dozens of colorful balloons. Couples swayed on the dance floor, their bodies touching as they moved to the music.

Aubrielle closed her mouth and swallowed.

John touched her arm. "Would you like me to take your coat?"

"Oh, yes. I'm sorry." She handed him her wool jacket, then looked over her shoulder at the singer. "I know that song."

John exchanged her coat for a metal number and slipped the tab into his pocket then showed them to their table near the dance floor. In the middle of the table stood a folded card, embossed with golden print stating RÉSERVÉ.

He seated Mae and Aubrielle and handed the card to the waitress. "Thank you, Bébé."

"*Bienvenu, mon cher.*" The dark-haired waitress turned her smile to Aubrielle and Mae. "What would the ladies like to drink?"

"Do you have a house wine?" Mae asked.

"Did you like the Sauvignon Blanc we had on Christmas Eve?" John asked.

"Oh yes." Mae nodded.

"I did too," Aubrielle agreed.

"Bring a bottle of Sauvignon Blanc with four glasses." John sat beside Aubrielle.

Henri arrived at the table as Bébé was leaving and they shared a brief intimate smile. When Bébé had gone, Henri grinned at Mae and Aubrielle. "It is so wonderful to see you, Mae. I told *Monsieur* Bonet you would be here tonight." He relaxed into the chair beside Mae. "He plans to come by and compliment you on your croissants."

"Aubrielle told me you come to the park each morning to buy them."

"It's true. I should have never suggested he try them. Now he insists he can have no other bread with his morning café."

It wasn't long after their wine arrived that Maurice Bonet stopped at their table. "*Madame. Mademoiselle. Monsieur* Larson" His black tuxedo, olive skin tone and slick black hair made him stand out among the other guests. He tipped his head to both women. "I am Maurice Bonet, and I am delighted to meet you." He held out his hand to Mae. "*Madame*, would you do me the honor of a dance?"

Mae's eyes opened wide. "Yes, I would. Thank you, *Monsieur* Bonet."

"Call me Maurice, *ma chère*." He tucked her hand around his arm and escorted her away from the table.

John rose and took Aubrielle's hand. "Shall we?"

Aubrielle hesitated. "I'm not much of a dancer." She shook her head and grinned.

"You'll do fine." He led her through the crush of couples to an open spot near the band. He took her in his arms and swayed in time to the music. "Not so bad."

"It's like a fairy tale."

The song ended, and John twirled her away from him, then pulled her back into his arms. "I love you," he whispered next to her ear. He pulled away, still holding her hand and spoke to the songstress on the stage.

The woman nodded and grinned at Aubrielle as she backed away from the microphone.

"Wait for me here. This won't take but a moment." John mounted the steps to the stage and stopped in front of the mic. "Good evening, everyone. *Bonsoir, mesdames et messieurs.* Welcome to *La Fleur Chantante* on this last night of 1939." John spoke easily to the crowd, nodding to people he knew in the audience.

The dance floor had cleared except for Aubrielle. Self-conscious, she put her back to the tables and focused on John.

He gave her a wink before he continued. "Please join me in thanking our host *Monsieur* Maurice Bonet for this New Year's celebration. The outstanding house band that plays for us every night. The waitresses and staff who make your evening comfortable, and our beautiful and talented guest singer, Toula Grange."

The loud applause startled Aubrielle, and she glanced at their table.

Maurice Bonet sat beside Mae. A wide grin stretched across his face.

The waitress, Bébé, whispered to Henri, who nodded and laughed, never taking his attention from Aubrielle and John.

As the applause faded, John held up his hand. "There's about an hour left until midnight, and the party will continue until you are ready to depart." He took a breath and his gaze found Aubrielle beside the stage. "There is only one thing left for me to do before I turn the microphone back over to our beautiful singer."

He wouldn't.

John hopped down from the stage and lifted her hand as he sank onto one knee.

In Aubrielle's daze, the room whirled about her. The only motionless place in the maelstrom was where they stood. His hand held her secure in the storm.

His dark eyes flecked with strands of gold, asked the question of her before his lips even moved. "Aubrielle Cohen, will you marry me?"

* * *

John Larson

John waited on one knee. His hands held her cold fingers. His gaze never left Aubrielle's pale face.

Why does she hesitate?

Aubrielle's cheeks had gone from the initial pink blush to an alarming shade of white. Her free hand trembled at her throat.

He stood and pulled her into his arms. "You don't have to answer now," he whispered into her hair. "I should have waited. I should have asked this question in private."

The club erupted into cheers and whistles, mistaking his embrace for confirmation she had said yes.

She gasped and coughed, shaking her head. "No," she managed

before she coughed again.

"Are you all right?"

"Yes." She cleared her throat. "Speechless."

The songstress took the microphone. "Congratulations John and Aubrielle." She raised her hands and clapped.

The crowd responded with renewed enthusiasm.

"Ask everyone to dance," John called to Toula over the applause.

She gave John a nod that she'd heard, then opened her arms to the crowd. "Let's have all our couples on the dance floor for this next romantic melody."

John took Aubrielle in his arms and moved in time with the music. "You look better," he whispered beside her ear.

"I've caught my breath. I think the cigarette smoke bothers me. I'm not used to it."

He put his hand on her waist, and they danced close as the dance floor filled. "I'm so sorry I put you in that position."

"You can't take it back."

John furrowed his brow. "Take it back?"

"Your proposal. I won't let you."

"I pressed you too soon." He moved to the tempo of the music, but his heart beat triple time. "You're not ready."

She ran her hand from his shoulder to his neck and tugged his head closer. "My answer is yes. Of course, I'll marry you." She chuckled. "I would have said so before, but I couldn't find my breath."

John rolled his head back as relief flooded through him. "Yes!"

Several couples dancing close to them startled and stared.

John took her shoulders and dropped a swift kiss on her lips. "I love you." He offered another kiss to the side of her mouth. "You've made me happier than I can say." He wrapped her in his arms, pulled her to his chest, and lowered his mouth to hers.

"Save it for the honeymoon," an older gentleman called to John.

John laughed as Aubrielle's face colored. He took her hand and her waist and danced across the small floor to their table.

Mae and Maurice Bonet were missing.

Henri raised his glass as the couple approached. "Congratulations, *mes amis*."

"Thank you." John held the chair for Aubrielle. "Where is Mae?"

Henri pointed onto the dance floor. "*Monsieur* Bonet appears quite taken with her."

The waitresses deposited streamers, confetti and *serpentins* horns at each table. Sprigs of mistletoe had been passed around all evening. Their table had four or five ribbon-adorned sprigs.

As midnight approached, Toula counted down into the microphone. The audience came to their feet and joined in the count.

"*Trois, deux, un—Bonne année!*"

The intimate club rang with cheers. Streamers and confetti filled the air, and the balloons released from the netting.

Aubrielle blew into her horn, laughed and turned to John. "*Bonne année, mon amour.*"

"Happy New Year," John whispered as his mouth claimed hers.

Amidst the joyous celebration, a prophetic conversation, spoken many years ago, replayed in his mind.

"After the depression, there will be another world war." His friend with knowledge of the future had lowered her head.

He'd known her secret. A passage through time. And she'd known his. The curse of immortality.

They'd talked by the corral on a dusty and hot summer day. He'd hooked a boot heel over the lower rung of the split rail and watched the horses as she whispered her warnings of the future.

"I wish I'd paid more attention in World History," she'd said with an apologetic half-smile. "But I didn't, so I can only give you generalities. Germany and Russia attack Poland, then the entire world will pause, like the dead air before a tornado. The inactivity will last for around six months." She'd shaken her head and shrugged. "Maybe more. I know it's less than a year. After that, the German army will sweep south and east, taking most of France in its grasp. It'll happen fast. A blitzkrieg. They'll bomb whatever they can't occupy."

She'd lifted her heavy blonde curls to catch a breath of air along her neck. "During the war, the safest place to be will be America." She shook her head. "Well, except for Hawaii, and whatever you do, Jim, once this war starts, don't go to Japan."

Chapter 31

Aubrielle Cohen

Aubrielle held Éclair's lead as she turned the pony cart into the *Champs-de-Mars*. Tulips bloomed in the flowerbeds. Their petals damp with morning dew. The trees, skeletal and dark yesterday, shimmered with the pale green of tender buds. Squirrels and birds chatted overhead as she walked to her usual selling place. Late April had left the bitter winter winds behind. The scent of damp earth and fragrant young blossoms drifted past her on a warm spring breeze.

She wedged a block beneath the wheel and lifted the tarp from her bread display. Behind the stand set a paper-wrapped package of croissants. Mae sent a dozen of the flaky pastries with Aubrielle to the park every day for Henri to take to Maurice.

Aubrielle tugged her stool from the cart and placed it beside Éclair.

There's likely a note tucked inside the package to Monsieur Bonet.

The sparkle in *Tante* Mae's hazel eyes this morning lifted Aubrielle lips with a delighted grin.

As she waited for the morning's first customer, her thumb played with the diamond ring on her left hand. She and John had argued again last night after he'd asked her to leave France and return with him to America.

His details about how they would accomplish such a move were always vague, like his fear of a German invasion. His unreasonable alarm grew daily as news of the war in Norway continued.

The Nazis will never get past the Maginot Line.

The Germans knew it too, so they invaded Norway. France was safe.

Then why is John so frightened?

French and British troops guarded the border with Belgium. Paris would never be at risk. And even if his fears were well-founded, John should know she could never leave *Tante* Mae.

Aubrielle looked up as a shadow blocked the morning sun.

A gentleman stopped to look over the loaves of freshly baked bread and baguettes. "Those smell delicious, *mademoiselle*."

"They were baked fresh this morning. The loaves may still be warm." She rose from her stool.

"Are you here every morning?" As the man reached to select two loaves, he turned his head revealing a dark discoloration along his jaw. The red-purple patch extended down his neckline.

Aubrielle placed his purchase in a bag. "Most mornings. *Oui*." She didn't want to stare at the birthmark, or burn scar, but she had seen them somewhere before. "I'm sorry, but haven't we met?" She collected his coins.

"It's always possible, *mademoiselle*. I've lived in Paris for some time." He took his bag of bread from her hands. "Perhaps we passed in the park or spoke at the market." He pointed to his scar. "I'm a hard man to forget."

"That must be it." Aubrielle's cheeks burned with embarrassment.

The man tipped his hat and turned away. "If these taste as good as they smell, you shall certainly see me again."

"*Merci*," Aubrielle called over her shoulder as she reorganized her display.

A steady stream of morning customers kept Aubrielle busy, and the strange encounter with the scarred man slipped from her mind.

Near noon, Henri crossed the wide parkway. "Good morning, Aubrielle," he called and touched his cap. His shirt sleeves were rolled up, and one finger held his jacket draped over his shoulder. "What a beautiful day."

"You're in a good mood." She retrieved the package for *Monsieur* Bonet.

"I have to be. Bébé told me she loved me last night." His grin widened. "Ah, springtime."

"You blame the season for her affection?" Aubrielle raised an eyebrow as she handed Henri the wrapped croissants.

"What about you and Big John? Have you set a date yet?"

"No. Not yet." Her bright smile faded. "But we will soon."

"I best get these back. *Monsieur* Bonet is waiting for them, I know." Henri kissed both sides of Aubrielle's face then waved as he walked away, whistling at the birds in the trees.

By mid-afternoon storm clouds were building. When the wind picked up, she covered her remaining goods and unblocked the cart. She had just turned Éclair around when she saw John enter the park.

He waved and double-stepped across the walkway. "Heading home before the storm?" John took Éclair's lead and leaned down to kiss her lips.

Aubrielle wrapped her arms around his waist, beneath his light jacket. The warmth of his body felt luxurious on her chilled arms. She remained beside him, tucked inside his coat beneath his shoulder as they exited the park. "Will you be able to stay for dinner?"

"Of course." He kissed the top of her head.

When they returned home, Aubrielle helped John settle Éclair into his stall behind her old home. Mae had rented the converted garage from the new owner next door.

As John and Aubrielle climbed the back steps to Mae's kitchen, raindrops pelted their heads. Aubrielle uttered a small shriek at the cold droplets and ran in through the back door.

Inside, Mae's kitchen was fragrant and filled with the sound of sizzling sausages and laughter.

"*Bonjour,* John." Maurice Bonet called from his seat at the table, wine glass in hand. He rose when Aubrielle followed John into the kitchen. "*Bonjour, mademoiselle.*"

"Maurice stopped by, and I asked him to remain for dinner." Mae moved the skillet to an unlit burner and turned off the flame. "Tonight we shall have *boudin blanc* and the last of the fall potatoes." She gestured to the empty chairs. "Please sit. Dinner is ready. I know the men need to be off to work."

* * *

John Larson

John held Aubrielle's chair as she sat beside Maurice at the table, then John claimed the corner seat for himself.

Mae placed the skillet with sausage and fried potatoes on a trivet on the table. "Help yourself."

From the front room, the radio newscaster reported the latest information on the war effort. British troops had begun to pull from central Norway. There were reports of early civilian evacuations as Germany tightened their grip.

John clenched his jaw and stared at the empty plate. Nothing he said swayed Aubrielle's determination to remain with Mae. Her faith in the French fortifications remained unshakable. A glint from her neckline caught his eye. The Star of David shimmered in the light. One didn't require knowledge of the future to know how Hitler felt about Jews.

Why won't she listen to me?

After dinner, Maurice kissed Mae on the cheek. "Thank you, *ma chère.* Seeing you is my greatest pleasure."

Mae blushed and tucked her chin. A delighted smile spread

across her face. "Please, come by again. Anytime. You are always welcome."

Maurice looked at John while he adjusted his hat. "Would you like to ride to *La Fleur* with me?"

"Yes, thank you."

Maurice winked at John and Aubrielle. "I'll wait in the car. It's parked out front."

From the back porch, John watched Maurice disappear between the buildings.

"I'm happy for Mae." Aubrielle took his hand. "For them both."

"I know. Me too." As he turned to kiss her, his glance caught her necklace and he paused.

"What is it now?" she asked. Her tone sharp with annoyance.

He straightened and looked down at her narrowed eyes. "Do you have to wear your father's necklace?"

Her eyes widened. "Now you're worried about my jewelry? What will be next?" She folded her arms and moved away from him. "Improper footwear?"

John exhaled between pressed lips. "You know what's happening in Poland." He leaned toward her, matching her anger and pointed north. "You understand what the Nazis are doing to those who offend Hitler. The Roma Gypsies. The Jews. *You know.*"

"Hitler isn't here, John." She tossed her head and looked over her shoulder. "Only you are, with your never-ending fear." She looked up at him, anger furrowed her brows. "Don't make Maurice wait for you."

He reined in his anger and softened his voice. "Aubrielle, my concern is for you."

"Good night, John." She ducked inside and yanked the door closed.

John watched her silhouette retreat from the door. "Damn it." He ran a hand through his hair and hurried down the steps.

After the club had closed, John sat at a table with Webber and Henri.

Henri pulled his necktie loose and came to his feet. "Good night, *mes amis."* He stopped suddenly and turned to John. "I forgot to tell you. Marcel said he saw Karl yesterday."

"Where?" John sat forward. "Where did he see him?"

"Near the market you went to with Aubrielle. Asher's was it?"

John nodded. "Did Marcel speak to Karl?"

Henri took a step back. His glance skipped to Bébé, who waited beside the stage door. "No. He only caught a glimpse of Karl through the shoppers." he took another step back. "But I thought you'd want to know."

"Thanks, Henri." John rose and pulled his jacket from the back of the chair. "Have a good night, Web."

"Toi aussi, John."

John changed out of his work uniform in one of the small dressing room behind the stage. He hung the black suit on the rack beside his name.

Outside, he inhaled the fragrant spring air, chilled in the early hours before dawn. He caught a cab and made good time home. At that time of the morning, traffic was light. The rain which had sputtered on and off all evening had stopped but left the streets wet. The pavement reflected every set of headlights they passed.

As he climbed the stairs to his apartment, he couldn't tear his mind from Karl Reimer. *Where were he and his men hidden?*

Once inside, he pulled off his tie while he navigated through the dark apartment. He slowed near the front window to check if Aubrielle's light was on. It wasn't. The darkness in the window across the alley tugged at his heart.

I push too hard.

He unbuttoned his shirt and tossed it over the kitchen chair as he walked to the bedroom and stopped.

Aubrielle's scent, a light musk mingled with a delicious fragrance all her own, filled his senses. From the window, a street lamp cast its shaft of light across his bed and caressed her bare shoulder while she slept.

John removed the rest of his clothes and slipped beneath the covers.

Aubrielle blinked sleepily and rolled to her side, allowing him more room, then snuggled close, angling her leg across his. "I used your key again."

"It's your key." He kissed her lips then tucked her head against his shoulder. "I didn't expect you tonight, though."

"I know." She ran her hand across his chest. "But I needed to tell you I'm sorry."

He kissed the top of her head and pulled her tight against his body. "I'm sorry too. I push you too hard."

"Your concern is for me. I know that."

"I couldn't live with myself if anything were to happen to you."

She tipped her head back as her hand slipped low across his stomach and found the evidence of his desire. "I love you," Aubrielle whispered. She took him in her grip and lifted her face to his.

He gasped softly then lowered his mouth to hers. "And I love you. Only you."

Chapter 32

John Larson

May 14, 1940

John straightened his tie and brushed a speck of glitter from his lapel. Bonet's latest acts fluttered around like messy little birds. He pushed the dressing room curtain aside and brushed another bit of sparkle from his suit sleeve.

The small troop of five dancing girls chatted in costume beside the backstage stairs. Their eyelids glistened with glitter. Their costumes, stockings, and shoes sparkled. Their dazzling attire left a trail wherever they went.

I'll leave my suit in Henry's room until their contract is over.

John edged around them and entered the club. He was later than usual. *La Fleur Chantante* had already opened their doors for the Tuesday night crowd.

Webber manned the entrance tonight, directing newcomers as they entered the venue. Each time the door opened, a gust of rain followed the guests and their umbrellas inside.

John circled the catwalk and stepped up to join Henri, Marcel, and *Monsieur* Bonet at their elevated booth. "*Bonsoir.*"

"*Bonsoir,* John. Have a seat." Bonet sipped his Bordeaux. "Have you been to see your young *fiancée*? More importantly, did you speak with *Madame* Moroney? Did she mention my name?"

"*Madame* Moroney always asks after your health." John slid into the booth and chuckled at Bonet. "She begged me to give you her regards."

Behind Bonet, Henri scrunched his eyes closed and shook his head.

John's grin grew wide.

"*Une belle femme*," Bonet replied with a sigh. He took another sip of his drink. *"Elle est magnifique."*

Despite *Monsieur* Bonet's good mood this evening, patronage at *La Fleur Chantante* continued to decline. Germany's advance into Belgium and the Netherlands had caused troop redeployment for those soldiers stationed in Paris. A good third of Bonet's business came from servicemen, both French and British. The thin crowd this night proved that point.

An hour later, the lights dimmed, and a spotlight lit the stage.

The band paused, and the small crowd hushed as the curtains split in the middle and drew open. The vaudevillian dancers pranced forward in their sparkling costumes, bowed, and then linked arms as the band struck up a lively tune.

"I miss Toola," Bonet muttered. He clipped the ends of his cigar and lit the stogie.

Webber, still at the club entrance waved, toward their table.

John gave Web a nod of acknowledgment and leaned toward Bonet. "Someone's coming up." He stood, buttoning his jacket and waited by the steps.

A uniformed officer glanced at John and came to a halt, one foot on the stair. "John Larson?"

John's brow lifted in surprise. *"Oui.* I am John Larson."

"Un télégramme pour vous, monsieur." The young officer held out an official tan envelope.

"Merci." John took the telegram from the young man's outstretched hand.

The officer gave a nod, did an about-face, and returned to the exit.

Webber looked from the messenger's back to John and shrugged.

"What does it say?" Henri asked.

John glanced up from the folded missive as he returned to the booth.

"Who's it from?" Bonet blew smoke toward the ceiling.

John sat and turned the document over. The seal held the official stamp of the *Bureau de la Sûreté nationale*. "I think it's from François," he guessed out loud. His thumb slipped into the opening above the seal and hesitated.

François and Billy had disappeared into the hospital the night they rescued François from Karl Reimer. The next day, no one had any record of their arrival. They hadn't been heard from since. For François to send a missive now left a block of ice in John's gut.

Bonet looked over at the letter. "Our missing friend has been detained?"

"I don't know." John broke the seal and opened the telegram. Inside, the message had been written in English with blue ink. "It's from Billy," he told them.

"Are they all right?" Henri walked around the booth to the front of the table.

"I'll read it." John held the letter flat and angled it toward the table lamp. "In good health, we send our regards. We depart soon for the Azure Coast and urge you to consider a holiday retreat to the south. William Bane"

"That's it?" Bonet dropped his cigar in the tray and raised his glass. "A smuggler's holiday plans announced by a telegram from *la Sûreté nationale*. Absurd."

John looked up at Henri.

"Let me see." Henri held his hand out for the telegram. "At least they're both well and leaving for the French Riviera. It sounds as though they would like for you to join them."

John handed the telegram to Henri. "François and Billy plan to leave Paris. I suspect they have information about the war we do not."

An uneasy tingle on the back of John's neck intensified, clawing its way down his spine. He gasped as a sharp shiver shook the foundation of his soul.

Dear God, no.

Movement inside the club ceased. Held captive by an ancient curse. By a call.

Aubrielle.

The waitress beside their table had lifted a glass of wine from her tray. Her motion froze. Her smile, fixed and unmoving.

The violinist held his bow poised above the strings, halted in mid-stroke. The music silenced.

The dancer's twirl hung suspended. Her toes dangled several inches above the wooden stage. Glitter spun away from her dress and hung motionless in the air.

Inside John's head pain expanded, crushing all his other senses.

Then movement resumed. Sound returned. The agony in his head diminished to a single blistering point on the side of his skull. He blinked at Henri through panicked tears and came to his feet, gripping the table as a wave of dizziness washed over him. "I've got to go."

"Are you ill?" Bonet sat forward.

Marcel came to his feet and searched the club for an immediate threat, then stared with concern at John.

Henri's hand steadied John's shoulder. "What's wrong?"

"It's Aubrielle."

* * *

Aubrielle Cohen

Aubrielle wiped the wineglass dry and put it away in the cupboard. Without pause, she reached for a plate and ran her dishtowel over the wet ceramic.

Mae had retired to the living room after dinner. By unspoken agreement, whoever cooked did not have to help with the dishes.

Instead of the music Aubrielle preferred, Mae had tuned in the National News. The war declared last fall had finally begun in earnest.

John's fear of the war must have affected her. She startled and dropped Mae's plate when a knock sounded at the back door. The platter shattered into shards at her feet.

"Are you all right, dear?"

"Yes, *Tante* Mae." She peered through the open curtains on the door.

A man waited on the landing. His back to the glass.

"Who's at the door?" The chair squeaked in the front room.

"I can't tell." Aubrielle tossed the dishtowel over the clean dishes in the sink, wiped her hands on her apron and looked again through the glass.

The man turned slightly, and their gazes met. He waved apologetically and shrugged. The dark mark on his chin and neck were visible in the light from the hall.

"It's a customer from the park." She'd trusted strangers from the park before, and the memory still burned. Aubrielle hesitated. "Should I see what he wants?"

Mae came down the hall and studied the man through the door. "I don't see why not. Perhaps he wants to place an order for tomorrow morning."

The man smiled and waved at the women through the glass.

Aubrielle stepped forward, unlocked and opened the door. "*Bonsoir. Puis-je vous aider?*"

* * *

John Larson

"I've got to go." John shrugged off Henri's hand. "Something's happened to Aubrielle."

"How would you know that?" Henri asked.

"Marcel, you're in charge until I return." Bonet slid from the booth with the grace of a much thinner man. He tossed Henri the keys to his car. "You shall drive. You know the quickest way."

The three men threaded their way around the tables and rushed through the back rooms. Maurice Bonet parked his vehicle close to the rear entrance.

Henri turned the ignition. "Ready?" He glanced at Maurice.

"*Oui. Allons-y!*" Maurice moved to the middle of the back seat and leaned forward between John and Henri. "Mae is with young Aubrielle."

Henri couldn't drive fast enough for John. The stinging needle above his brow throbbed out the seconds. "Here! Turn here."

Henri took the turn a bit too fast, and the tires squealed. Streetlights reflected off the wet pavement, but the windshield remained dry.

The car slid to a halt in the middle of the *ruelle* behind the bakery. The back door to Mae's home stood open.

John raced up the steps and into the house.

A smear of blood marked the wall. A plate lay shattered on the kitchen floor.

Maurice huffed into the house behind John. "Where are they?"

Over the voice of the newscaster, they heard a muffled thump.

John tried to open the washroom door, but the latch wouldn't budge. "Mae?" he yelled. The sting on the side of his head told him Aubrielle was gone.

Another muffled thump, and John stepped back, kicking the handle and shattering the frame. The door swung open.

Maurice pushed past John and fell to his knees beside the bathtub.

A knotted dishtowel had been forced into Mae's mouth and tied behind her head. Her nose bled over the white cloth. She lay on her side in the tub. Her hands tied behind her back. Her furious eyes rimmed with tears.

Maurice untied the gag, tossed it aside and worked the knotted twine around her wrists.

The urge to follow the point of pain marking the path to Aubrielle tore at John's mind as his sight locked with Mae's.

"He came for Aubrielle, John. He forced her to tie me up." Her fierce anger faltered, and she uttered a sob as Maurice lifted her to her feet. "He had a gun."

"Who had a gun?" Dread punched John in the stomach. He knew. *He knew.*

"I don't know." Mae clung to Maurice as he helped her from the tub. "Aubrielle said she knew him from the park." She hugged Maurice then her eyes went wide. "He had a birthmark or scar on his neck and face." Her hand trembled as she held it to her neck.

"Karl Reimer. *Le salaud.*" Henri pressed past John and handed Maurice a washcloth. "Where are you going?" He called at the empty doorway.

"To get Aubrielle," John replied over his shoulder.

"John. Wait." Henri followed him onto the back porch. "I'll go with you."

"No. Maurice and Mae need you here. I can find Aubrielle." He started down the steps, then turned to Henri. "If you can leave Paris, do so. Go south, like Billy said." He reached out and grasped Henri's hand.

How much can I tell him? What will he believe?

"France will surrender to Germany by midsummer. There will be German troops in Paris, Hitler himself, by this time next month."

"John, how can you possibly know this?" Henri gripped John's hand, his brows drawn together in dismay.

"I just do." He returned to the porch and wrapped Henri in a hug. "Take care of yourself," John whispered. "Take care of Mae and Maurice."

"You won't be back?" Henri called. "John?"

Seized with a sudden premonition of horror, John ran down the steps.

Nescato or Hitler. Which would be worse?

It didn't matter. Whichever evil Karl raced toward would mean Aubrielle's death.

I can't lose her now.

He hesitated at the gate and looked up at his apartment window. *There are things I need.* He dodged past Bonet's car, rounded the building and took the stairs to his apartment two at a time. From beneath the bed, he pulled the two Thompson submachine guns. Both had a half magazine remaining. He rolled the weapons in a sheet.

He opened the top dresser drawer and stared for a moment at the hand-carved box beside his gun and holster.

The box is too big, but there are things I can't leave behind.

Inside were his ships papers for John Larson, and his identification papers for the British citizen John Locke. He slid both into the inside pocket of his jacket.

He picked up the leather bag and weighed it in his palm. The treasures it contained were irreplaceable, links in a chain trailing back across centuries.

An engraved silver band Alyse had worn for over 40 years. A brass key, with the number seventeen, etched into the head. The tarnished key to the house in Denver and more.

He shoved the pouch into his trouser pocket, along with a handful of francs, and then replaced the lid on the box. He checked the gun clip then slid the revolver beneath the belt at the small of his back. The leather holster he wrapped around the sheets and carried the weapons bundle out the door.

In the alley, Maurice helped Mae into his car. "I am taking her to the hospital. She fainted after you left." He eyed the bed sheets and holster in John's arms. "Make him pay."

"I intend to." He bent and looked through the car window at Mae.

She rolled down the window. "Bring her home, please, John."

"I'll try to come back." He pressed his lips. "But if we can't get back to Paris, I'll take her to safety. I promise. Thank you, Mae. For everything."

Mae covered her mouth with her hands and nodded, unable to speak as tears raced down her cheeks.

"*Bonne chance*, John Larson." Maurice gave his shoulder a pat then moved quickly around the car.

"I'm going with them," Henri said.

"Here." John dangled his keys from his fingers. "Take these. Let the butcher know I've left. Take the food and clothes if you want them." He paused and gave Henri a meaningful stare. "There's a box in the dresser that means something to me. I'd like for you to have it."

"Thank you, John." Henri took the keys. "Good luck, *mon am*i." He folded himself into the car's back seat and closed the door.

John watched Maurice drive down the alley and turn onto the street. As soon as the car wasn't visible anymore, John raced between the buildings toward François's truck. The old vehicle remained parked across from Mae's bakery, fueled and maintained should François or Billy return for it.

John slid the sheet-shrouded submachine guns across the truck's bench seat and climbed in. The old vehicle roared to life while a bee-sting compass-point pounded urgency against his skull.

Chapter 33

Aubrielle Cohen

The scarred man forced Aubrielle to kneel on the floorboard of the back seat of his automobile. He ran the cold barrel of his gun along her neck then laughed as he pushed her head to her knees. "Keep your head down and your mouth shut until I say otherwise. *C'est compris?*"

Her wrists, tied together with the same coarse twine he'd forced her use on *Tante* Mae, were sticky. Her hands smelled of blood. *Mae's blood.*

She couldn't get the image out of her mind. The constant reproach repeated in her mind.

I knew better than to open the door. I knew better. I knew.

As soon as she had, the man stepped past her, and struck Mae hard with his fist. It slammed into Mae's surprised face, knocking her to the floor where she lay still, bleeding from her nose and mouth.

Before Aubrielle had been able to manage more than a gasp, the man held a gun to her head and began giving orders.

Folded over her knees, she watched the brief slant of light illuminate her tight prison before it moved back into darkness, until the next streetlight.

The carpet beneath her nose reeked of spoiled wine and urine.

Nausea twisted in her stomach.

Why had he taken her?

There were other men in the car. The driver and a passenger in the front seat, her and the marked man in the back. The three men spoke sparingly, mostly grunts of acknowledgment or brief questions about direction. They headed north.

Once the light from the streetlamps ceased, and the cab remained dark, her kidnapper spoke, as though he read her mind.

"You must wonder why you're here."

Amused laughter came from the front seat.

Aubrielle swallowed. The pain along her thighs and back from the uncomfortable position made it hard to take a full breath. She shook her head.

"Come now. You have questions. I know you do." He gave the leather seat beside her ear a pat. "We are out of the city. Sit up here with me."

She attempted to straighten her spine, to raise her shoulders, but the muscles in her back seized and cramped.

"She tries my patience already." The marked man grabbed her arm and yanked her up, wrenching her shoulder.

Her legs straightened as he pulled her onto the seat by his side. Her limbs felt dead and disconnected from her body, appendages too heavy to lift. The cramping pain in her back and shoulder masked the touch of his hand on her breast. Until he pinched.

She gasped and tried to pull away, but her legs wouldn't move. She could only bend forward.

He pushed her down on the seat, her head near the door, and ran his hand up her leg.

Even in the darkness, she was close enough to see there were no handles. No way to open the door or window. No way to escape.

He yanked her skirt up and ran his hands over her hips.

"Stop it. Stop." Aubrielle kicked out, and tiny stinging knives flashed along her legs as blood flow returned.

He grabbed one of her legs and flipped her onto her back,

putting her ankle between his ribs and the cushion. He pushed her other leg against the back side of the front seat with his foot, spreading her legs wide.

"If you're going to fuck her we need to stop. Bruce will wreck trying to watch." The passenger turned in the seat. "Besides, I want *cette petite chatte,* too."

"You said we weren't to kill her," the driver said.

"No. We can't kill her. He can't follow us if she's dead," the marked man replied.

"How will he know?"

"He'll know. The baroness told me he must find her when her life is threatened. He can sense her."

"If we're not going to kill her—"

"We're not, but Baroness Nescato will. She'll gut this little French fish like a flounder." His hand ran up the inside of her thigh, and he flipped her full skirt over her face. "Make no mistake. Her life is in terrible danger."

"No!" Aubrielle screamed and kicked wildly. She freed her leg from beneath his shoe and swung it toward his head.

He knocked it away and laughed again.

She batted the skirt from her face and used her elbows to drag herself away from him across the seat.

He held one of her legs pinned between himself and the seat. He leaned over and ran his tongue along her naked thigh.

Aubrielle shrieked and hit his head with her tied hands. "No. No. No."

"So feisty." He grabbed her wrists and yanked her upright. "I like it when you scream."

The car careened off the road for a moment, bouncing along the ungraded shoulder, then back onto the gravel.

"I told you we need to stop. Once we all have our turn with her, we will continue."

"He'll be coming," the scarred man said, and licked his lips. "He always comes for you, but you wouldn't know this, would you?"

The car slowed. "If we go too far we'll run into French and British troops."

"We only need to keep ahead of John Larson. Once our panzer division makes it through the Ardennes, they will sweep across France to the channel, separating us from him. How Larson reaches this little bitch after the baroness has her is of no concern to me."

"What does the baroness want with her if she's only going to gut her?"

"Nescato doesn't want this little bitch. She wants John Larson or whatever name he's using now. The baroness confided to me she has searched for this man for nearly two thousand years."

The driver turned down a dirt road as they laughed from the front seat.

"You said this baroness was a young beauty. She sounds like an old hag."

"A very old hag."

"She's a witch and never ages, just like her mate, John Larson."

Aubrielle's adrenaline fueled thoughts could make no sense of their conversation.

John's mate? Two thousand years old? A witch would gut her?
Panic robbed her of rational thought.

The vehicle stopped, and both men in the front seat got out. The back door opened, and the marked man slid out of the car, his grip never lessening on her wrists.

Aubrielle fell to the ground as he dragged her from the car, but he yanked her back to her feet. "Walk."

"Up in the headlights, so we can watch." The one they called Bruce walked ahead of them.

Karl gripped her above the elbow and pushed her ahead of him to where the driver waited.

When they reached the light from the headlights, he spun her around and ground his mouth down on her lips so hard she tasted blood. Then he shoved her backward.

Aubrielle stumbled, desperate to stay on her feet.

Rough hands grabbed her and yanked her wrists up and over his head. When he straightened, both of her shoulders popped. Her back to his stomach, she dangled down the man's chest. Her tied wrists secured behind his neck, her toes barely touching the ground. He pulled her tucked shirt out of the waist of her skirt and ran his calloused hands up her bare skin to her breasts.

She could smell his fetid breath at the side of her face.

His fingers slid beneath the elastic of her brassiere and pulled up, freeing her breasts to his hands.

She kicked him and screamed as he bit down on her ear.

A single gunshot echoed in the night, and her assailant froze.

In front of her, a bullet hole appeared in the side of the driver's forehead. He stared back into her eyes as he fell.

Her attacker shoved her arms from around his neck and pushed her to the ground. "Where? Where?" He dodged out of the beam of the headlights and into the darkness.

Aubrielle didn't see where Karl went or hear his response if he made one. She balanced on her elbows and knees as she stared into the eyes of a dead man. Panting with terror, her vision spun, and she lowered her forehead to the dirt, her bound wrists stretched before her. *"Sainte mère de Dieu, protégez-moi!"*

"John." She whispered his name, unsure if it was a prayer, a wish, or a talisman against evil, she only knew he was out there. If she could stay alive, he would come for her.

The crack of a gunshot nearby brought her head up. Kneeling in the headlamp beam made her an easy target.

Move.

She struggled to her feet and staggered to the side of the car, out of the light and into a void of darkness. She squeezed her eyes shut and blinked, hoping to gain some night vision, but her eyes couldn't adjust swiftly enough.

Out of the black, an arm circled her neck and pulled her upright.

The barrel of a gun pressed against her side. "Back into the light. I want him to see you."

Who would see her? John?

She tried to inhale past the arm around her throat as the man pulled her back into the light.

In the middle of the headlight beam, Karl stopped and put the gun to her head. "I know it's you, Larson. If I'm going to die so is your little Jewish girl. Show yourself."

John moved in front of the headlight, his outline black against the bright beam.

"Drop the machine-gun," Karl demanded.

The weapon fell from his hand.

"If you hurt her, I'll kill you."

John!

Tears of relief slid from the corner of her eyes, yet something was different. There was a bloodless resonance in his voice. A flat and haunted inflection. Daunting. Deadly.

"I've already hurt her, what can you do?" Karl laughed without humor. "Take another step and I'll put a bullet through her brain."

John stopped walking forward. "And then what would happen to you?"

"I would die. So what? Everyone dies, John Larson." Karl pulled her back a step. "Everyone except you and Baroness Nescato."

"There are worse things than death." John's voice dropped low. "I'd be happy to demonstrate how truly painful it can be to remain alive."

Karl barked a laugh. "Fuck your threats. You are nothing compared to Nescato. She is absolute evil." He waved his gun in the air. "She is—"

John drew his sidearm and fired.

Aubrielle's abductor fell back, taking her with him. Off-balance she fell, although Karl no longer held her neck. She landed on her side, half on top of Karl. Before she could push away from the dead man, she was lifted to her feet.

John pulled her to his chest and held her close. "Are you hurt?" He held her away and studied her. "He said he hurt you."

She shook her head. "He scared me—threatened me. That's all." Now that she was safe, and the men who abducted her were dead, she couldn't stop the tears. She sobbed and held her breath as John untied her wrists, then she was again pressed against his chest, surrounded by arms.

"I about lost my mind," he murmured into her hair. "When the engine in the truck failed two miles back, I thought I'd lost you forever. I grabbed one of the machine-guns and ran."

"How did you find me?" She pushed back and tried to study his face in the shadowed light. "And Mae. Did you find Mae?"

"Yes we did, and she'll be fine." He pushed the hair from her forehead, then cupped her face with both hands. "As for how I found you, your heartbeat called me." He pulled her close again.

She leaned her head against his chest. "I want to go home." She wrapped her arms around John's waist and relaxed into the warmth and safety of his body.

Chapter 34

John Larson

John kissed the top of Aubrielle's head then looked at the sky. Last night's rain clouds had cleared, and stars filled the heavens. To the east, a glimmer along the horizon hinted at dawn. "We should go."

Aubrielle adjusted her clothes. "The marked man said there would be Germans behind us. He thought they would stop you from reaching me."

"If there were Germans to the rear, I didn't see them. But I was closer to you than Karl realized." John lifted his chin and looked north.

The Germans advance through Belgium.

His head turned to the south.

Hitler or Nescato. Her fate would be the same with either demon.

"He talked about a panzer unit coming through the Ardennes." Aubrielle brushed her skirt, then captured her hair and twisted it to the side.

"The Ardennes Forest is directly east of where we are now. If German tanks are sweeping south, we won't make it back to Paris. And if they come west..." his voice faded.

"They'll come straight at us," she finished his thought.

John met her gaze. "We'll go north. There's a small town not far from here. We can pick up supplies, food at least—maybe buy petrol and try to find out what's happened."

"Then where?" She rubbed her arms and John tucked her back beneath his coat.

"After that, we'll go to the coast. We should be able to find a ship in Calais."

She looked up at him. "Leave France?"

"Yes. I have resources in Great Britain. I can keep you safe there."

He walked her to the passenger door, placed the small machine-gun on the backseat, and then circled the vehicle closing the doors. The Renault continued to idle as he sat behind the wheel and closed the door. The gauge showed half a tank of petrol.

That won't be enough.

He offered Aubrielle a confident smile as he backed out of the dirt lane and returned to the pavement.

* * *

Aubrielle Cohen

Aubrielle stared at the side John's face in the soft red glow of dawn as they drove north.

I have to ask.

"Are you cold?" John laid his arm across the back of the seat. "Sit close. I'll keep you warm."

She didn't move. "John, the man who took me, the one you called Karl, spoke of more than troop movements."

John cast a brief glance at her. "Tell me."

"Who's Nescato? Karl planned to take me to her. He said…" She swallowed. "He said Nescato is your mate. That she would kill me, and she is two thousand years old." She tried to scoff at the absurd notion, but her laugh stuck in her throat.

John didn't smile. He drew his arm from the back of the seat and gripped the wheel with both hands. "You don't have to worry about Nescato. She won't get her hands on you."

"She's real?" Aubrielle's voice rose in disbelief. "Are you married to her, John?"

"No," he replied, his voice sharp. He gave her a brief look, and his voice softened. "I rejected Nescato, years ago. We never mated."

They never mated?

She tapped her nail beneath the window.

Another bizarre response.

The sky had lightened enough to see the pristine French countryside roll past. A peaceful illusion.

How do I balance the scales where John's concerned?

She watched him from the corner of her eye. "How many years ago?"

He began to speak, then made a low growl in the back of his throat. Lips pressed, he gripped the steering wheel so hard his knuckles turned white. "There is nothing I can say. No explanation will ever convince you I speak the truth."

"Why?" she whispered. Tremors shook her legs. She rubbed her hands up her arm to calm a sudden chill.

"Nescato is a witch." He looked at Aubrielle. "An evil, vengeful woman who cast a dark and hate-filled spell." His eyes returned to the road. "She cursed me—*cursed us*—because I didn't love her. I could *never* love her. My heart already belonged to another."

Aubrielle's stomach clenched. "John—"

"My heart belonged to you. I love you. I always have. Loved. You."

"John, we only met last fall." She covered her mouth and choked back tears. Tears of terror, of relief at her rescue, and finally, tears of confusion. The world lost its balance. Reality shifted.

"No." John's voice held both regret and apology. "I met

Aubrielle Cohen last fall. That's true. But I have loved you, and every incarnation of your soul, for two millenniums."

She turned away from him and stared out the window as the sun rose. "More magic."

* * *

John Larson

John drove in silence. With no way to prove his words, he had nothing to offer. He glanced at her.

She sat huddled against the door, staring out the window.

Late morning found them near the town of Arras. As he turned onto the main route into town, a French lieutenant stepped from beside his vehicle and in front of their car. He waved his hands above his head for them to pull to the side of the road.

"He doesn't look happy," Aubrielle said.

"They've secured the town." John caught her watery gaze and lowered his voice. "I'm going to tell him I'm British. There will be fewer questions. Don't act surprised."

The car rolled to a stop and John cranked down the window. "Good morning, Lieutenant. How may I help you?" he asked with a strong British accent. He cast a quick glance at Aubrielle.

She stared at him, eyes wide and brows raised.

The lieutenant looked across at Aubrielle then into the back seat. He sprang back, drew his revolver, and pointed the gun at John. "Exit the vehicle, *monsieur*. Hands in the air where I can see them."

"Easy, Lieutenant." John reached through the window and opened the door from the outside. "We're not trying to hide anything."

The French officer ignored John's statement. "Turn around. Put your hands on the top of your automobile." He patted down John's sides with one hand, pulling the revolver from its holster. "Where did you obtain these weapons?"

"The hand-piece is mine. The Thompson—" John looked over his shoulder at the lieutenant, "isn't mine. A friend with the *Sûreté nationale* left it in my care."

"Where was this?" The officer lowered his gun but remained several feet away.

"In Paris."

"You came from Paris this morning?"

"No. We left Paris last night." John turned and faced the officer.

The lieutenant holstered his weapon and handed back the revolver. "Show me your papers."

John pulled the identification for John Locke from his jacket. "John Locke of Essex."

The officer shuffled through the paperwork and handed it back. "What are you doing in France at this time *Monsieur* Locke?" He looked again through the window at Aubrielle. "And who is your companion?"

"This is my fiancée, Aubrielle Cohen." John smiled at Aubrielle. "We came across to administer her late father's estate. It took longer than expected. We hoped to make it to the coast and depart for home, but I'm afraid we're about out of petrol."

"All the petrol in Arras is conscripted for military use. The nearest port is Calais, but the Boches are on the move." The lieutenant lowered his voice. "They've broken through at Sedan bypassing the Maginot Line." He shook his head as he took the machine-gun from the back seat. "This will stay with me."

John nodded. "That's quite all right." He closed the back door while the French officer inspected the Thompson. "Are we free to go?"

"*Oui.*"

John slid behind the wheel. "Is there a place we can purchase supplies?"

"Down the *rue* is Jo's Café. There is a small market next to Jo's, although you may be disappointed. Most of the shelves are now empty."

Allied vehicles and troop carriers choked the roadway as they pulled into town. John parked in a *ruelle* down from the café. As an afterthought, he tossed the keys onto the front seat.

"What are you doing?" Aubrielle asked over the top of the car. "Someone may steal it."

"They won't get two miles. It's out of gas." John took her arm, and they crossed the street making their way to the restaurant. "We'll have to find another way to Calais." He entered the crowded place while Aubrielle waited beside the door.

French and British officers filled the chairs. Enlisted men lined the wall, eating where they stood.

John stopped the harried waiter as he passed. "Are you serving civilians?"

"*Non*," the waiter replied. "Displaced and *réfugié*s eat next door."

Refugees?

John glanced out the window at Aubrielle.

Is that what we've become?

She spoke with a French officer, her smile cautious.

The officer nodded to something she said while he waited in line to enter the café.

As John threaded his way to the door, a detonation in the distance rattled the dish display on the wall.

The waiter dropped his tray and uttered a short shriek.

Across the room, a British commander came to his feet. "You are safe. Allied forces are collapsing the bridges to slow the German advance."

Aubrielle stared at John through the window, wide-eyed.

He hurried from the café and took her arm. "The explosions are from our troops. They're destroying the bridges."

"Where are we going?" She jumped in surprise as another detonation, closer this time, rattled windows along the walkway.

"Next door."

The shelves inside the market held only non-edible items. Folded blankets and empty baskets.

A young husband and wife with a tiny babe spoke in hushed tones to a tall, middle-aged woman wearing a white bib apron. She directed them to an area with several empty chairs, and then she looked at John. *"Puis-je vous aider?"*

"Yes. We've been stranded in Arras on our way to Calais. The waiter next door directed us here."

"An Englishman." The woman grinned showing her crooked teeth. "My name is Joséphine." She indicated the chairs in the corner as another explosion rattled the market. "Oh!" She blanched then chuckled, patting her chest. "If that keeps up my last nerve will surely give out. As I was saying, I have a vegetable soup ready. As for transport to Calais, the older gentleman in the corner mentioned Calais as well. Perhaps you could pool your resources."

"Merci." Aubrielle murmured. She held John's arm, exhaustion darkening her face.

John helped her to a chair along the wall.

The young mother nursed her baby in the furthest chair as her husband spoke with the older man at the other end of the seating area.

"I'm going to ask about transportation to Calais." John picked up her hand and kissed it. "You should try to get some sleep."

Aubrielle nodded, relaxed her head on the table and closed her eyes.

The older man and the young husband were discussing payment.

"I wish I could take everyone, but space is limited. I have my family to consider as well."

The young man's head hung as he returned to the nursing mother.

"John Locke." John held out his hand in greeting.

The balding man took his grip. "Gabe Lefèvre." Curly white hair circled his bald head, and blue veins traced across his reddened nose.

"When do you leave for Calais?" John sat beside Gabe.

"In the morning." He raised a bushy white brow. "Are you interested in joining us?

"Yes." John lowered his voice. "I overheard you discussing payment. What's your price?" His gaze strayed to Aubrielle. *Any cost.*

"Anything that would help us. Blankets. Food. Lacking those things, silver or gold."

John pulled the pouch from his pocket and withdrew the silver ring. Engraved on the inside were the words: *Today Tomorrow Forever—A&J.* The outside of the ring had tarnished to a dark gray. He rubbed the metal on his trousers, read the inscription he knew by heart one last time, then held the ring up for Gabe's inspection. "Will this do?"

Gabe took the ring and studied it. *"Oui."* He nodded "This is more than enough." He glanced at the young couple, then back to John. "It would, in fact, pay for all five of you."

"Thank you. I'll let them know."

Chapter 35

Aubrielle Cohen

They didn't leave the next morning. Or the morning after. For three days they waited in Arras as the town filled with Allied forces and supplies dwindled.

"It's time." Gabe's command woke the small group before dawn. "Bring your bags and blankets. Hurry."

Aubrielle filed out of the market holding John's hand, their blanket over her arm. A gift from Joséphine. The store owner had given a blanket to each family, along with a small cloth bag with bread and cheese.

In front of the market, Gabe's elderly wife and adult son watched them through the truck window.

Caleb, Gabe's brother, and a cousin shared the bed of the truck with the refugees from the market.

Aubrielle had met Gabe's family over the course of the three-day wait as the brothers gathered supplies and traded for petrol.

No greetings were necessary as they climbed into the back of the truck. John stepped in last and settled beside Aubrielle.

Outside of town, the truck slowed behind a column of soldiers.

"Why are they leaving?" Aubrielle whispered to John.

"They may have been ordered to support the ports," John replied. "There are three along the channel. Boulogne, Calais, and

Dunkirk. They'll fight hard to defend them."

"And we're going to Calais?" She glanced at John as the sun broke the horizon and bathed the passengers in a pink light.

John kissed the side of her head. "Anywhere along the coast where we can find a ship will do."

Behind them, a woman walked alongside a mule cart filled with household goods.

In the afternoon, Aubrielle held the baby while Rhea, the new mother, slept beside her husband.

Aubrielle closed her eyes, resting her head against John's shoulder, only to be jolted upright. She glanced at the young mother.

How can she sleep?

The ruts shook the truck again, and she sighed.

Their progress was slow. They could travel no faster than the families and soldiers walking ahead of them.

Caleb complained continuously about their pace, but there was no recourse. "We've gone less than thirty kilometers," he exclaimed.

"Hush, Caleb," his brother told him. "You don't have to walk. Be grateful."

"I'll be grateful when we're on a ship."

The next day they advanced less than the day before. Two vehicles ahead of them broke down, one after another. John and Caleb pushed the cars from the road, amidst the owners' angry threats. They wanted Gabe to siphon some of their precious petrol into the dry tanks. The argument had lasted well into the night.

Before dawn, explosions followed by gunfire jarred the group awake. Flame-colored clouds reflected the fires below, shadowed by dark smoke. Occasional tracer rounds streaked across the sky.

"*Mon Dieu!*" Aubrielle whispered. "Is that Arras?" Her chest tightened as her heart rate spiked.

Is this real?

Despite the Allied troops in Arras and the sound of detonations as they collapsed the bridges, the war had seemed distant. Not an immediate threat to their lives.

Not until now.

"The other side of Arras. They're defending the city." John stood in the bed of the truck and watched the battle rage for several moments before he picked up their small bag of supplies and vaulted over the side. "We need to get off the road." He reached up for Aubrielle.

"You're leaving?" Gabe got out of the cab and stared at the firefight near Arras.

"We move slower than the soldiers." John motioned for Aubrielle to hurry and glanced over at Gabe. "And there's no cover along the road. We're an easy target."

Aubrielle tossed John their blanket, then swung her leg over the side of the truck.

The blanket over his shoulder, John helped her to the ground.

"We'll take our chances with the truck," Gabe said. He dug in his pocket and held his hand out to John. "Take this back. You may need it if you find a ship."

"Merci." John slipped the item into his pocket, then gripped Gabe's hand. "*Bonne chance.*"

"*À vous également,* John."

"What did he give you?" Aubrielle carried the small satchel as they walked away from the road.

"I had given him a ring to pay for our passage." John took the bag from her and clasped her hand. "He returned it."

"I've never seen you wear jewelry." Aubrielle looked back at the truck as they passed the last group of travelers who had camped to the side of the road. "Do you think we'll see them in Calais?"

"I don't know." John lifted branches out of her way as they passed beneath the trees. "I hope so."

They walked through the woods until the sound of battle faded behind them.

John spread their blanket on a thick bed of leaves.

Aubrielle cuddled beside him, wrapping the quilt around them both.

"Leaving the road was the best choice," John said.

Her head tucked beneath his chin, she spoke into his chest. "I know."

Over the next days, they encountered other people fleeing north and west. The displaced civilians grew in number as they traveled closer to the coast, as did the aircraft.

The drone of airplane engines overhead had been with them all afternoon as they wound their way, single file, beneath the shelter of the trees. Their small group had grown in number to nearly a dozen. No one had food. No one spoke.

As they reached the edge of the copse, John held her back. "Wait."

She followed him to the side as the men behind continued across a fallow field. "Why do we wait?"

"The planes. I don't know if they are British or German. I don't want to take the chance—"

They both looked up as the sound above grew louder.

"Which is it?" Aubrielle asked. "Can you see?"

The steady hum of the engine changed, and a high-pitched whine grew sharp as the aircraft dove toward the field. Soil erupted across the clearing just before the sound reached them. A sharp rat-tat-tat, followed by cries of terror from the people beside them.

John pulled her behind him. "Get down." His body sheltered hers, his back to the enemy guns. Strafing fire shredded the leaves around them as the gunner took aim at their cover in the trees.

After what seemed an eternity, the aircraft flew south, the sound of their engines faded.

John checked Aubrielle for injury, but the deadly rounds had missed them.

Sightless eyes stared up at her from the man who had walked behind them on the path. Of their dozen companions, five lay dead in the field, three men and two women. Within the shelter of the trees, there had been one death and three injuries.

With no means to bury the dead, they could do nothing except continue and hope rescue awaited along the coast.

As they walked in the night, Aubrielle caught her first scent of the sea tainted with smoke.

Out of the trees and across a dirt field was the sea road. Burned and broken vehicles clogged the roadway in both directions.

In the darkness, they threaded through the abandoned cars and stood on the sand. Her first sight of the ocean filled her with emptiness, as though they stood on the edge of the world. The empty blackness of the sea and sky extended to infinity. The froth on the waves reflected in the firelight as they rolled, pink and gray, onto the shore. To their north, a city burned.

"What town is that?" Aubrielle wiped tears from her face. The wind had changed and blew smoke across the beach fouling the air and stinging her eyes.

"I don't know," John said.

"That would be the oil tanks at Dunkirk burning." A short heavy-set man with mud caked to the side of his face pointed toward the billowed smoke. "They'll burn for days."

People passed around them in the light from the massive fire. Displaced civilians like themselves. Some walked north toward the flames. Others traveled south.

There must be a hundred lost souls, like us. Aubrielle clung to John's side.

"We've come up from Gravelines." A thin woman approached them from the road. "The army came through the town. They told us to leave. German tanks were approaching up the coast from Calais. You'd best keep going." She pointed toward the flames.

Aubrielle looked up at John.

His arm tightened around her shoulder. A line had wedged itself between his brows over the last days. It grew deeper as he peered west, across the sea, toward Britain. "We're too late." He swallowed and shifted his gaze to hers. "I've failed you."

They took shelter with a small group of people along the canal, east of the sea road. A few people talked in the dark, exchanging tales of what they knew, or what they'd heard, or what they guessed. The British were in full retreat. The Germans had cut France in two, trapping the army between the panzer units to the south and the Belgium forces along the northern border.

Aubrielle fell asleep listening to the voices of the lost.

Near dawn, John shook her awake. "Troops are moving down the main road toward Dunkirk."

"Whose troops?" Alarm tinged her voice.

"British, I think. Thousands of men."

"Should we go?" Aubrielle slipped on her shoes. The sole of her left shoe had come unstitched and flapped when she walked, scooping up dirt beneath her toes. An annoyance compared to the blisters on the heel of her right foot. They'd burst and bled yesterday.

"We can't stay here." His voice had lost the defeat it held last night. He helped her stand, then gripped her hands as she limped. "Let me see."

"There's nothing you can do."

He slipped off her shoe and inspected the bloody heel. "When did this happen?"

"Yesterday, but I'm fine."

He tore a strip of cloth from the tail of his shirt and wrapped her foot then slipped her shoe back on over the fabric. "Tell me if you can't walk. I'll carry you."

"Of course." *He's exhausted.* She touched his face as he knelt before her. "I love you, John."

He kissed the palm of her hand and helped her to her feet.

She took a step, then hopped and uttered an exclamation as the hard leather bit down on her raw flesh.

John scooped her up in his arms, cradled against his chest. "I can't watch you walk in such pain."

When they reached the road, Aubrielle caught her breath. For as far as she could see, men marched toward Dunkirk. "My God!"

Several civilians gathered beside her and John at the road's edge.

"Will they make a stand?"

"Where are the German tanks? Have they stopped?"

The questions continued, but there were no answers.

At a break between groups of soldiers, John carried her across the road. "There won't be room for us at the harbor," he said.

Aubrielle stared over John's shoulder. East of the sea road, the oil tanks in town still burned, billowing black smoke into the morning sky. To the west, the port of Dunkirk had also sustained heavy damage from the German bombs.

Endless lines of British and French troops marched toward the damaged port and pressed forward into the water.

"There are ships in the channel," John told her. He looked back along the lines of men still moving toward Dunkirk. "We'll never reach the ships. There are too many men waiting along the mole and wading into the water." He turned around, searching for another solution.

"Where will we go?"

"East, along the coastline." John made a decision and turned his back on the lines of men entering Dunkirk. He followed a group of men and French troops along the water's edge. *Châteaux* dotted the beach between them and the sea road as black smoke blew across the sand.

"Where are they going?"

"From what I overheard, there's a landing point up the beach. Bray-Dunes." John's breath had grown labored, and he walked some distance before he spoke again. "They say small boats can land there."

Chapter 36

John Larson

They were mistaken.

The long shallow beach prohibited even the smallest boat from coming ashore.

John carried Aubrielle to the large *château* that faced the water then lowered her legs to the ground. "See the small boats beyond the beach? Even the flat-bottomed rowboats will hang on those sandbars at high tide."

"How will we reach them then? Swim?"

More displaced civilians ran down toward the beach toward the uniformed Frenchmen at the waterline watching the boats.

John ran his hand along the back of his neck and looked back toward Dunkirk. A large ship appeared anchored near the long stone jetty. It would be evacuating soldiers.

Have I made a mistake and bypassed her best chance to escape?

"John, look." Aubrielle pointed at a woman following the group of civilians.

In late pregnancy, the woman struggled to keep up with the group as they crossed the sand.

"I see her." He squeezed Aubrielle's shoulders. "I'll be right back." He crossed the beach with his long strides to the pregnant woman.

"Let me help you," John said as he reached her.

She had fallen to her knees in the sand but looked up at him and nodded.

He pointed to Aubrielle beside the *château*. "My fiancée is there." He gripped her arm and helped her to her feet. "There's more cover near the building until we decide what we'll do next."

She latched onto his arm with a firm grip and a grateful smile.

Several servicemen ran past them shouting plans to bring automobiles down to the beach.

"That might work." John watched the men as they ran around the side of the building toward the sea road.

"What might work?" Aubrielle helped the woman into the shade beside the building.

"Those men." He pointed as four more ran past. "They plan to drive vehicles into the channel far enough to form a pier and reach the small boats."

"Is that possible?" the pregnant woman asked.

Aubrielle shared a long look with John. "We're fine. Go. Help them. If we stay on this beach, it will be certain death for all of us."

John hugged her. "Stay close to the building." He released her and ran after the last group of soldiers. Their plan was desperate, but they were out of options.

This has to work.

* * *

Aubrielle Cohen

"I'm Aubrielle." They settled against the building and sat on Aubrielle's blanket from Arras. "When are you due?" she asked.

The dark-haired woman gave a sharp laugh. "My name is Lucie, and I was due last week." A protective hand caressed her round stomach. "I give thanks each day that he or she has decided to make me wait. I pray the baby will hold on a few days more."

The first car rounded the *château* scoring deep tracks in the soft sand. The driver passed the first sandbar before the tires slipped sideways and spun in place.

Soldiers watching near the water line ran to assist. They pushed the car into the water. With each incoming wave, the front of the car lifted and tried to wash backward.

"They've stopped," Lucie commented.

After a quick discussion over the top of the half submerged auto, the men dove beneath the waves.

"What are they doing?"

Aubrielle shook her head. "I've no idea."

Another vehicle rounded the *château*. Four men, including John, ran beside it. Each time the car stuck in the sand the men forced it forward. When it stalled, they pushed the vehicle into the surf behind the first.

"When's high tide?" Aubrielle asked the small group that had gathered near the edge of the *château*.

"After dark," a hollowed-eyed elderly man said from across the gathering. "Not long. It's almost sunset now. There will be another before noon tomorrow."

Had John carried her that long? The day had muddled in her head.

I must have slept as he carried me.

"How do you know this?" challenged a stout woman with dried blood on her neck.

The man pointed at the building behind them. "The wife and I were the caretakers here. We came up from Lille every summer." His chin quivered, and he wiped his nose.

A third car careened around the building and onto the beach, and then another. With the first pier completed, the men began another a hundred yards to the west.

The old man had been right. The sun hung low, a strange red ball coloring the sky through orange striped smoke-clouds.

The big ship had sailed from Dunkirk and been replaced by another. *At least some are getting out.*

John returned to the *château* when it became too dark to work. Wet, chilled and exhausted, he leaned against the building and shivered.

Aubrielle sat beside him. "Lie down and rest."

"We'll need to go out to the boats when the tide comes in." He pillowed his head on her lap.

She covered him with their blanket and rubbed his arm. "You'll wake when it's time."

In the dark, she listened to the waves as they crashed closer. The tide had risen, and the water swept near.

As though the Germans knew their plans, planes returned with the tide. They dropped flares attached to small parachutes. The lights hung suspended, like a hundred tiny moons, and extended from Bray-Dunes to Dunkirk, lighting the waterline.

Several dozen men ran to the improvised piers. They made their way to the end, which was well beneath the water now. Waist-deep, they waited for the small boats to pick them up.

"This is going to work," John said. He gripped her hand and they crossed the beach.

The old man and Lucie followed behind.

Aubrielle's heel stung as the raw flesh pulled away from the shoe, but she tried not to limp. John would pick her up again, and exhaustion etched his face.

I can walk.

As the salt water washed over her shoes and licked against the opened blisters on her heel, she caught her breath at the pain.

John climbed on top of the nearest vehicle and held his hand out for her.

The sharp whine of a dive-bomber echoed from the darkness overhead accompanied by shouts from the beach. Explosions lit Dunkirk, back-lighting the large vessel at the jetty.

John clenched his teeth. "Damn them." He slipped into the

water and lifted her above the surf. His long legs fought against each receding wave, and as they passed from the water's edge, an explosion rocked the beach.

Aubrielle landed on her back in the wet sand. The breath knocked from her lungs. Above her hung a thousand tiny lanterns floating in the sky. Then John was there, sheltering her with his body. She couldn't hear his voice, but the rat-tat-tat of machine-gun fire pierced her muffled hearing.

John pressed her into the sand, curling around her until he covered her completely.

She was suffocating.

One ear buried in the sand, the other to John's chest. The glow of a single flare floating above the waves became her focal point, the only thing she could see, and then her lungs released, and she inhaled.

Time slowed to a standstill while death swept the beach.

After a long while, John rose onto his hands and knees.

She turned her head and said his name into a vacuum that stole sound.

He frowned at her. The line between his brows was back. His lips moved, but he had no voice.

Then her ears popped, and a piercing whistle slowly faded. Sound returned.

"Aubrielle?" John gripped her shoulders and pulled her upright. His hands ran through her hair checking for injury. "Are you hurt?"

"No." She placed her hands on both sides of his face until his eyes locked on hers. "I'm all right, John."

Behind him, the second vehicle-jetty had completely dissolved. Not even flames remained.

He pulled her to her feet, and they ran to the relative safety of the building. One by one the hanging flares failed. In the end, only the burning ship in the channel outside of Dunkirk glowed in the night. Even the stars were gone, blanketed by smoke.

When the sun rose, the men pulled the dead up the beach away from the high tide line. Some they pulled away from the water had been killed last night. Other corpses, bloated and grotesque, had washed ashore with the tide and remained.

The second pier built from vehicles had taken a direct hit. Both the boats and the bodies that had been in front of Aubrielle and John were gone. Blasted into the channel.

Like the sun, the water slowly rose again.

While they waited for the tide, Aubrielle sat with Lucie

The pregnant woman curled herself over her stomach and cried until the tears stopped, then she rocked herself, her stomach wrapped in her arms.

John walked through the waiting men, talking with soldiers. When the water reached its high point, he returned where Aubrielle waited with Lucie.

"I've spoken with most of the men near the water. We're going to get the women off the beach and into the boats first."

Aubrielle counted six including herself and Lucie. "Now?" She observed the water. The choppy waves in the channel had calmed.

"Yes." He helped Lucie to her feet and escorted them toward the water. Three French officers flanked the other women and John made a path to the makeshift pier.

Like they had attempted last night, John climbed onto the roof of the second submerged vehicle, then lifted Aubrielle to the hood. "Are you steady?"

Aubrielle nodded and looked into the channel. Three small boats had turned and headed toward them.

Behind her, John helped Lucie onto the vehicle.

"John!"

John looked to the beach, then out at the boats. "Well, I'll be damned."

Aubrielle made her way to the end of the pier and held Lucie as the rest of the women walked toward her.

The men in the boat used their oars to halt their progress at the end of the vehicles. They wore unfamiliar uniforms wet from the choppy waves in the channel.

The younger man in the back of the vessel called to John, a huge grin on his face. "You make a big target up there, John. They can see you from Dover."

"What the hell are you doing here, Bosun Sweeney?" John smiled, the first time in days. "Where's the *Giselle-Marie*?"

"Master Keats awaits us in the channel." A white-haired man with a matching beard offered his hand to Lucie. "Churchill put out a call to all civilian vessels requesting assistance. Keats answered the call to evacuate Dunkirk." He passed Lucie to the man behind him, then reached for the next woman. "I never dreamed we'd find you here."

The women filled the small boat.

Last to board the small vessel, Aubrielle held John's hand, refusing to let go. "Get in with me, please."

"I can't, love. My weight will swamp the rig." He looked at the white-haired man. "Take care of her, Mister Rice."

"I will, John."

Her wet hand slipped from John's. "No. Let me stay with John."

"Easy, miss. You'll need to sit, or you'll tip us over." He gently pressed her down onto a cross-board seat. "We'll come back for John."

"Promise me." She gripped his jacket. "Promise you'll come right back here and get him."

"On my word," the old sailor replied. He lifted the oar and nodded to his partner. "My name is Kenneth Rice."

"Aubrielle Cohen."

The small boat rocked as they stroked away from the pier. Overhead, the sound of aircraft clenched her stomach. This time, they were above the clouds, their guns firing in the air. "What's happening?"

The bearded sailor looked up. "The Royal Air Force is keeping the Luftwaffe busy."

Aubrielle couldn't tear her sight away from John.

He remained on the makeshift pier helping other men climb into small boats. He was easily the tallest man on the man-made dock. Then clouds blew between them and the beach, and he was lost from view.

"Fog?" Sweeney asked.

"Or smoke. We'll take either," Mr. Rice replied.

Through the mist, a solid hull rose, and the men turned the boat. "Ladies, this is the hardest part. You'll need to climb that ladder to the deck."

The small boat bobbed beside a rope ladder with rounded wooden rungs for footholds.

"*Merde!*" one of the women whispered.

A tall blonde-haired girl rose and gripped the ladder. "This is nothing." She stepped onto the board and climbed. At the top people waited and helped her onto the deck.

"The quicker we unload you, the faster we can go back for your men."

Aubrielle gripped Lucie's hand. "What about her?" She looked to Ken Rice.

"Pete, can you climb behind our young mother-to-be?"

"Aye, sir." He stowed his oar and shifted closer.

The second woman had reached the top, and one followed halfway up the ladder.

"I'll be fine," Lucie whispered to Aubrielle. "I'm very strong."

Aubrielle nodded, glanced at Kenneth Rice, then rose to take her turn up the Jacob's ladder. At the mid-point of the climb, her arms started to tremble. Just when she thought she would fall, strong hands reached for her and pulled her onto the deck.

Moments later, Lucie stood beside her.

Pete Sweeney called across the deck. "John Larson's on the beach. We're going back for him. Let Master Keats know."

Aubrielle pushed her way to the railing and watched Pete and Kenneth paddle away from the big ship.

A line of smaller boats had formed, and the ladder filled with men climbing to the deck. Across the water, smoke and fog marred her view. She counted the boats as they dislodged men. Five. Fifteen. Thirty.

The surreal calm of the channel's water returned to its normal choppy state.

"Excuse me, miss." A stocky, thick-necked sailor nodded to Aubrielle. "You'll need to come away from the rail. The master has ordered us back to Dover."

"What?" Aubrielle knocked the sailor's hand away. "We can't leave yet."

The sailor directed her forward to the base of the wheelhouse.

Lucie sat, her back against the metal housing.

Aubrielle pulled from his grip. "We can't leave John."

"The master said to get the civilians away from the rail. Please, sit with your friend."

Aubrielle dodged his grasp, ducked around another sailor and ran to the rail. She looked down at the ladder as Pete Sweeney looked up.

"Where's John?" Aubrielle called, then slapped at the muscular sailor who tried to pull her away from the rail. "Let me be!"

"You need to come away from the rail, miss."

"I'll take her, Taylor. She can be a handful."

The sound of John's voice squeezed all the pent-up emotion from her eyes. As soon as Taylor released her, she spun toward John. Her toes left the deck as she jumped, wrapping her arms around John's neck.

John caught her and limped away from the rail. "Shh, my love. Why are you crying?" John set her on her feet and brushed at the steady stream of tears on her cheek.

"You're injured." She pushed back and stared at his torn and bloody slacks.

"It's not as bad as it looks. I took a round just before Ken and Pete returned. They fished me from the water."

"I thought they were leaving you." She pointed toward the rail. "I waited and counted boats. Then that big sailor said we were leaving and told me to stand back."

She gripped his waist and cried. Tears of anger. Tears of relief and exhaustion.

John leaned against the wheelhouse and held her close. "We're on the *Giselle-Marie*, among friends. We'll be all right."

Pete made his way across the deck and stopped before them. "Master Keats wants to see you, John."

"Now?" he asked.

"Now. You know the way."

Chapter 37

John Larson

John knocked on the master's office door.

"Come."

Inside, Master Keats sat behind the desk in her officer's uniform. Her auburn-gray hair braided in a crown around her head. "I see you've rejoined us, Mister Larson."

"Yes, sir. Fortunate for me."

Her brows drew together, and she rose to her feet. "They didn't tell me you were injured."

"I took a round in the leg just before Mister Rice returned to the beach. We were under heavy fire, ma'am. He and Pete pulled me from the sea."

"You'll have our medic look at that."

"Yes, sir."

She walked to the front of the desk and leaned against it. "Tell me, did you find who you searched for in France?"

A muscle near his mouth twitched. "As a matter of fact, I did." He pressed his lips to hold back the grin, but when his gaze met her laughing eyes, he smiled.

"So I heard, Mr. Larson. Rumor also tells me she wears an exquisite engagement ring." Master Keats folded her arms, her smile genuine and happy.

"Yes, sir."

"Congratulations, John," she said. Her enthusiasm faded along with her smile. Long thin brows drew together as she lowered her chin. Unlike her usual confident tone, she spoke in a quiet voice with her eyes closed. "I have a family member." She swallowed. "Someone close to me that I haven't been able to contact. I fear he's—"

"Your brother?"

Master Keat's head came up. "Do you know what has become of François?"

"I think I do."

Impatience flashed in her eyes as she searched John's face.

"He sent me a message two weeks ago." John stroked the unfamiliar growth of hair on his jaw. "He planned to leave Paris and travel south to the Azure coast. He urged us to do the same."

Her chest rose and fell. A deep sigh escaped her nostrils. "Then I have hope." She looked up, blinked and covered her mouth in time for a tear to trickle down her thumb.

"I wish I could tell you more." John raised a hand of comfort to her shoulder, but she pulled away.

"You've given me a direction to search, and I thank you." She wiped away the evidence of her emotional relief.

John remained straight and tall and gave the respect the master deserved. "Your brother is an intelligent man. I'm sure he made it to safety."

Her gray eyes crinkled at the edges, and she managed to regain her smile. She cleared her throat. "At this moment, Mr. Larson, I have a full crew. Your old bunk is not available. However, the passenger suite is vacant. I suggest you retire to the small cabin immediately with your bride-to-be before this crowd discovers the empty room."

"Thank you, sir." John nodded and turned to go.

"Will you be leaving us in Dover with the rest of the evacuees?"

John looked over his shoulder.

Master Keats pushed away from the desk and faced him. "After Dover, we'll set sail for Boston. The war effort still needs us." She shrugged one shoulder. "You'd be welcome to remain in the passenger suite for the voyage if Boston is your destination."

"Honestly, sir, I hadn't thought we'd have a choice. Let me speak to Aubrielle and I'll let you know."

"Is that her name? Aubrielle?"

"Yes, sir. You'll like her."

"I'm sure I will, Mr. Larson. Glad to have you back on board." She dismissed John with a nod and stern instructions. "See the medic as soon as you leave my office."

"Yes, sir."

John paused outside the master's closed door. His relief that he and Aubrielle had escaped the coast of France to the relative security of the *Giselle-Marie* was profound. And yet his gut still churned with anxiety.

While Nescato lived and hunted him, there would be no real safety. What her ultimate goal was, he could not imagine. Certainly, she must know the loathing he carried in his heart for the witch. Perhaps she hoped to end both their cursed lives.

Aubrielle's and Sweeney's laughter echoed up the metal stairs.

For now, John's only concern would be Aubrielle's happiness and well-being.

When the emptiness of the in-between claimed him once again, John would turn his thoughts to hunting Nescato. Until that time, he had a life to live with the woman he loved. A woman who deserved all the affection and protection John could provide. He balled his fist against the metal housing.

No specter from our ancient past will find us or harm Aubrielle. This I swear.

* * *

Aubrielle Cohen

They sailed into the setting sun, a bright cool day on the North Atlantic with following winds.

Aubrielle had been surprised when John suggested it, but now that the day had arrived, she couldn't have been happier with their decision. *America. And this.*

Master Keats had invited Aubrielle to her quarters and the two women bonded over their love of beautiful clothes. Master Keats, who asked Aubrielle to call her Giselle, had an entire wall filled with gorgeous dresses and gowns.

"I dress up whenever we are in port. It's been so long since I've worn more than my Captain's uniform. I'm sure we'll find something here for you to wear. We're close to the same size."

Kenneth Rice, the tallest man on board next to John, loaned him a suit. "The finest I own." Ken had whispered to Aubrielle. "I hope it passes muster.'

"I'm sure it will be fine, Ken. You're very generous."

The crew wore their dress uniforms. John's closest friends among the crew formed an honor guard on each side of the passage from the steps to where John stood with the ship's master.

Aubrielle beamed at them as she descended stairs from the forward housing. She wore the evening gown she and Giselle had chosen—white lace over a beige silk under slip. The V-neck draped with layered white lace folded back over her shoulders. She'd never felt so elegant.

I wish Papa and Tante Mae could see me. She pressed her lips. *I will not cry.*

At the end of the aisle of seamen stood John and Master Keats.

John took her hand and leaned forward to kiss her.

"Mister Larson," Master Keats sharp voice stopped him. "You will kiss the bride at the proper time, Seaman."

John faced the ship's master and grinned. "Yes, sir."

"Then let's begin." She paused and looked at the men on the ship, and then her attention focused on John and Aubrielle.

"John and Aubrielle, today you celebrate one of life's greatest moments and give recognition to the worth and beauty of love, as you join in the vows of marriage.

"The night I met John, I asked him to tie a fisherman's knot. He informed me that he could not, for a fisherman's knot requires two lines. He was correct."

She handed John two single lines of hemp rope.

"My late husband once told me a fisherman's knot was also called a lover's knot. Under pressure, this fastening will increase in strength to form an unbreakable bond."

While Master Keats spoke, John tied both ends of the lines together in a loose knot and handed one of the ropes to Aubrielle.

"The knots at each end of the double line represent the two of you." Master Keats nodded to John and Aubrielle.

"Pull," John said to Aubrielle.

Her face lit in delight as the double knots at each end slid together and met at the center of the ropes. Two lines had become one.

The master's voice rose as she looked over the assembly on the deck of her ship. "This is a bond that will not break. Like your love, the knots strength will increase and endure each trial." She waited until all voices were silent and all eyes fixed on her before she continued.

"John, do you take Aubrielle to be your wife? Do you promise to love, honor, cherish and protect her, forsaking all others and holding only unto her?"

John squeezed Aubrielle's hand and looked into her eyes. "I do."

"Aubrielle, do you take John to be your husband? Do you promise to love, honor, cherish and protect him, forsaking all other and holding only unto him?"

"Yes, I do." Aubrielle blinked at her tears, her smile wide with happiness.

"I assume there are no rings."

"I have her ring." John reached into his pocket and withdrew a silver ring, polished to a glossy shine.

"When did you get that? It's beautiful." Aubrielle held out her hand. "Can I see it?"

"There are words inside." John gave her the ring.

She held it up and read the inscription. "*Today Tomorrow Forever—A&J.*" Stunned, her gaze sought his. "It's perfect. How did you manage this?"

"We should finish," Master Keats whispered. "Place the ring on her finger, John, and repeat after me. "Wear this ring forever, Aubrielle as a symbol of our love, for like this ring, our love will have no end."

John repeated the vow and slipped the ring onto Aubrielle's finger. A perfect fit.

"Aubrielle, if you would repeat your vows after me."

"I wrote my own vows," Aubrielle said, never looking away from John's face.

"Of course, you did." Master Keats closed her book and nodded to Aubrielle. "Please proceed."

"I love you, John. But it's more than that. I love how I've blossomed, who I've become, because of you. You've brought both love and magic into my life." She wiped a tear, but continued, looking into his eyes with a watery smile.

"I never want to live without those things or the beauty of your love. I am yours, and because of you, I believe in an eternity where I always will be yours. If there comes a day when I don't recognize you, please know I'll still love you. You'll only need to take my hand, and the magic will be reborn."

John lifted her hand and kissed the rings on her fingers. "May I kiss my bride, Master Keats?"

"Yes. Please do, Mister Larson."

John tipped Aubrielle's chin up and touched his lips to hers. In a whisper meant only for her ears, he said, "I make you one last vow, my love. I will always answer when you call."

Also by C. Marie Bowen

Soul of the Witch

The Original Series
Passage
Prophecy
Paradox

Coven Moon
Prodigy
Pyromancer
Patriarch – *Coming soon*

J.L.'s Timeless Quest
Aubrielle's Call
The Corsair's Tempest
Hawthorn and Mistletoe

The Hunter Chronicles
Hunter's Gamble
Hunter and Lily Graham
The Kid in Black
Penelope's Heart (The Kid in Black ~Part 2) – *Coming soon*

About the Author

Not your ordinary paranormal romance.

Discover nail-biting suspense with paranormal romance author C. (Connie) Marie Bowen. She weaves her supernatural characters into a collection of tales linked to her award-winning novel, *Passage*, the first book in her Soul of the Witch series.

Although many of Ms. Bowen's characters have their own series, they all exist in the same persistent universe. For example, Hunter, of *The Hunter Chronicles,* and J.L. of the *Timeless Quest* are a major contributor to The Soul of the Witch series.

Coven Moon, Connie's new series, will encompass the original Soul of the Witch series, serving as both a prequel and a continuation.

Born in Denver, Colorado, Connie grew up with an appreciation for her western heritage and the love of a good ghost story. Writing from an early age, she dabbled in poetry and short stories. She loves music and plays both the piano and the accordion.

She now lives in the greater Chicagoland area with her husband and two rescue pets—Abigail and Rousseaux.

Visit her website: *CMarieBowen.com* to learn more.

www.ingramcontent.com/pod-product-compliance
Lightning Source LLC
Chambersburg PA
CBHW060546180626
46817CB00002B/750